SHARDS OF GLASS

SHARDS OF GLASS

AMANDA LYNN PETRIN

Get new release updates and exclusive content by signing up to my mailing list.

Cover by JF Dubeau.

For my family, who raised me to believe I could do anything...

Family Tree

Harrises
Jack Harris
Sierra Glass
Christopher Glass
Tobias Harris
Haylie Harris
Sarah Glass
Matt
Jared Glass
Kyle Glass
Rachel Glass
Katie

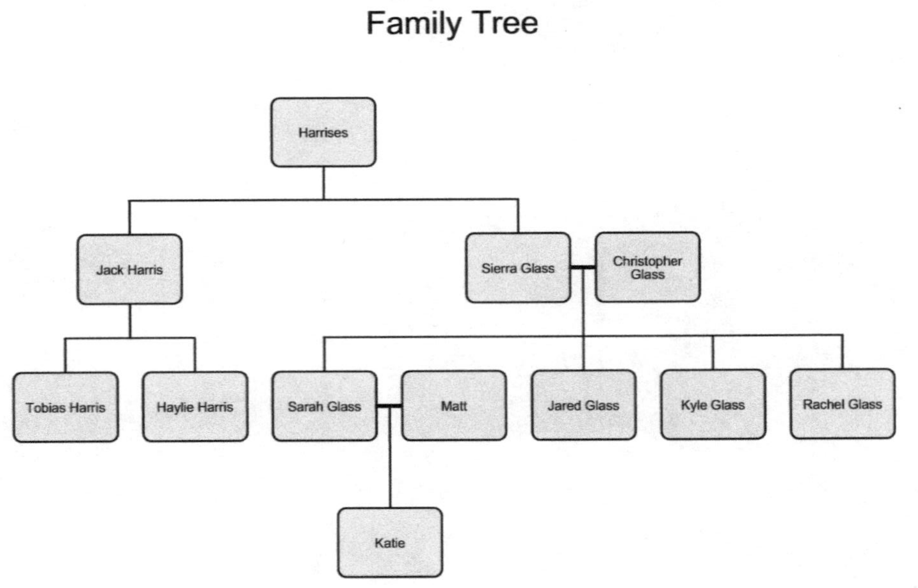

PROLOGUE

I watched, transfixed, as the rain poured onto the windshield. It was easier to concentrate on that than to think about what just happened, to try and look past the rain, at the building that looked so calm while my imagination ran wild. All I could hear was the way the drops pounded on the roof. The rest of the world was quiet while the three of us sat in the van and waited. None of us dared to put our thoughts into words. I could tell that even though Kyle wasn't saying anything, he was as terrified as I was.

When mom ran into the building, I was the one who reached out and grabbed onto my brother's hand, but he was holding on pretty tight now too, and not just to make me feel better. He was looking for the same comfort I was.

I bit my bottom lip to stop the tears, because crying would mean I thought something bad had happened, and I was not ready to go there.

"When is nana coming back?" Katie, my four-year-old niece broke the silence. Even she felt how serious this was, because she never stopped talking, unless she was eating or sleeping, and even then, it was debatable.

I turned away from the school and watched her try to understand what was going on. She held on to her little yellow soccer ball as you would a stuffed animal.

I realized I was looking at her like she was speaking a foreign language, so I tried to come up with an answer, but I couldn't.

"She'll be back in a few minutes sweetie, don't worry," Kyle, who was usually the funny one, assured her with a smile even she could tell was fake. Still, she nodded and accepted it, because we had never given her a reason not to trust us before.

Katie went back to looking out the window, but Kyle fixed his green eyes on me, the fear in them telling me he was just as worried as I was. My niece was young enough to think the loud noises were thunder, even though there was no lightning. As for me, I flinched every time we heard a gunshot. The silence unnerved me, but the sounds that ripped through the rain and chilled my bones were so much worse.

"Is she okay?" Katie asked after another series of gunshots. She was used to noise, because our house was normally bursting with all kinds of arguments, telephone conversations, loud music, video games, TV shows, and some occasional singing. This noise was different though, and I couldn't tell if the rain was muffling the screams, or if I was imagining them.

I couldn't tell how long it had been since my mom went into my high school, but it felt like hours. I knew it was actually less than ten minutes, because I couldn't hear sirens, and we had called the cops as soon as she left us. Katie asked us questions every minute or so, whenever she got the courage to disturb the silence, and we took it in turns to tell her nana would be okay, that she didn't have to be afraid.

"Is nana coming back?" she asked when the rain and gunshots stopped. This time, no one answered her. It wasn't that we couldn't find the words. We just knew, or rather felt, our assurances would be untrue. I couldn't tell you the exact moment it happened, or which gunshot did it, but we both knew that at some point between the last reassurance and Katie's final inquiry, our world fell apart.

THE LAST SUPPER

That afternoon...

"She should have stayed with him. She loved him, and he was perfect. You can't beat Ryan Brooks," I said as the credits rolled. Mom had the day off, so we spent the last day of summer vacation in her bedroom, watching movies. We made a half-hearted attempt to go outside after the first one, but it started raining so we felt justified watching two more.

"Sometimes loving someone means you have to let them go," mom sided with the movie's heroine, like they shared wisdom my fifteen-year-old self had yet to acquire.

"Isn't that when keeping them caged is selfish?" I asked.

"They don't have to be caged, Rachel. And he was happy at the end." Mom checked her watch before turning off the TV.

"She was alone," I argued.

"She was fulfilled by other things." Mom pressed her forehead against mine and smiled, closing her eyes, then pulled away. "This was a perfect afternoon, but I have to make supper." When she got up, she let the cool September air into the blankets, so I reluctantly got up as well.

"We could ask Sarah to bring us takeout," I suggested.

"I promised Katie pasta." She ruffled my hair. I tried to get away, but after a day spent lying in bed, I doubt it made any difference to the knots that settled in my long brown mess of curly hair.

"I'll come help you in a minute." We were at the bottom of the stairs when the doorbell rang, but I could see Alex through the frosted window.

"I'll make garlic bread," she smiled, knowing it was his favorite and there was a 95 percent chance he would stay for supper.

"You walked here?" I asked when I opened the door and saw him. Alex's light grey t-shirt was almost black from the rain, and his spiky blonde hair was lying flat against his head.

"It's barely raining," he shrugged it off.

"You're crazy," I shook my head and let him come inside.

"I'm not staying. I was on my way home from the arcade and it started raining." He gestured to himself as evidence of the downpour.

"You came for shelter?" I raised an eyebrow, then reached up to pass my hand through his hair to shake out some of the water. Alex was my best friend, basically my only friend other than family, so I treated him like one of my brothers and he did the same.

"No, I left my raincoat here last week," he admitted. "Thought it might be more useful if I actually wore it."

"It usually is," I agreed. "We're having spaghetti if you want to stay." I handed him his jacket from our closet.

"You're killing me here." He shook his head with reproach, then more forcefully when he realized his hair was wet enough for some drops to reach me.

"Not nice," I warned.

"We're doing family supper. Rain check and leftovers?" he asked.

"I might start charging," I warned without conviction. He

probably had supper at our house as often as he did at his own, and I always brought way too much food for my lunches, so he rarely brought anything.

"You know you love me." He gave me a hug, which was more to press his soaked t-shirt against my dry one than to show affection.

"Still not nice," I smiled in spite of myself.

"I know. I'll call you later. Maybe we can go to the drive-in tonight? One last hurrah before school starts tomorrow?"

"Sounds like a plan," I said before he headed back out into the rain.

"How many people?" I asked my mom when I walked into the kitchen.

"Is Alex staying?" He often hung out with Kyle or Katie while I helped my mom cook.

"No, he left. We might go to the movies tonight, to say goodbye to summer." I grabbed a handful of utensils.

"It'll be four of us then." I put back the extra cutlery while she added basil and oregano to her spaghetti sauce.

"Sarah isn't staying?" I asked of Katie's mother, my big sister.

"She has an overnight shift at the hospital."

I went to the dining room and set the table. The smells from the sauce wafted in and it was heavenly, like every time she made pasta. A few years ago, Sarah asked mom for her spaghetti recipe. At first, we laughed, because Sarah's the sibling we don't allow in the kitchen until after the meal is done, so she can help with the dishes. Mom eventually shushed us, and Sarah found out what I already knew; there was no recipe. Mom put whatever vegetables or leftover meat we had in the fridge into a big pot and added spices and random ingredients until it tasted right. It made sense that this was how she cooked, because it was also her philosophy in life. Mom often did something crazy or impulsive, then figured out how to make it work. She was great at taking everything as it came and never backing down.

Uncle Jack said he wasn't surprised when she enrolled in the police academy, because she would defend you until her last breath, especially if you were family, but even if you were a stranger. Kevin, her partner that we call her work-husband, thought this made her soft, because she sometimes got too attached. Then again, she holds the record for the least repeat offenders. My entire childhood we had people from rehab centers, juvenile detention facilities or foster care who would come for a few meals or stay a night on our couch. They often showed up years later and thanked her for giving them a chance when they needed it most.

"Smells delicious." I heard Kyle, so I went back to the kitchen. He spent his day playing football under the rain in a muddy field, and it showed.

"Go wash up for dinner." Mom frowned in spite of the compliment, but it had nothing to do with the mud stains on his cheek.

I shrugged when he looked at me, so he nodded, understanding he wasn't forgiven, and went upstairs to change.

"Can I help with anything?" I tried to distract her, as she stared off in the direction Kyle had taken.

She shook her head to snap out of it and acted like everything was fine. "Just the table sweetie." She smiled at me, but I wasn't fooled.

"Of course." I kissed her on the cheek and got back to work.

"She's still mad at me?" Kyle came to help me in the dining room, where his books were scattered across half of the table. Each one had a complicated math problem he was working on, that I hoped I would never have to deal with. He was a special case, as you could tell from him immersing himself in school before his semester even began. Sarah was the same way, absolutely loving anything to do with science. Or studying in general, which is how she has extensive knowledge on all of our appliances. Don't get me wrong, I love reading. And school. And I get way too excited over everything we learn in history class. But numbers are Kyle's thing, and I like to read fun books when school is out. Then again, no one in my family was even remotely interested in the Philippa Gregory novels I finished over the summer. The big difference between me and my brother was that everyone knew I was one of the weird kids who liked school, while he graduated as homecoming king, with most of the school thinking he was a lovable-yet-clueless jock. He somehow convinced his fellow classmates he was in detention whenever he went to see his math teacher for extra credit, or more challenging problems.

"What do you think?" I knew better than to get in the middle of it, but I definitely had an opinion. The fight between him and mom was a pretty big issue around the house, and the major reason mom wanted to stay home and cuddle even before the weather got dark and gloomy.

"It's not like what I did was completely out of the blue. Mom's a cop. Grandpa's pride and joy was being a decorated war hero. Uncle Jack joined at eighteen and will never leave. We celebrate Veteran's Day and Memorial Day like other people do Thanksgiving," he pointed out. "Support our Troops stickers have been on every car in our family for as long as I can remember." He wouldn't dare say any of this to mom, but he was right. Our family was big into risky jobs and service. Luckily, we've managed to come out unscathed so far. Grandpa died of old age in his sleep, after a long career and reluctant retirement. Uncle Jack spent years flying in, out of and around war zones before taking a position training the next generation. He sometimes missed the action, but he wanted to be closer to his kids, Haylie and Toby. Plus, he already had more than a lifetime's worth of stories to go with the medals he earned.

"But this is you," I argued. "Uncle Jack looks like he was born to wear aviator sunglasses and fly combat planes, but you look like you should be playing college football and joining a fraternity. I will support you no matter what, and I can pretend I'm on your side, but I don't want you to go either." Out of my three siblings, he was the only one who still lived at home with me. We walked to school together, we had movie nights...I wasn't ready for him to leave me, especially not for a war zone where he could get hurt.

"They're not sending me overseas any time soon. I'll spend the year playing football, going to college...I can even join a fraternity if it makes you happy. I just belong to the NAVY now," he teased.

"I'm not laughing," I reproached his smile. "You can't joke this under the table."

"I know," he assured me with a look to the kitchen.

The table was set, so I went in and found mom lost in thought over a plate of spaghetti. She grabbed another plate and filled it when she heard me come in.

We brought the three plates out and mom set them down before the door opened.

"Sorry we're late, Katie's soccer ran over," Sarah called before I could see her. My sister and I were almost identical, except she was a little taller, and her eyes were green while mine were blue.

"I've got it." I went back to the kitchen and took out a Tupperware for Sarah and a plate for Katie. I put so much sauce on Sarah's that you had to look from underneath to see the noodles, but I only put a drop on Katie's, just enough so she could argue if Sarah said she didn't eat any vegetables.

My sister had Katie a week after she turned twenty; old enough so she could convince herself it wasn't a teen pregnancy. She and her husband, Matt, moved out last year, to a house that is less than five minutes from us, but they're here for supper almost every night. Kyle and I are the ones who pick Katie up from daycare, so she can hang out with us until Sarah or Matt finish work. She basically still lives here, which suits mom just fine. She loves having us close, which was a part of the reason she saw Kyle enlisting as such a betrayal.

"You won, right?" Kyle asked when Katie sat beside him.

"It was just a practice." She smiled when she saw the plate I put in front of her, then grabbed the parmesan cheese and proceeded to cover every inch of it until you could no longer see the pasta.

"Easy there," Kyle laughed. He took the cheese away and ruffled her hair, but his plate was only slightly less white.

They talked about her soccer, and mom went to get herself something to drink, which let Sarah get the gossip from me.

"How is she taking it?" she leaned close and whispered. Mom had ears everywhere.

"Worse than when Jared moved to California to fight forest fires, but better than when you told her you were pregnant," I whispered before mom came back.

"I think I was pretty decent when my nineteen-year-old daughter told me she was pregnant," she waited until she sat to let us know we weren't whispering low enough.

"I was in college and very mature for my age," Sarah defended herself, but it wasn't much of an excuse. "We wanted to get married anyway and it all worked out in the end," Sarah smiled at Katie and was going to add more, but mom cut in.

"You can't just act without thinking about the consequences and hope you'll be able to figure it out later."

Mom had described herself, which Sarah was about to point out when we realized this had nothing to do with her and Katie.

"Is that what you think this is? You're mad I joined the NAVY because you think I didn't think it through beforehand?" Kyle took the opportunity to bring up the topic we were trying to avoid.

"No, I am mad because it was a ridiculously stupid thing to do. You never asked my opinion or talked to me about it. I didn't even know you were interested in the NAVY until I saw your invitation to basic recruit training," she reproached. He got back on Friday and the tension had been uber-present ever since.

"You signed the consent forms." He looked guilty even as he tried to defend himself. He'd used Jared's trick for absenteeism slips.

"You tricked me into it, Kyle! You knew I was busy and I'd just signed Rachel's report card. I never, in my wildest dreams, believed you would slip something like that into my hands without talking to me. We're a close family that talks about things and doesn't make huge decisions like this on their own." Her voice was raised from hurt and fear, not anger, which made it so much worse.

"It's not like you can't take it back."

"You don't know how close I am to doing that," she threatened.

"Why don't you?" he was defeated and looked ready to apologize and promise he would never leave.

"Because if I do that, what's to stop you from waiting until you're eighteen to leave me for good?" she fought to keep the tears at bay. I didn't even need a whole hand to count the times I had seen my mother cry.

"I can wait. I can go to Virginia Tech as a regular student. Or see if the scholarship at Skidmore is still there. I won't be mad. And I would never leave you forever," he caved. The most shocking thing about the recruit training wasn't so much that he was joining the military. It was that we all thought he had accepted the scholarship to Skidmore and we had another four years with him at home.

"You'll resent me for it. I talked it over with Jack and he says they won't send students to Iraq, especially ones that are underage. It's four more years of training and seniority so you know what you're doing and are safe once you get there."

"You're okay with it?" Kyle was as shocked as the rest of us. Except for Katie, who was still eating, we all turned to face mom, our mouths agape and our eyebrows scrunched. If you had asked me to place a bet yesterday, all my money would have been on Kyle begging Skidmore to take him back.

"As much as I hate it, I understand this is partially my fault. A very small part, but...I raised you to know your grandfather and uncle were heroes. It was only a matter of time before one of you chose to follow in their footsteps. This Reserve Officer Training is smart...it just hurts that you tried to do it so sneakily behind my back." She was calm and vulnerable now.

"I knew you would say no if I said I wanted to enlist."

"Would that have been so bad? To wait a little longer?"

"No, I just...I wanted to help. When Uncle Jack brought me to the base last summer, there was a kid who was sixteen and cheated his way in with a forged birth certificate. He wanted so badly to make sure no one else lost their family like he had, and I don't know, he got to me. Because of Ted."

Mom took a breath and all I could picture was the images on the screen of Ted's plane crashing into the second tower while mom tried frantically to reach him on his cell phone. He was the only guy mom brought home after my dad left, and Kyle had definitely gotten attached. We all had, but Kyle was the only one who sometimes called him Dad.

"Next time, talk to me. Whatever it is. Your job is to convince me, not hide it from me. You've always come to me for everything else," mom reminded him.

"I will," he promised.

"You know I love you Kyle. No matter what."

"I love you too, mom."

She sighed, relieved, before looking around the table. "Who wants ice cream?"

"Me!" Katie shot her hand up.

"I have to get to the hospital, but she can have one scoop," Sarah said, kissing her daughter.

"When does Matt get back?" mom asked.

"Friday," she sighed. He was in Hong Kong to deal with

clients, which made me want to get into copywriting, but he acted like it was a burden and he would rather be home.

"Be careful," mom said after her goodbye hug.

"Thanks for dinner," Sarah told me of the Tupperware, before she hugged me as well.

"You scream, I scream, we all scream for ice cream!" mom and Katie chanted, so I rolled my eyes and followed suit.

KYLE SAT in the passenger's seat and changed the radio station. I smiled at how seamlessly he and mom got back into their conspiratorial world of inside jokes and favorite Real World contestants. My mom is my best friend, but Kyle is a mama's boy through and through.

"Nana?" Katie asked, but mom couldn't hear over the radio and their animated catching up. "Nana," she tried again, louder, but to no avail.

"Let them catch up a bit. They haven't talked in a week," I reminded her.

She pouted, but ultimately decided I was right. We couldn't hear a word they were saying, but their laughter told me things were going back to normal.

WE WENT to the Friendly's a few blocks from our house and took the same booth we've sat in since my parents moved here. I wasn't personally there for Sarah's first birthday, but I've seen the pictures.

"Rachel, how can you eat that? It looks like something your... it's gross." Mom stared at my cookie dough happy ending covered in peanut butter and marshmallow toppings with disgust, her mint chocolate chip completely forgotten. She stopped herself short of saying it was something my father would eat, because she knew how much I hated it when anyone mentioned him, let alone compared me to him. Mom didn't seem to actively hate him anymore, but we still had to change the channel if ever his face came on the screen. I couldn't forgive him for bailing on us either. He left one night nine years ago, while we all slept, and I haven't seen him since. At least not in person.

"It's delicious. Want to try some?" I offered.

"Oh, please don't!" She backed away from my spoonful like it was a disease, but she was laughing. "I love you, even if you eat the weirdest things," she assured me.

"That's good, because I love you, even though you wear the weirdest sweaters," I reciprocated.

"Your grandmother made this for me." She pointed out the blue S for Sierra stitched into the right breast of her peach sweater. Blue pompoms were glued half-hazardly to the front of it.

"It's still ugly," Katie said with a guilty smile, so mom pretended to be offended and turned to Kyle, who reluctantly nodded.

"But I wouldn't want to try Rachel's ice cream either," he tried to redeem himself, as did Katie, who nodded vigorously.

"You guys are horrible. Are there any of my sweaters you won't tease me for? Sarah still hasn't told me where she hid the one with the snowman."

The sweater in question was particularly unsettling, but it was also a mom and Sarah thing. They constantly mocked each other's clothes, or hid them on each other, like mom's sweaters and that time Sarah tried crop tops in junior high. Shoes were the complete opposite. They have the same size feet, so Sarah went years without buying a single pair. She simply wore mom's. Things have changed now mom sticks to her black cop boots and Sarah wears crocs at the hospital.

"Even if you found a cool one, we'd still have to tease you for wearing it on the first of September," Kyle pointed out. Even with the rain, it was hot and humid outside. Everyone in the restaurant had shorts and t-shirts on, while she was bundled up in an oversize sweater.

"It's chilly," mom argued. With the ice cream I just finished and the restaurant's air conditioning, I maybe got her point.

ONCE EVERYONE WAS DONE, we sprinted to the car to avoid the rain. I got there first and called shotgun, leaving Kyle in the back beside Katie, whose car seat claimed her spot.

"What's going on at your school?" mom asked when she saw the parking lot filled with cars.

"New student orientation," I shared.

"And you didn't tell me?" she asked.

"We're not new. It's the same welcome speech you've heard the last twenty years," Kyle exaggerated a bit, but this would be her tenth time.

"That doesn't mean we shouldn't go. There could be new clubs or activities." Mom had already turned into the parking lot. She was the type of parent who went to every PTA meeting and volunteered to chaperone every class trip and school dance, even when she had done it all with the three first kids. She would probably do the same once Katie got to high school.

"Katie won't sit still for three hours to go over—" I stopped when mom slammed on the breaks, giving us all a jolt. I tried to see what jumped out at us, but mom rolled down her window rather than explaining.

When I heard the terrified voice of Diana, a junior who lives on our street, I thought mom was going to yell at her for not paying attention. Instead, she asked, "What's wrong?"

"He shot her. He shot her and then the others came and..."

I looked behind me at Kyle, to see if he heard the same thing.

"Slow down honey." Mom got out of the van, so it was hard for me to hear the rest of the conversation through the distance and the rain. Mom nodded a few times, already in cop mode.

I thought I misunderstood Diana, but mom poked her head

in and said, "I need you to radio Kevin. Tell him there are multiple shooters at the high school and they've opened fire. We need ambulances and a hostage negotiator."

"Where are you going?" Kyle asked, but we already knew the answer.

"Stay here until they arrive. And you wait in the van. Don't you dare come inside." She looked pointedly to Kyle.

"But mom," I argued.

"This is what I do, babe. It's okay," she told me before running in.

All we could do was wait...

2

THE AFTERMATH

"Kyle, can you get them out of here?" Kevin asked my brother while he tried to manage the chaos. Less than a minute after the cops finally rushed into the auditorium, there was a series of gunshots, then nothing but screams as a flood of people stormed the parking lot. We got out of the van to search the crowd while students and teachers ran past us to the families that arrived with the sirens. Kevin was posted outside to control the crowds and take names, but he looked older and more serious than I had ever seen him before. "Please?" he added when none of us moved. It wasn't that we wanted to be a part of it, we just wanted to know what happened. For now, the best way to do that was to listen to the terrified witnesses sharing their stories to the cops.

"Where is she?" I asked Kevin. No one in a position of authority was giving any information. I knew protocol dictated that you notify the family before releasing names to the rest of the world, but I needed him to tell me mom was managing the crowds inside, or apprehending a suspect, anything that meant she wasn't among the fallen.

The consistent story was of three shooters with a specific list of people to kill. More than once, the shooters pointed a gun at someone, only to let them leave as they shot someone else. Apparently, when the cops went in, the shooters shot themselves, which accounted for those final gunshots. Still, no one was clear on how many people they shot, and even the ones who had been inside weren't sharing names.

"Please, Rachel, I don't want Katie to see this," Kevin pleaded with me. As Katie's godfather, he would want what was best for her, but Katie was also the same age as his oldest daughter, Abby. I looked over to the doors of the auditorium and saw that people were no longer running out on their own, but with the help of paramedics and stretchers. The first few had talked animatedly about their ordeal while being wheeled out, but the more recent ones were in body bags.

We lived in a small town, where everyone knew mom, so any cop, paramedic or student could have told us where she was, but they all walked by like they didn't see us. I had hoped Kevin would be different, since he was her partner and Matt's best friend and we have always considered him family.

I could tell he was concerned about us, and I didn't want Katie to see the dead bodies, but all we needed was a straight answer and I would take her away. The only outcome worse than this not knowing would be to have the horrible feeling in the pit of my stomach confirmed.

WE FINALLY LISTENED to Kevin and stood away from the action, by the trees we sometimes had lunch under. I had Katie in my arms, so Kyle put his arm around me. It was partly for comfort, but also to make sure I wouldn't run off to get answers.

Katie wasn't asking about nana anymore, but she traded her soccer ball for a teddy we found in the back seat.

Kyle let go of me when Bridget came out of the cafeteria doors. They're in the off-stage of their on and off relationship, ever since he enlisted, but the second she spotted him, she ran into his arms. She cried those silent tears that come when the pain is too great for sounds. She tried to tell us what happened, but all she could manage was "We were in the bathroom when we heard the gunshots so we stayed and…" before sobbing.

Any hope I had of her filling us in died there. Even if she had seen anything, she was nowhere near coherent.

"It's okay, you're safe now. You're okay," Kyle tried to reassure her, but his stoicism was failing, and the tears poured down his face as well. I had only seen Kyle cry once, at Ted's funeral, before he buried it all deep inside.

I went back to staring at the doors and waited for her to come out.

"I CAN HAVE someone bring you home." Kevin found me as I moved away from Bridget, to a quieter spot for Katie. He was worried I was inching closer to the school, but I didn't want to go anywhere. My chest felt tight and I kept trying to breathe, but it was like no air was coming in. The tears were so hard to push down, because I couldn't believe what they weren't saying, because it hurt, and because the only thing in the world that I wanted right now was my mommy.

"My mom can bring us home," I told him. He looked at me in a way I did not like, before Katie reached out for him.

"Rachel…"

I wanted to stop him as much as I wanted to know, but in the time it took him to build up his courage, my attention was brought back to the school.

"This one's alive!" a paramedic called, excited for the first stretcher in quite some time to not contain a body bag.

I was fine away from it all before, but now I ignored Kevin's request and got close. I could see there was someone on the stretcher, but it was impossible to tell who is was; boy, girl, teacher…nothing. I knew it was selfish of me, that the other parents and students in there didn't deserve to die either, but I prayed it was my mom. I promised God I would be good and pay more attention in church and be a good Samaritan and help the orphans and do whatever it took if it could be my mom who would live. I needed her for so many things...for everything. I was nowhere near ready to lose her. I don't think I would ever be.

It wasn't hard to get away from Kevin, since he also tried to get closer and see who it was. At first, it was hard to push through the mob gathered around the stretcher, but then it got easier as I saw a bit of the person on it. My stomach dropped when I realized it was a boy, not my mother. Then I saw the light grey t-shirt going dark from blood instead of rain, and knew exactly who it was.

"Alex!" I bridged the last few steps to get to him and understood why the crowd parted to let me through. Alex was the kind of kid the whole town knew and loved, but ever since he moved here when I was seven, the two of us have been nearly inseparable.

I kept thinking that he wasn't supposed to be here. We'd decided to skip the assembly this year, and he had a family supper and we were going to go to the movies...but there was no mistake that it was him. I couldn't imagine who would do this to him, because he was friends with everyone, regardless of social circle. I froze when I saw where the paramedic cut his shirt open, and the small holes that so much blood was pouring out of.

She covered the wounds with gauze and a second paramedic was applying pressure, so I made sure I was out of her way and took his hand. This was harder than expected, because the tears, that I was no longer able to fight, were making everything go out of focus. I was terrified to ask the paramedic if he was going to be okay, because I was pretty sure he wasn't. There was so much blood that she needed to put more and more gauze, but it still came through.

Alex looked up when he felt my hand on his. He looked so happy that it was me, but the eyes that met mine knew this wasn't good.

"Rachel." He struggled to smile, but his voice was weak.

"I'm right here," I assured him.

"I'm so sorry." He fought tears. "I tried so hard, but he..." he fought to get the words out, but he stopped when he coughed up blood. He was so pale. I wanted to run away and pretend this wasn't happening, but I couldn't imagine leaving him. I held on to his hand as if I could comfort him, when he was the only thing that kept me vertical.

"It's okay, Alex, whatever happened, it doesn't matter. It wasn't your fault. I forgive you. It's okay." I had no idea what to tell him. He tried to lift his hand, so I helped him bring it to my cheek. I held it there with mine and gave him a sad smile, the only kind I was capable of. The paramedic looked at me and tried to decide if she should send me away or let me stay with them.

Alex got agitated, then calmed down when I repeated, "It's okay, I'm right here," so she let me follow them to the ambulances.

"It's so cold Rachel," he confided with a look of pure terror in his eyes. I wanted to tell him he would make it through, but he could always see through my lies. "This is some last hurrah," he joked, but neither of us laughed. He squeezed my hand and my heart ached.

"I love you Alex," I told him before he coughed up more blood and struggled to breathe. I wanted to close my eyes and escape, but he kept his eyes locked with mine, as if they were the only thing he could see clearly, so I did my best to stay strong. He would not be alone.

"I love you too. Always," he got out before his mother screamed.

I looked up and saw her coming towards us, her face an absolute mess of tears. She recognized the look on mine as a confirmation of her worst fears and brought her hand to her mouth, frozen on the spot.

Alex coughed again, so I came back to him. I wanted to tell him how much he meant to me, but I couldn't find my voice.

Mrs. Sims got to us as they were about to lift him into the ambulance. She went with her son, and my heart stopped when he let go of my hand, that was now covered in his blood. I knew it was because the stretcher moved too far away, that he wasn't gone yet, but I also knew I probably wasn't going to see him again. I watched them shut the ambulance doors and drive off, then turned around once I could no longer see them in the distance. I hadn't decided if I wanted to run away or crumble to the ground, but instead I collided with Kyle, who must have followed me. All of the strength went out of me as he held me in his arms and let me cry heart-wrenching sobs I didn't think I would ever be able to stop.

I DON'T KNOW how long we stayed like that until Kyle tensed up.

"What's wrong?" I tried to turn to see what was bothering him, but he held me tight, so I couldn't. "Kyle, let me see," I asked with a conviction I pretended to have, because I was actually dreading what I would find. Unless it was my mom with an exhausted smile, ready to apologize for giving us such a scare.

"Okay." He released me, but the paramedic had already zipped the body bag he wheeled out on his stretcher.

"She's in there, isn't she?" My tears had slowed, but they came back with full force. Kyle wrapped his arms around me, so I could lean into him as we watched them wheel her past us.

"KYLE, RACHEL...COME ON," Kevin called from beside the cop car he usually rode around in with mom. I was relieved to see he still had Katie in his arms, but hated the way she seemed to be taking it all in, rather than being the center of attention she usually was.

"I'm going to drive you guys home now, okay?" he used his authoritative voice, but still ended it with a question. He would let us walk home, or stay there, if we insisted.

"Can I borrow your cell phone?" I saw the green finger prints on his forearms and realized he had been off-duty like mom when we called. He came for us.

"She's not picking up. The nurse's desk was slammed, but she thinks Sarah is in surgery." Kevin motioned to Katie, who must have wanted her mom after I abandoned her. He opened the back door for Kyle and me.

"Matt's still in..."

"I called him, he's trying to get a flight back," he assured me.

"We have the van," Kyle argued with Kevin's original statement.

"I'll have someone drive it over," Kevin told him. "Come on."

I opened my arms to take Katie into the backseat with me, while Kyle headed for the passenger's.

"Kyle," Kevin stopped him after looking me over, so my brother came back and took Katie from him.

"What was that?" I followed Kevin as he reached into his glove compartment. "What's this for?" I was confused when he handed me a wet-nap, until I saw the blood that stained my hands. Alex's blood. "Oh my God. I'm so sorry." I looked to Katie in the backseat.

"It's okay, she probably thinks it's finger paint." Kevin hugged me, both because I needed it and so Katie wouldn't see the mess I was in.

It took two more wet-naps before my hands were mostly clean, but I could still see the blood all over them. Kyle put Katie in the middle seat between us, but she cuddled up to me as soon as I sat down.

The ride to our house was quiet while we processed things and numbly thought of nothing. I held Katie close to me and focused on running my fingers through her hair like mom used to do for us whenever we had trouble sleeping.

I could see Kevin check on us every few minutes in the rearview mirror, but I focused on my simple gesture and let it occupy all of my attention. If I let myself think of anything else, I would think of them, and the tears would fall, and I couldn't do that in front of Katie.

"Is mommy home?" Katie asked when we drove past their house.

"Can we try again?" I asked Kevin, so he handed me his cell phone.

I dialed the number, needing to hear her voice, but it went straight to voicemail.

"Again," Katie asked when we pulled into the driveway. The five-minute drive had seemed like forever, but now was over way too soon.

"She's in surgery sweetie." Kyle opened his door as I obliged Katie and tried one more time.

"Hello?" my sister sounded happy. My relief at hearing her voice disappeared as soon as I realized I would have to tell her. I couldn't just ask her to come home and put the pieces together without telling her why they fell apart.

Kyle knew this, so he took Katie in his arms and left me alone in the car with Kevin, who got out of the driver's seat and came to sit beside me in the back. He took my hand in his for moral support.

"Hey." I tried to build up the courage, but my tears were back.

"Rachel, what's wrong?" her voice was laced with concern.

"It's...can you sit down?" I remembered the way mom made me sit on the couch before she told me that daddy wasn't working late, that he left us and was not coming back.

"Rachel..." she was worried now as well, but there was a lot of noise behind her. "Hold on a sec, multiple traumas just came in and I can hardly hear you."

I waited while she tried to find a quiet place.

"Are you okay? Do you need me to come get you?" She still thought this was a 'me' problem I needed her help with.

"You need to come home." To where it wasn't just me on the phone with her, what might as well be a million miles away.

"Are you out with Alex? Why didn't you call mom?" she was trying to figure out what was going on and I was not helping.

"There was a shooting," I shared, but Sarah got distracted.

"These kids all go to your school…Alex's dad…wait, did you say a shooting?"

"At the school," I agreed.

"Is everyone okay?" she asked, but I could already hear the tears that were ready to fall.

I shook my head as Kevin gave my hand a squeeze, before I realized she couldn't see me. "No," I admitted.

"I think they just brought Alex to the…"

"Sarah," I cut her off.

"You went to get ice cream, not to the high school."

"It was on the way home."

"Just tell me Rachel."

"Mom…mom went into the school to help and no one would tell us anything, because they all knew, but…"

"Are they bringing her here?" We both knew that was a roundabout way of asking the real question.

"No." I was squeezing Kevin's hand so hard I might have broken something.

"I'm on my way," she understood.

"I don't think you should drive," I argued.

"I'm not letting you be alone right now," she said forcefully. "Is anyone else hurt?"

"Kyle, Katie and me are okay." I bit my bottom lip.

"But…" she pressed while Kevin tried to tell me something with hand gestures.

"They shot Alex. And there was so much blood." All I could hear were tears on the other end as Kevin wrapped his arms around me and took the phone.

"I have a guy bringing the van over, so I'll have him pick you up on the way." That explained most of the hand gestures. "I'll stay as long as you need." He tried to be strong for her, for us, but he was failing. We were his family, and he had lost mom too.

WHEN HE HUNG UP, he radioed in the new directives, then gave me a few moments to somewhat compose myself. I was dreading going into the house, because I knew it would still be the same, waiting for her to come home, but she wouldn't. Nothing would ever be the same.

Kyle clearly felt the same way, because he waited for us in the doorway. He handed Katie to me, knowing that holding her was the only thing that could make me feel even remotely better.

Kevin waited, without saying anything or using his key, knowing we weren't ready. Finally, Kyle took a deep breath and opened the door. We stared inside a few moments before walking in, straight to the living room, where we collapsed onto the couch.

NO ONE SAID ANYTHING, or even moved until Kevin's phone rang. He ignored the first couple of rings, then took it out. "I'll put it on silent."

"It might be Michelle," I argued of his wife, who must be panicked for him.

"I'll be right back." He headed for the dining room.

"I'm thirsty," Katie whispered, reminding me that we needed to take care of her until Sarah came. We couldn't be the broken orphans we felt like.

"Is water okay?" I asked, since Sarah didn't let her have anything else this close to bedtime. If she hadn't nodded, I would have given her absolutely anything she asked for on the off chance it would make her feel better. I went to the kitchen and poured her a glass, then saw the mess we left in the kitchen and on the dining room table. We had put our plates in the dish-washer, but hadn't bothered to do any other clean up before leaving for ice cream. I brought Katie her glass of water, then came back to clean.

I wasn't particularly fond of doing the dishes, or cleaning in general. Sarah and I usually traded off cooking and cleaning. Still, characters on TV always cleaned when they were stressed, so it must be soothing when you've gone through an emotional breakdown.

The theory worked for at least a second, because I was busy thinking about how much I hated cleaning instead of focusing on what happened, but everything reminded me of mom. Not just because I had so many memories of her in there, and she was the one who made the supper and used all the dishes I was cleaning. It was how this afternoon, she stood at the counter I was standing at now, stirring the spaghetti sauce, cutting the crusty bread, grating the cheese...she was alive. She would never do those things again. She would never tell me how much she loved me. I could never tell her that she was the greatest mom in the entire world and I would give anything to have her back.

I felt the tears coming again so I brought my hand to my temple and took a deep breath, trying to get a hold of myself, but it didn't exactly work. I breathed in, then out, went back to the dishes, bit my bottom lip until I tasted blood, scrubbed like my life depended on it...none of it helped. The cleaning actually did the opposite, but it wasn't like anyone else would do it.

"What are you doing, sweetie?" Sarah came into the kitchen. I hadn't even heard the door open.

"We didn't clean up after supper," I explained as she took a cloth from the drawer and wet it.

"You hate cleaning," she said, bringing the cloth to my face and neck, where I must have had blood caked from when I held Alex's hand there. There was something comforting about looking like a mess when I felt like one, but I regretted being oblivious to it while holding Katie earlier.

"It beats what we have to do once it's done." My eyes were watering and biting my lip couldn't keep the tears at bay anymore.

Sarah put the cloth down and shook her head at me, since she was crying too. I stopped pretending I was strong and buried myself into her, needing the hug more than I knew, but she did too.

We stood like that for at least five minutes, both of us sobbing and trying to figure out how we could ever get through this.

Eventually, we pulled apart and I went back to the dishes. She grabbed a new cloth and dried the clean ones. "I talked to Reverend Connors and he's making the arrangements for Thursday." She said it matter-of-fact, like we were talking about restaurant reservations.

"I'm sorry you had to do that." I couldn't imagine how hard it must have been for her.

"Nothing is going to be easy or happy for a long time," Sarah told me. I was also of the opinion that I would never be truly happy again.

"Alex didn't make it, did he?" I tried to act like it was old news that wouldn't affect me, but I was drawing blood, and everything was blurry.

"He didn't even make it into surgery." She came close, but I kept scrubbing.

"Yeah, he didn't look good when they brought him out. He was really pale and the blood was everywhere," I was repeating myself, but I couldn't help it.

"Was he conscious?" Her hand hovered near me, but she understood that holding me would break the floodgates.

I nodded. "He wasn't making much sense though. He said he was sorry and he tried, but he didn't say what. He looked so scared and small...I told him I loved him, and he said the same, but I couldn't tell him that he's my best friend and my family and how much I mean it..." I took a deep breath and wiped the tears with the back of my hand. "When does Matt get in?"

"Rachel..."

"Kevin said he was trying to get a flight."

"He's on standby for a flight that would bring him back tomorrow afternoon." She let me change the subject, but I knew it wasn't over.

"We still have to let everyone know," I brought up the task none of us wanted to do. I would hate myself forever if Jared found out on the news, but I couldn't go through it again.

"Don't worry, I'll do it," she said because she was the adult and felt like she had to, not because she was capable.

"Just because you're the oldest doesn't mean you're alone, or that you have to do everything. I can help." I regretted it the second I said it, but I knew I had to. I couldn't make her do it alone.

Once Sarah and I brought the kitchen back to its pre-dinner state, we went to the living room, where Katie had fallen asleep on Kyle. Other than that, they were exactly as I had left them an hour ago.

"Kevin said to call if we need anything," Kyle shared.

"Was she okay?" Sarah sat on her daughter's other side and brushed the hair from her face.

"She hasn't said much."

"No questions?" Sarah pressed.

"Not since she stopped asking when nana was coming back." Kyle swallowed, and I think Sarah flinched.

"Did you tell her?"

"No, but I'm pretty sure she knows." We dropped the ball on that one.

"I'll talk to her in the morning," she decided. "We can call after I put her to bed." The last thing we wanted was Katie waking up during one of the conversations we were about to have, but I think Sarah also wanted to delay the inevitable.

"She can sleep in my room. I still have the night light." I didn't use it anymore, since she told me reading books with it after I was supposed to be asleep would make me need glasses, but I never bothered to unplug it.

"That'll be nice." Sarah brought Katie upstairs, so I sat beside Kyle. He wrapped his arms around me and let me lean into him, but we didn't speak.

SARAH TOOK her time on the stairs, tip-toeing as if she didn't want to wake Katie rather than not wanting to make the phone calls. When she finally reached the couch, the three of us just stared at the phone on the coffee table.

"We can call immediate family tonight, and the others can..." I stopped short of saying they could hear it on the news, but I couldn't handle us being the ones to tell more people than was absolutely necessary. I was surprised no one had called us yet.

"Uncle Jack can tell Haylie and Toby. We can just call him and Jared tonight," Sarah broke it down to the bare minimum. Years ago, our cat accidentally ate our neighbor's pet hamster. Jared nominated Sarah to tell them, because she wanted to be a doctor and needed to practice telling people the worst news of their lives. It was funny to watch her squirm at the time, but there was nothing funny about the dread and determination on her face now.

WE CALLED JARED FIRST, with the phone on speaker so none of us would have to do it alone.

"Hello?" Toby answered. When Jared decided he didn't want to just be a regular firefighter, that he wanted to fight forest fires in California on top of the whole burning building thing, Toby moved there with him. He'd just got back from this super prestigious cooking program in Paris and had a friend who owned a catering company. He goes back and forth from wanting a Michelin starred restaurant, to wanting a food truck he can drive across the country.

"Hey," I spoke up when no one else did.

"What's up munchkin?" We could hear the smile in his voice. I turned to Sarah for reinforcement.

"Is Jared home?" she asked.

"Is everything okay?" he was annoyingly perceptive.

"Can you put us on speaker if he's there please?" I used all the politeness I could muster, which was nothing like how I usually talked to him. I was too busy trying not to break down and cry that I couldn't tease him and tell him all the awesome things he was missing out on over here. I could already hear the crack in my voice.

"Rachel, what's wrong?" I hated making him worry, but it would be worse once he knew. I was about to suggest we tell Toby and let him deal with Jared when another phone came on the line.

"Rachel, what happened?" Jared armed himself with authority, like when mom would try to get us to admit to something that either we or another sibling had done. It worked every time.

"There was a shooting at LG High tonight," Sarah told them. We were holding hands, way too tight for comfort. Kyle was in between, an arm around each of us, notably silent.

"Is everyone okay?" Toby asked. They could tell someone was hurt, and badly, but they wanted to know who and whether they would get better without specifically asking.

"It's mom," Sarah managed, while Kyle rubbed her back and held her close.

"How bad is it?" Jared used his calm, firefighter under pressure voice, but I knew it was the last question before he'd break.

"She's gone," I said through tears before hearing one of the phones drop to the floor. The words took so much out of me, but Sarah hadn't recovered.

"We'll be there as soon as we can," Toby assured us before hanging up. It scared me because Jared was usually the unbreakable one. Then again, I also felt a lot less breakable when I knew mom would be there to put my pieces back together.

I pressed the hang up button on our end, then sunk back into the couch so Kyle held both of us to him. I pulled my legs up and literally retreated into the fetal position. "Let's get this over with," Sarah sniffed and straightened up.

UNCLE JACK'S line was busy, so we called Haylie, and got the same reaction as Jared. Luckily, she had Peter, her fiancé, there to comfort her. He hadn't been on the call, but he saw her drop the phone and came on to ask us what happened. Sarah and I looked at each other, knowing we couldn't say it all over again, but Haylie told him to tell us they were coming, so he focused on her instead.

We'd just hung up with her when the phone rang, making us all jump. We stared at it a while before Sarah answered it on speaker. She kept her finger on the hang up button in case it was a media outlet, which we expected would happen as soon as they released the names.

"Kevin called, are you okay?" We all let out a breath when we heard Uncle Jack's voice. He was shocked and heartbroken, but kept it together better than we were. The three of us looked at each other with no idea what to say. Sure, we had no bodily harm, we weren't physically involved in the shooting, but we were nowhere near okay. "I'm sorry, that was a stupid question. I asked the admiral for emergency family leave and he said I could have as much time as I need. I should be home before morning." His house was across the street from ours, so we all grew up together, but he had been taking assignments in different places since Toby and Haylie moved out.

"Be careful," I said, not just because I wanted him to, but it was what mom said every time we left the house.

"I will," he promised.

"Is Mackenzie with you?" Kyle asked of Jack's soulmate. It was weird to call her that, but there wasn't a better word. They weren't dating and had never been more than friends and coworkers, but they were also in love with each other. Have been for decades. You could practically see the sparks fly when they were in the same room together. She came to all of our family functions or any time he needed a date, ever since his divorce eleven years ago. That was right before my dad left us, so with him gone and Jack's wife not the maternal type, mom sort of adopted Toby and Haylie, while Uncle Jack became our father figure. Even when Ted moved in, he was always careful not to entirely take over, because he knew it was Jack's shoes he would be filling.

"She's still in Turkey. I haven't told her yet." Mom had not kept it a secret that she was pulling for the two of them. "I'll see you soon."

We said our goodbyes and hung up.

"You can sleep in my room too," I offered when Sarah stopped on her way to the basement, where her old room was. It meant freedom when she was a teenager, but I was pretty sure tonight was the exception where no one wanted to be too far from everyone else.

When we reached the top of the stairs, Kyle gave us hugs that lasted a lot longer than usual. I paused in front of mom's room, hoping I might hear her moving around inside.

Sarah put her hand on my shoulder and guided me to my room, where we both cuddled into the bed without bothering to change our clothes. We kept Katie in between us, and Sarah ran her hand through her daughter's hair while I wrapped my arm around her stomach. Feeling it rise and fall with her breath comforted me more than it did her. I don't think I could have slept alone.

We stayed in the dark what felt like hours, staring at each other while the storm raged again outside. There was a soft knock I thought came from outside, until my bedroom door opened.

"You girls okay?" Kyle whispered, in case we were asleep.

"Come on in." Sarah was the one facing the door, so she lifted the blanket behind me.

"I was just making sure..."

"Make sure from here," she cut off his excuse.

"You shouldn't be alone," I agreed.

"But that's what we are," he said simply.

3
THE CALL

"Rise and shine, princess." I woke up to Uncle Jack on the edge of my bed. He looked at me with compassion as he lifted the hair from my face, but his puffy eyes told me he had also been crying all night.

"It wasn't a nightmare, was it?" I had to make sure.

"No, sweetie. It happened, and it won't get any easier for a long time," he warned me from years of experience in losing people he cared about.

"The others are downstairs?" I got out of bed and tied my hair into a ponytail. I somehow managed to sleep through all three of them waking up and leaving me.

"Kyle woke up when I came in so he's sleeping on the couch downstairs. Sarah got up with Katie about an hour ago."

"When did you get in?" I asked.

"Around four o'clock this morning? I figured you guys could use the sleep."

"Did you get any?" He looked exhausted.

"I made coffee, but I'll take a nap later, before I crash," he assured me. "Katie's helping me with my world famous French toast. It should be ready in twenty minutes." He kissed the top of my head, then went back to the kitchen so I could get ready.

I wished he would have let me stay in bed to sleep until it was all over. Instead, I took a quick shower and convinced myself the sticky stuff behind my ear was honey, rather than more of Alex's blood. I put on a pair of sweatpants with mom's precinct t-shirt and went downstairs.

KYLE WAS in the living room with a forgotten mug of coffee, mesmerized by the footage and images on the morning news. I got that he was curious and wanted to know, but I would have preferred to forget about it.

The screen went from an interview back to the reporter, that one you always see when a big tragedy occurs, the kind you think only happens somewhere far away. He looked exactly like he always looked, like this was just another day at the office, rather than the end of my world.

"The death toll is still at ten, with nine pronounced dead at the scene and Alexander Sims, a student, who died shortly after arriving at Glens Falls Hospital from multiple wounds." It was surreal to hear Alex's name on national television. I wanted to call him, to tell him he was famous and tease him, but I couldn't. Because this wasn't his name in the newspaper for beating me in a spelling bee. This was because he was gone. "Alexander was the younger brother of Philip Sims, who is believed to have been at the head of the group of students who opened fire on their teachers and classmates before taking their own lives." My heart tightened when they first mentioned Phil, because I realized I had no idea who the other eight were, though I was sure I knew every single one of them. I thought they were saying his name because he was one of the fallen, which I guess he was, but the rest of the statement didn't make any sense. Phil wouldn't bring a gun to a high school and shoot people. He was more the type to stand up to bullies than to be one.

"Eight students and two teachers are still in critical condi-tion. One of the victims, an off-duty cop named Sierra Glass, was flagged down by a student and went into the school without any backup or protection. She managed to handcuff one of the shooters before another took her down. We have some footage that was taken during the tragedy."

The screen switched to a chaotic film of the inside of the auditorium. It was pandemonium, with everyone crying or screaming. I recognized Michael Stewart, a stoner who didn't go to our school anymore, but sometimes hung around with Phil. He was standing at the doors, letting some people go to another room, but making others stay. The camera had an excellent view of Phil talking to Alex, the gun in his hand so out of character. It seemed like they were both trying to convince the other to leave, before Alex saw something and turned away. Phil looked in the same direction, but whatever it was scared him. He lifted up the gun at his side, that I couldn't believe he even knew how to use, and pointed it at something. Or more likely someone. Michael came over from the door and did the same, looking a lot more confident. I saw Alex mouth "No!" before jumping between the guns and whatever they were aiming at. I would have done the same, convinced Phil wouldn't hurt me, but Michael had pulled the trigger. There was shock on Alex's face before he fell to the floor. Phil looked horrified and pushed down Michael's gun, that was still firing, before finally going over to see if Alex was okay. Michael was the only one left on the screen, scared yet determined, before the person filming showed what the guys had been aiming at. I could see Corbin, Phil's best friend, on his knees with his hands zip-tied behind his back. My mom was on the floor next to him, her peach sweater turning red from the blood pouring out of the bullet holes. They fit right in with the blue pompoms, until they got bigger and bled together.

I breathed in sharply and brought my hand to my mouth, only slightly hyperventilating when I let the breath out and tried to take another one. Kyle realized he was no longer alone and turned the television off, but the damage was done.

"I'm sorry, I wanted to know what happened," he came over and explained.

"It's okay. At least now I know," I assured him, but I didn't believe a word of it. I would have very much preferred not knowing. Not seeing Alex getting shot or mom covered in blood. On top of the pain, now I felt guilt, because he might not have stood in front of the gun and caught speeding bullets, lots of them, if they weren't intended for my mother. And now I didn't have either of them.

"Breakfast is ready." Uncle Jack came in with a pan and an egg lifter in his hands. He could see we were upset, but I wasn't expecting anyone to look even remotely okay today. Even Katie, who was wearing her cooking apron and following Uncle Jack around, was not smiling.

I took a moment to compose myself for Katie before Kyle and I followed Uncle Jack into the kitchen. We carefully avoided mom's seat, although Uncle Jack had set it. Sarah brought the plate and utensils to the seat on my other side.

"Eat up." Uncle Jack hoped our favorite breakfast food would make us feel at least slightly better.

"I made a list of everyone we still need to call. I didn't want to wake people up, but I think it's on the news now," Sarah said through a mouthful of bacon.

"You need to swallow first!" Katie reproached.

"Very true. And daddy's still on standby at the airport, so we don't know when he'll be here."

I wanted to be surrounded by family, but I could imagine Sarah was looking forward to being the one who fell apart, instead of the one who was supposed to be strong.

Uncle Jack wolfed down his food and went to do dishes at the sink. I finished my plate and brought it over, about to help him, but a piece of paper on the counter caught my attention. "This is your list?" I asked Sarah.

"Yeah. I think I'll go home with Katie and get some things, so we can stay here for a while. Then we can power through when I get back."

"I'll get it started while you're gone." Uncle Jack looked to Katie, knowing it would be best to finish before she got back.

"Thank you." Sarah grabbed her purse and headed out, so I finished the cleanup with Kyle while Uncle Jack made calls in the living room. In this case, dishes were definitely better than the alternative.

We made ourselves tea and coffee once we finished, selfishly hoping Uncle Jack could get through the entire list. He was at it for almost an hour before his cell phone rang, so he went to the backyard to talk to Mackenzie. You could usually tell it was her because he couldn't stop smiling, but today she was his rock like he was trying to be ours. He came with the intention of protecting us from the hard things and was doing a pretty good job so far.

Kyle followed me into the living room, where the list was down to a few names, all people Jack did not get along with. Upon close inspection, I saw the top of the list was actually instructions Sarah wrote out.

"Let them know what happened.
Don't beat around the bush, say DEAD.
Comfort until they can actually understand the funeral
information."

She had the address of the church and a nice hotel, as well as a list of people who would stay here with us. 'Dad' was at the bottom of it with a question mark.

I checked the three names left to call and saw a great aunt who never forgave Uncle Jack for not inviting her to his wedding, one of mom's high school friends who'd broken his heart, and Christopher Glass, with a note that read 'West Coast'. I would have changed my last name to no longer be associated with him in any way, but mom kept it, even after their divorce and the years she was with Ted, so I did too. It was weird, having his number in front of me when I had once spent an afternoon with Alex, calling every Glass in the phonebook to try and find him. My dad left us in the middle of the night when I was six years old, without a word or any way to contact him.

"We can call aunt Enid and Doreen, but I'm not touching that last one," Kyle warned.

Katie would be back soon, so we went for it. We used speaker phone, I made Kyle tell them what happened, then I gave soothing reassurances until they calmed down enough to write it all down.

"I'll take Katie to the park, so Sarah can do the last one," Kyle decided. "She actually likes the monster."

I would have followed him, because he made a good point, but my eyes caught the 'dad?' on the list of people sleeping here and I knew she would invite him if she called. I couldn't deal with him sleeping here on top of everything else. I understood that marriages fell apart, but to spend nine years with absolutely no effort to try and win me back or change my mind; he didn't deserve any better.

I dialed the ten-digit number with my hands shaking and my heart pounding. He might decide not to come. Or he might be snobby and unreachable, like that Hollywood cliché, in which case he wouldn't even take my call. I could cross his name off without feeling guilty, because I had made the effort, then forget about him.

Unfortunately, that wasn't the case.

"Hello?" a woman answered, half-asleep. That was why Sarah emphasized the West Coast.

"Does this number belong to Christopher Glass?" I wondered if it was the wrong number or if she was his new and much younger wife. They occasionally appeared together in the Star Tracks of People magazine.

"How did you get this number?" I got the feeling she was about to hang up and maybe block my number.

"From my sister?" I waited, but she needed more. "I really need to talk to him, please. It won't take long." I'd rehearsed it with Kyle for the other calls. With my nerves, I was sure I could get it out in less than thirty seconds.

"He's busy right now. I can take your name and number and have him call you back," she offered, but I had my doubts.

"It's Rachel Glass," I told her. "He can reach me at..."

"Rachel?" she said like she knew me, which I knew she did not. "Wait a minute." She didn't put the phone on hold, so I could hear her moving around, possibly nudging him, saying, "It's Rachel...I think so...I don't know."

I was about to hang up, more out of fear than anything else, when he said, "Rachel?" I recognized his voice instantly, not so much from my childhood, but from prime-time TV every Thursday, when I pretended to be asleep or doing homework in my room. I would never admit to watching his show, especially not to having seen every episode, but I couldn't help it. "Rachel?" he repeated, so excited to hear from me, which I was not expecting. "Is that you, honeybee?" Uncertainty laced his words now that I was taking so long to reply, but his old nickname had me biting my bottom lip again. I willed myself to recite the words I had so carefully rehearsed in my mind before dialing, but no sound came out. "Rache?" I could picture him pulling the phone from his ear to look at it and make sure I hadn't hung up.

"It's me," I said in such a low voice I didn't think he could hear me.

"It is so good to hear your voice. I was surprised when Tracy said it was you, since it's been so long, but your call just made my day," he continued rambling, because I still wasn't saying anything, and the silence would have been unbearable.

I took a breath to prepare myself and then went for it, a lot colder than the previous calls we made. "My mom died last night in a school shooting. There's a funeral on Thursday at 11 am at

Reverend Connors' church. If you come, there's a motel right beside the cemetery, so you can be in and out in no time. But you also don't have to come." It was mostly said in the same breath before I went quiet, so he could reply.

There were a lot of partial words, like "what..." or "are you..." sounds before I couldn't take it anymore. It might be his acting, or he may truly be shocked and in pain, but I didn't want to care.

"Goodbye." I hung up feeling like a terrible person my mother would be ashamed of. I knew I was horrible to him, but part of me wanted him to hurt as much as I did.

"WE'RE MAKING LUNCH." Sarah poked her head out from the kitchen, with Katie in her arms.

"No you're not." I tried to act normal.

"Uncle Jack's cooking, we're supervising," she amended before the phone rang.

"I've got it." I picked up before she could say anything, so she went back to the kitchen. "Hello?" I fully expected it to be him, to yell at me for how blunt I was and the way I hung up, which was the only reason I volunteered to answer. I didn't want Sarah to know what I did.

"Hi sweetie." My heart stopped when I realized it was Alex's mom. I was ready to fight and be mean to him, but she was crying, and I was having trouble not doing the same.

"Mrs. Sims." I walked over to the staircase and sat in the middle of it. "I'm so sorry." She lost both her sons, and with the names released, she would never be able to walk around town without someone glaring at her for what Phil was a part of.

"I have no words to tell you how sorry I am for what my son has taken from so many people, for what you are going through right now. I had so much trouble working up the courage to call you..." I couldn't exactly argue, so I stayed silent. "If you hate me like everyone else must, I understand..."

"I don't hate you Mrs. Sims. I don't understand what

happened, or how Phil got involved, but I don't think you did anything wrong," I assured her.

"I wish I could take you in my arms and make it all go away. I know you're not okay, but...are they taking care of you?" she asked.

"My uncle drove back this morning and everyone else is on their way." No one could do anything, but at least I wasn't alone.

"I also called to let you know about the funeral. It'll be a small family affair, but I thought you would want to be there."

"Of course." I couldn't imagine not being there.

"We're only having one funeral...for both of them. I can't go through it twice," she warned, which got more silence from me. "I understand if that changes your mind and I don't think Alex, or anyone else would blame you."

"I'll be there." I put my hand over my heart and rubbed it as if that could make it feel better.

"It won't be in the papers, we're calling to let everyone know so there won't be any...so only the right people come," she sounded heartbroken. She gave me the details and apologized some more, then I tried to find words that wouldn't come before she finally told me, "Take care honey," and hung up.

"What took you so long?" Katie saved me the seat beside her. "I had him make yours with the white cheese instead, but now it's cold."

"I had some phone calls," I said loosely, focused on the grilled cheese instead of my siblings. Kyle looked guilty, but Sarah made me feel terrible.

"I guess you sent him to the hotel?" she looked around the room and figured out who I called.

"The motel on Fairview." I took another bite, but I could feel her disappointment.

I caught Kyle's smile, but Sarah was furious. "You sent him to the run-down motel in front of the cemetery?"

"That's cold," Kyle was impressed.

"Rachel, he's our..." Sarah was in full-on reproach mode, but she stopped that particular statement when I glared at her. She put her sandwich down and looked at me, incredulous.

"Come on, let's eat," Uncle Jack suggested. He usually got us to do what he wanted by using his military voice. This time he just sounded defeated, but we listened. "Can we agree to disagree on the matter?" I got the feeling he didn't make the call because he was on my side, not because he didn't want to wake him up with bad news.

"I'm sorry. I know it was wrong. I just think this is hard enough as it is, and I don't want him here. In her house. With us. If you're over it, that's great for you, but I'm not. I can't." I did not want to fight with her.

"I'm sorry too. You shouldn't have had to do that. I'll call him back and let him know he can stay at my place, since we'll be here." She put her hand on my shoulder, then went to make the call.

"I would have done it," Uncle Jack said once she was gone.

"I couldn't risk you inviting him here," I admitted.

"I would never do that to you. And I don't think Sarah would either." Kyle and I looked at each other like we weren't so sure, then went to the backyard with Katie.

❧ 4 ❧

ARRIVALS

When we came in from the backyard after an intense game of freeze tag, Uncle Jack was asleep in the lazy boy. "Why is he sleeping in the middle of the day?" Katie asked from Kyle's arms.

"He drove all the way from Virginia last night," I reminded her.

"Is that far?" she asked, so we went to the coffee table and I took a sheet from my sketchbook to show her.

I was halfway through a rough map of the east coast when a big, black escalade pulled into our driveway. A lot of cars had driven by and slowed, but they all kept driving when they saw our blinds pulled shut.

"Who's that?" Katie asked, then rushed outside before we could answer.

WE GOT to the porch as Peter Hartley, my cousin's fiancé and the lead singer of Hartley, stepped out of the driver's seat. It hit me that I had never seen him sad before. I saw him drunk once, at mom's Cinco de Mayo party, and he got angry when we visited and the paparazzi came too close to an eighteen-month-old

Katie, but he was never sad. Most of the time he was joking with Kyle and you couldn't wipe the smile off his face. He was always saying he was the luckiest guy alive and he 100 percent believed it. Today, for once, his customary dark jeans and black t-shirt perfectly reflected his mood. His hair had none of its usual products and his face was inches away from crying. He didn't look up to see us though, he went straight over to the passenger's side, where Haylie climbed out. Her auburn hair was up in a ponytail and she wore her Harvard sweats.

"She's dressed like you are." Katie looked from me to my twenty-three-year-old cousin. I looked down and saw we were both in black sweatpants with grey t-shirts, only mine carried the Lake George PD's logo instead of an Ivy League school's.

"Uncle Pete!" Katie ran over once they got close, so I went to Haylie.

"I can't believe she's gone," she told me with tears in her eyes as we hugged.

"Me neither," I agreed before Katie came to hug her, so I went to Pete and we all came inside.

"Long time no see," Uncle Jack said when his daughter walked in. He'd woken up and got himself a beer since we left.

"Law school is intense." She hugged him, then took a seat on the couch, with Katie in her lap.

"When's the wedding?" Uncle Jack asked Peter, taking a sip of his beer.

"May 12th," Pete filled him in, although I'm sure they called him like they called us when they decided on it. Mom put it on the calendar in the pantry before she even hung up the phone.

"You'll get an invitation in the mail," Haylie added calmly, with none of her usual wedding excitement.

"Are you hungry? Thirsty?" I knew they'd had a long drive.

"Starving," Haylie admitted. The clock read 3:30, but time was passing so slow I was sure it should have said midnight.

. . .

WE ORDERED Chinese food and purposely talked about things completely unrelated to what we were going through. We covered Pete's new album, Haylie's classes, and asked Uncle Jack for the millionth time when he was going to make a move on Mackenzie.

"Other than my kids," he made a point to include me and Kyle, "she is the most important person in my life and I can't risk it." He stuck to his standard answer.

"Is she coming?" Haylie asked.

"She has another month in Turkey, but she sends her...her heart is breaking for you guys," Uncle Jack broke slightly, so Pete took over the conversation and told us all about the tour he was going on with his band.

"You going with him?" Kyle asked Haylie.

"I wish," she said before the doorbell rang.

"I'll get it." I was a few feet away when the door opened and my brother walked in.

"Jared!" I bridged the distance so he could take me in his arms and twirl me around. For the longest time, this was how I greeted and was greeted by the men in my family. Mom said it was my dad who started it with Sarah, but I chose to ignore that instead of stopping. I tried to put an end to it a few years ago, when I thought I was getting too big. They all assured me I would never be too big for their bear hugs, so they'd continue it as long as they wanted to, regardless of how old or big I got. I went with it because it made me feel safe, like a little kid who had yet to discover the world wasn't rainbows and unicorns. Jared held me close before he put me down and went to Kyle, giving him one of those hugs guys do, where they pat each other on the back lots of times. They did a few more pats to get a semblance of a hug out of it.

Toby came in once Jared was out of the way, and held me just as tight as my brother had.

"We also have a bunch of Chinese food." Sarah followed Toby in, so I helped her bring the containers to the dining room.

"I'll add some settings." We had ordered extra food for them, but didn't think they'd get here until we were done eating.

"We'll need to bring up the other table." Jared looked around and saw mom's seat was the only one left. We were a full house, even if it felt empty.

AFTER SUPPER, Haylie, Katie and I made cookies from scratch. Rather, Haylie had us measure out ingredients that she turned into cookies. Mom was great at anything that you made by taste, but baking required exact measurements that she didn't see the point to.

"They smell delicious," I said when Haylie opened the oven to take out our first batch, so I could put in the second.

"The one good thing my mom ever gave me," she said as if she didn't care, which Katie might believe, but I didn't.

"Her loss. Our win," I said of Haylie, and the cookies. We let them cool a bit before she put them on a plate for me to bring out.

"HAYLIE MADE COOKIES." I found some of the guys in the Adirondack chairs in the backyard and put the warm, gooey cookies in front of them.

"When is everyone else getting here?" Toby asked after a rather large bite of cookie.

"Matt finally got on a flight this afternoon, so he'll be here tomorrow," I shared.

"What about dad?" Jared asked me. I was confused as to how he could talk about him like he was a person now. I didn't know if their grief was making them forget, or if they thought mom was the only one he hurt, but I didn't ever want to talk about him.

"Tomorrow," I answered anyway, because I had all the travel information. Not his specifically, but it was the only flight coming in from LA. "He's staying at Sarah's."

"He didn't want to stay here?" Jared wasn't there for our earlier conversation, but Uncle Jack was on alert. Jared lived in LA, so maybe there was some reaching out or an apology, but it never reached me. Jared was usually better at reading his audience.

"This isn't his house," I got upset, even though I didn't want to. "He decided he wanted to leave us. If he wants to ease his conscience by coming to her funeral, fine, but I'm not making it easy and I will not call him daddy, or talk to him, or let him put a foot in her house." Once I started, I couldn't stop. I left him there, shocked, and went back towards the house.

PETER WAS SITTING on the swing set, so I went over and sat beside him instead of going inside. I had a tendency to cry when I was angry, and I was trying not to do that in front of Katie.

"Mind if I sit?" I asked.

"Go for it," he assured me, so I took the middle swing. It wasn't so much a swing set as ropes with planks of wood on a tree, but I liked sitting on them more than swinging anyway. Ted put them up for us kids the first summer he lived here, but he and mom probably used them more than anyone.

I was barely there a minute before Jared came and took the swing on my other side. The three of us sat there for what felt like an eternity before I broke the silence with "I'm sorry." I hated him even more for all these fights he was causing with my siblings.

"It's okay. I know you've always hated him, but...you might not have all the information." For the first time, I understood that they had forgiven him. They didn't forget what he did or decide to move past it...they justified it and forgave him.

"I don't care anymore why he left, Jared. All that matters is that he did. He kissed me goodnight and then he was gone when I woke up. Even if he had the best reason in the world for that... it was nine years ago. He's never visited, never sent cards, never called. I don't care what his excuse for leaving was, because he never came back," I defended why it upset me. How could they not get it when it was so simple to me?

"I have a show next month in New York City. If I can arrange to get you there, will you come?" Peter asked to change the subject when Jared wasn't saying anything, and I loved him for it. He became one of us almost immediately after he started dating Haylie three years ago.

I was about to tell him I would ask mom, but I couldn't. Then I realized that I had no idea who I should ask, because I didn't know where I would be living in a month, or who would take care of me. "I don't know who I'll be living with. Maybe," I told him, slightly disconcerted.

"Don't worry Rache, if no one else wants you, you can live with me and Toby in LA," Jared teased, but I knew the offer was serious.

"Or you can come on tour with me. We go back to Montreal during breaks, where winters are cold and have snow. Wouldn't you miss snow in LA?" Peter always teased Toby and Jared about moving to LA where it's hot and sunny most of the time. You would think it would be the other way around, but Peter absolutely loved his hometown, that he had us all come to, and was a huge fan of winter sports. I love looking out a snowy window on Christmas, but I think I could adjust to a city where you don't need a winter coat.

"Thank you," I told them with a smile, because I did appreciate it. But on the inside, I wondered if it would come to that, or if it would be worse. My best bet would be to move in with Matt and Sarah, help out with Katie, stay at the same school... only even that sounded awful. I could never go back into that auditorium. And how could I face school without Alex?

· · ·

Eventually we all went inside, where a few of us played poker.

"I raise," I said, pushing one of my chips into the middle of the table as Uncle Jack left us to take Mackenzie's call in another room.

"I fold," Pete sighed, not entirely convinced it was the right move. He wasn't much of a gambler, even when it came to plastic coins with no real value.

"I see your blue chip and raise you a red one," Jared said confidently, adding another chip without taking his eyes off Toby. They'd been having poker tournaments since they were kids. It went from being for random toys and candies, to girls' numbers, to whatever they were interested in at the time. The last game was always a chance for the loser to win it back, so they usually went home with exactly what they came with. They used to let me win whenever I played with them, but a few years ago they decided I was old enough to lose (or win) on my own merit.

"I see your raise and raise you a green one," Toby said smugly.

It went on like this for a while, with me matching every one of their raises, until they both looked to each other and folded.

"You could give your father a run for his money." Pete had followed the game with a new appreciation for my lying abilities once he saw the cards I was bluffing with. Toby's reaction had been to vehemently claim he let me win.

I looked at Jared because I could feel his eyes on me, expecting another burst of anger, but I ignored it. I also ignored Pete's second comment, when he told us that he'd been watching one of his movies when Haylie admitted he was her uncle. It was when Pete gave a running commentary of his films that I couldn't. Haylie never talked about her mom, so she probably didn't tell him about my dad either. Even if Pete didn't know that he wasn't supposed to talk about him, I still couldn't listen.

"I'm making teas, anybody want one?" I offered, getting up.

"I'll come with you," Toby beat Jared to it, so he had to stay with Pete. Which was better, because Jared could participate in the conversation without getting rude or upset.

"Still won't forgive him?" Toby asked me once we were out of earshot.

"It's not like he's begging me for my forgiveness and it's keeping him awake at night. He's off in his nice big house with his lovely wife and new son and his perfect life and he doesn't need us. The only times I've seen him since I was six was in magazines or on TV. My favorite was the one where he pretended to be nice, but he was actually a serial killer, who buried the bodies in his flower bed? I think it captured his true nature." I was a little bitter, but Toby was used to hearing me go on like this.

"Do you still take out the old home videos on your birthday?" He knew me better than I wanted him to. Watching those videos and his TV show were my most shameful secrets.

"Yeah," I reluctantly admitted. "This year I couldn't find our home videos, so I snuck into Sarah's room when I was babysitting and took her Flight Season One DVDs." There was a tear in the corner of my eye, but I purposely kept a smile on my face. He smiled too.

"How was the call?" I don't know if he heard, or just figured we were the ones who called him as well.

"His wife answered. I don't think she liked me, but then I said my name and she woke him up to talk to me."

"What did you say once you finally had him on the line?" We had gone through multiple scenarios of what I would potentially say if he ever showed up on my doorstep. At first, I just wanted him back. At one point there was a lecture about never doing it again. We stopped years ago, when I realized he wouldn't be coming, so the activity was pointless.

"I told him when the funeral was, then let him know he could stay at the crappy motel beside the cemetery." I knew it was uncharacteristically mean of me, even if we both knew he deserved it.

"Rachel," he reproached with the hint of a smile.

"You know what he did," I defended myself.

"I'm not blaming you. I just hope we have the story back-wards or something, because although you act like you couldn't care less if he rotted in hell, a trained eye like mine can tell he broke your heart, but you still love him with all the little pieces. Which is why you hate him."

"I thought you were a chef, not a shrink." I didn't bother arguing with his assessment.

"I don't know brains, I know you," he explained. "Come here." He held me close and pretended he didn't see the few tears that fell. I could say they were because of my mom and Alex and the shooting, but he knew. He also knew that a few of them were for him, no matter how hard I tried to deny it.

WE WENT BACK to the living room with our teas and I sat beside Jared, so he could wrap his arm around me and know we were good.

"I'll probably go see Bridget," Kyle answered Uncle Jack's question about everyone's plans for tomorrow.

"I need someone to drive me to a church tomorrow at ten o'clock and pick me up a little later," I blurted out. I hadn't found the right moment to bring it up, but I did need to get there.

"Is it about Thursday?" Jared asked, unable to say, 'the funeral'.

"No, it's about...it's Alex," I admitted, biting my bottom lip.

"I heard about him on the radio. I'm so sorry," Haylie said. I hadn't mentioned him other than to Sarah. It wasn't that his death wasn't affecting me; I simply reached a point where my heart was so broken you couldn't make the pieces any smaller. I felt both of their losses, but I couldn't deal with all of it at the same time.

"It didn't occur to me there were others," Jared admitted

awkwardly, having looked around, confused, until he understood that Alex was one of the victims.

"His mom called this afternoon and asked me if I could come. She knew a lot of people wouldn't." I swallowed at the bitter taste in my mouth. "She also wanted to make sure I'm okay. Whatever that means anymore."

"Why would she think people won't come? The church will be packed. Everyone loves Alex," Jared pointed out.

"She's only having one funeral for both sons," I said quietly. Everyone understood, except for Jared, who clearly hadn't watched the news, and Peter, who looked to Haylie. Peter had met Alex at least a dozen times over the years, but I wasn't sure we ever mentioned Phil.

"Alex's brother was one of the deranged mental cases who killed my mom, as well as his own brother," Kyle explained with clenched fists.

"Phil?" Jared looked at Kyle like he was crazy, but the rest of our looks confirmed it. Haylie closed her eyes and winced as if she had been slapped, but I knew it was psychological pain from seeing it in her head like I was. I wondered if it was better to imagine it than to have seen the footage. "And you're still going?" Jared asked me, more to make sure I was prepared for what might happen than to question my decision to go.

"He's my best friend." It was as simple as that. "And she's right. No one else will show. Which is terrible because I saw the footage this morning. Alex jumped in front of bullets that were aimed at mom. That's why he died. He deserves to have a billion people there and I don't think it's right to turn my back on him because he was related to a monster," I said with a determination I did not feel. I loved Alex and knew I had to be there, but I would rather stay here and avoid the outside world.

"I want to make sure you'll be okay if people do show," Jared explained himself.

"I won't be okay either way," I pointed out.

"I can drive you on my way to Bridget's," Kyle offered. Even with their off and on, there wasn't a doubt in my mind she would be my sister-in-law someday.

"Don't be ridiculous, I'll go with you," Uncle Jack assured me. I considered telling him he didn't have to, that I would be fine with Alex's parents, but I gave him a grateful smile instead.

Since Matt wasn't back yet, Sarah and Katie slept in my bed again. It was better than being alone, and I was emotionally drained by the time we called it a night, but it still took me hours to fall asleep.

5

ALEX

"Are you okay?" Kyle came and sat beside me while I waited for Uncle Jack, wearing the dress I wore two years ago for Ted's funeral. It was very close to no longer fitting, but I added a sweater and a pair of black tights to make it work.

"Yeah, of course." I adjusted my current meaning of okay to 'not currently about to fall apart'.

"I can come too. Drag Bridget or cancel on her. Alex was family."

"I'll be fine. Uncle Jack has the big, strong arms that keep bad things away," I teased. "And I don't know if Bridget would forgive either of those options."

"I get a free pass," he argued.

"She does too." I remembered how distraught she was in the parking lot. "Give her a hug from me." I gave him one as well, then let him leave.

"READY?" Uncle Jack asked when he eventually came down the stairs with Haylie, Toby, Jared and Sarah.

"What are you doing?" I asked. They were all dressed in black.

"The whole point of family is not having to do these things alone." Jared put an arm around me. I wouldn't have blamed any of them for not coming, but they had known Alex. And Phil. When Jared came home for Easter, Phil had taken him out for coffee to ask questions about being a firefighter in LA, and the application process. Not what you would expect from someone who was about to...you know.

"I have to leave at eleven to get Matt at the airport, but I wouldn't miss this," Sarah assured me.

"What about Katie?" I didn't want her there, even though she spent more time with Alex than most of them.

"Pete brought her to that indoor gym place. Otherwise he'd be here too." Haylie gave my shoulder a squeeze.

"Thank you," I told them before we headed to the van.

I HADN'T BEEN outside our yard since it happened, hadn't seen anyone since we left the school, so I stared blankly out the window while we drove. Everything looked the same, but it felt cold and dark, like the van, that used to hold so many happy memories of road trips and silly sing-alongs, but now only reminded me of being helpless, waiting in it while my mom died inside.

"We can stay in here until it starts," Sarah offered, putting her hand on mine. We were parked, but I made no effort to get out of the van and join the other mourners.

"No, sorry. My mind was elsewhere." I turned to face her instead of the window and gave what I hoped to be an encouraging smile. I pulled to open the door, but hesitated. Uncle Jack and Jared got out of the front seats, so I took a deep breath and stepped out, adjusting my dress while Haylie and Toby got out.

"You've got this." Uncle Jack put his hand on my shoulder

before the five of them followed me to the entrance of the church, where Alex's parents were waiting.

"Rachel, sweetie, I'm so glad you came." Mrs. Sims met me before we even reached the steps and took me in her arms. She gave me one of those big, motherly hugs mom would give me when I was having a bad day. Unlike the hugs I normally got from Alex's mother, this time she didn't let go. It was slightly awkward, because we had never been this close, but she needed a child to comfort and I could use a mom hug.

"I'm so sorry," I apologized again for her loss, and because she would still have one of her sons if he hadn't tried to protect my mom.

"My boy was a hero, just like your mom." She gave me one last squeeze, then took a step back. She looked at me wistfully before tucking a loose strand of hair behind my ear. "You look beautiful." She shook her head and sighed before turning to everyone that came with me.

"Thank you so much for coming." She gave them each a hug, then said, "It means a lot," tearing up before walking off to someone else who arrived.

"KYLE," I paused when we opened the church doors and found him there.

"It's the only black thing I had in the car," He explained the leather jacket he'd zipped up over his white t-shirt, paired with black track pants.

"I really was okay," I argued.

"I know, but I wouldn't have been."

"Off again?" I asked of Bridget.

"She wasn't ready to see people, but she understood."

"There's more people in there, right?" Haylie asked him as we were told to go inside. Sarah took my hand so I would follow her.

"Nope." I felt horrible for Alex, and his mother when the priest was the only one there. Alex's family always came to

Reverend Connors' church with us, so being here, in a different church, with a strange priest who'd probably never met Alex...it felt wrong. When he told us to take our seats, I saw the pew had been reserved for 'Alex's friends', but we were the only ones there.

"This isn't right. There should be more people." Jared was upset.

"It wouldn't have been the right people," I argued. Other than the seven of us, there was Alex's parents, his grandparents, a cousin from Arizona, and Phil's girlfriend, Alice, who was crying her eyes out in a pew marked 'Phil's friends'.

I gave a running commentary as they all came in, getting big eyes from Haylie when I told her who Alice was. I knew she was wondering the same thing as me. Did Alice know this was going to happen? Who she was dating?

I CRIED with Uncle Jack's arm around me and Sarah holding my hand the whole time Alex's cousin gave his eulogy. He managed to make most of us cry with the few memories he shared, but if Alex's death had been an isolated incident, I would have been the one up there, with a lifetime of stories to tell everyone how amazing he was. Losing my mom made the world go dark, but Alex was me losing my other half.

WHEN MR. SIMS went up to eulogize Phil, I almost forgot what he'd done and actually felt guilty for not wanting to be there. He kept bringing up things that happened years ago, like when Phil defended us from bullies in the park; memories I couldn't reconcile with the Phil who had murdered people.

"One day when Philip was in elementary school, there was a fire that destroyed the apartment building one of his classmates lived in. No one was injured, but they lost everything. My son came to me and said he couldn't imagine what it would be like to lose his home like that, so he went up to his bedroom and packed a box of toys. Not the old ones he didn't use, but even his favorite one, a basketball he'd received for his birthday. When he was done with his own room, he convinced his brother and other kids in the neighborhood to give away their toys as well, and asked me to drive him to the motel the displaced families were staying in. He put the boxes in front of the door without knocking and came back to the car. When I asked why, he told me that if it was him, he wouldn't want people making a fuss of it. That was my son." Mr. Sims talked through his tears. I suddenly felt like I couldn't breathe.

I BROKE AWAY from my family and walked out of the church as quickly and as quietly as I could. I sat on the steps and tried to take deep breaths before giving up and burying my head between my knees to wait for it to pass. It didn't, but I wasn't alone.

"I couldn't handle it either." Alice's voice made me look up. I hadn't noticed her sitting in a ball by the doors I rushed out of.

"I'm sorry for your loss," I said, but my heart wasn't in it.

"Thank you," she ignored the falseness. "I didn't know," she added, coming to sit beside me. "It's what everybody is wondering, but he didn't tell me."

"I didn't think you knew." I wasn't sure if it was a lie or the truth. We weren't close, but I spent a lot of time with her in the past year when we were both over and the boys had chores to do. Still, if I didn't see this coming for Phil, nothing would surprise me about her.

"He left me a letter, to explain it."

"What?" I hadn't been listening to the news, but I was sure someone would have filled me in if we knew why they did something so cold and unlike themselves.

"It was under my pillow when I got home. I don't think anyone wants to read what he wrote, or if they do it's to turn it around and twist it into something it wasn't."

"He killed a bunch of people," I reminded her, not sure how you could spin that to make it worse. Phil, Michael and Corbin weren't depressed or troubled. Not just from looking at them, but from having spent so much time with them and knowing Phil more than half my life. I went door to door with him for that toy drive, and waited in the back seat while he dropped them off.

"Your mom and Alex were accidents. He never would have wanted to hurt them."

"But he did," I argued, getting upset. The funeral was more appealing than this conversation.

"I know. And I will never forgive him. I'm not saying it justifies what he did, but at least I can see how Phil saw it."

"I don't care," I said, cursing the tears that now fell from anger. I hated Phil for everything he did that night, but also for the guy he seemed to be when I was growing up. Now I was disliking Alice for defending him.

"My mom says it helps to make sense of things. To understand," she offered.

"How lucky to have a mom to help you through this," I said through clenched teeth. I hated that I wanted to know. "What in the world could make what they did make sense?"

"They had a list. People who were doing bad things without getting caught."

"If only there was a cop he could talk to." She wasn't helping herself, but she also looked guilty. Not like she knew, but like one of the names might be on the list because of her. I shook the thought away and focused on what I knew. "My mom and Alex were the most decent people I know, who wouldn't hurt a soul. I could say they would lay down their lives for others, but I don't have to because they actually did." I felt bad for how I was saying it, and the way she kept reacting like my words slapped her, but she looked like she understood and would take it.

"Your mom and Alex must have gotten in the way, but if you

look at the other people who died…you know…" She could see the wheels turning in my brain, but I didn't want to go there.

"It wasn't their place," I told her before the church doors opened and she walked off to her car. I turned to the people coming out and saw Uncle Jack off to the side, looking like he'd seen the conversation.

"You okay?" he asked, putting his arm around me.

"She basically told me the shooters were vigilantes killing people who thought they were above the law." I was pissed, but he looked like the words cut him to his core, so I added, "Except mom and Alex. They were mistakes."

"I didn't pay attention to the others," he admitted. He lived here to be close to us, but he didn't join the community. "They were teenagers and teachers." He didn't look convinced. "What?" he asked when I shrugged.

"And parents…Mom got reprimanded a few years ago for trying to have one of them sent to jail even though no one was pressing charges. His wife and daughter claimed they were incredibly clumsy on a near-monthly basis."

"He was abusive," he understood.

"I've heard rumors about some of the others…bad things, but…it doesn't justify what they did," I argued before Mrs. Sims came up to me.

"Don't worry, it was hard for me too." She took me in her arms, which made me feel guilty again for hating her son, but I got the sense she hated him a bit too. Either way, she kept her arm around me until we got to the cars, where she hesitated, because she was bringing me to hers.

"I'll be right back," I assured her before going to the van, where my family was waiting.

"Is it okay if I ride with Mrs. Sims? You guys don't need to come," I assured them.

"Sarah left to pick up Matt, but we can get groceries to give you guys some time?" Uncle Jack offered.

There had been many comments on our lack of almond milk

and other healthy, 'granola' things mom would buy whenever she knew they were coming.

"That would be great," I agreed, getting hugs before going back to Mrs. Sims. My family was here for me, which was what I needed, but she needed someone to take care of, and she probably thought I would come alone.

I ALWAYS FOUND the idea of a wake ridiculous. I didn't see how eating and drinking together could help us grieve, or honor the person who died. The ones I had been to were either depressing or became a party, which I thought we should feel guilty for. We shouldn't go from being sad to laughing about the good times, right?

ALEX'S PARENTS asked me trivial things during the drive, an attempt to pretend everything was normal, but my heart sank when we got to the house. I thought I knew what to expect, having been to my share of funerals and wakes, but I hadn't known Alice had work, the grandparents drove home so they wouldn't be out after dark, and the cousin was on his way back to the airport. This left me sitting on the couch with Alex's parents, staring at enough food to feed an army, that no one was touching.

"We appreciate you coming, Rachel," Alex's father told me. I could see it was hard for him to say, and to deal with everything, but he meant it.

"Alex was my best friend," I said simply.

"I always thought the two of you would end up together," Mrs. Sims smiled through her tears. "I know you always insisted you were just friends, but I knew that someday you would realize it was more and then I would have my daughter and the two of you would live happily ever after."

"Nicole," Mr. Sims warned, pulling his wife close.

"It's okay," I said, even though it wasn't.

"He loved you so much," she tried to hold the tears back.

"They boys have some things they won't be using anymore, and they're still good, some of it is new, if you want to look around..." he tried to change the subject, but it took him nearly five minutes to get the words out. The look of revulsion on my face didn't encourage him to go any faster. I didn't mean to look so appalled, but I couldn't imagine going through their things, or even going into his room without him now. It seemed wrong.

"We understand. We thought it would be better to give it to you than to some stranger," his mother explained.

"I'm sorry, it wouldn't feel right," I told her.

"We didn't think you would. We're thinking of giving it to Goodwill. That's what the boys would have wanted," she said. "But there were a few things we couldn't stand to give away," she tried to make me understand, so I looked to where her eyes kept darting and saw a box on the floor in the corner. It was closed, but not sealed, so I could see the material from Alex's letterman jacket poking through the top. He would have been wearing it the other night if it was nice out. He would rather spend the day out in the rain with only a t-shirt than to wet his team jacket.

"I can't take those," I told her.

"Of course you can. Alex would have wanted you to. They're all things he has forgotten at your house a million times. Some of it is actually yours." The look on her face was so hard for me to deal with. It was breaking her heart to part with these things, but it was too painful for her to look at them. Giving them to me was a compromise, where she wouldn't have to see them every day, but they'd be with someone who understood how much they had meant to him. I understood then that no matter how much I argued, the box would magically find its way to me.

"Thank you," I reluctantly gave in as the doorbell rang.

· · ·

Mrs. Sims was at the door before her husband or I even had the chance to stand. By the time we got to the vestibule, she'd already ushered the newcomers in.

"We have sandwiches and salads and cake and everything," she told them.

"Thank you, so much, but we have to get home. My daughter's asleep in the car," Matt told her instead of saying this was the last place he wanted to be. Mrs. Sims didn't want to be alone.

"I'll go grab my purse." I went to the living room and took my bag from the floor, then came back to find Alex's dad handing the box to Matt.

"Don't forget your box," he told me.

"Thank you," my brother-in-law said, confused.

"Come by any time Rachel. You're always welcome," Mrs. Sims told me when I hugged her.

"Did everyone else leave?" Matt asked once he was in the driver's seat. The box was in the back with me, Katie was nowhere in sight.

"There were seven people other than us at the funeral, including the priest," Sarah told him.

"No one came back. Just the three of us," I shared.

"No wonder she didn't want us to leave," Matt sighed.

"I think it's hard to be alone in a house that used to have two teenage boys in it," I defended without getting into it.

Matt was usually the one who drove us home when Alex and I babysat Katie. He always dropped Alex off first, then we would listen to Bob Seger until we got to our house, with both of us singing along to every word. We barely had time for one song, but today he was driving so slow we could have played three. I wasn't looking forward to getting home and seeing she wasn't there either.

. . .

ONCE MATT PARKED in the driveway, he came around and gave me a big hug. "I'm so sorry kid," he told me.

"Me too."

Sarah and I took his luggage and had him take my box, which was a bad idea because it was not the type he could carry in one hand when Katie ran into his arms.

We let them catch up and brought his luggage down to the spare bedroom, where Sarah and I plopped onto the bed.

"Let's stay here for a week or two?" I suggested.

"Until everyone forgets what happened and the pain is a little less intense?" she wrapped her arms around me, completely getting it.

"This can be our fortress of solitude." I got a smile from Matt, who came in to get something from his bag.

"But then we'd miss the funeral," she sighed and got rational on me, but kept running her fingers through my hair.

"Would that be a bad thing?" I asked.

"Don't you want to say goodbye?"

"Funerals aren't for saying goodbye. We just went to one and I don't have any closure. I feel worse because they shoved everything I'm missing in my face. Eulogies remind you of what you've lost."

"They suck," she agreed. "But we still have to go."

"I can't wait for it to be over."

"Look on the bright side, sweetie, everyone will be here. Even your dad is coming." Matt tried to cheer me up, handing me a bag full of different flavored KitKat bars from his trip. He knew how important family was to me, and how much I loved it when we all got together. But the argument collapsed when he mentioned *him*.

I made an odd grunt of disgust as Sarah gestured for him to zip it. "Thank you for the chocolates, and I'm glad you're home. I missed you." I gave them each a hug before going upstairs.

. . .

I WENT to my room to change into normal clothes, but the box was right there on my bed, staring at me, so I brought it to the floor and opened it. I put the letterman jacket aside, not needing to look at it to know exactly what it said, or how the material felt, but then I decided to put it on. Maybe it could help with the chill that settled in my bones.

A sweater I had left in his room was the next item, but when I lifted it out of the box, Alex was there, smiling up at me. It was the same picture that usually stood on his nightstand, of the two of us at a barbecue, holding melting ice cream cones and grinning with his arm around me and mine around him. I held the picture close to my heart, then carefully took out his lucky ball cap, and the brown teddy bear he used to hide whenever I came over, so I wouldn't know he slept with it. At the bottom of the box was an old, worn and frequently read copy of The Lion, The Witch and the Wardrobe. It had been our favorite book. We spent an entire summer searching through every wardrobe and cupboard in both our houses, and any other ones we could find, looking for Narnia.

6

THE NIGHT BEFORE THE END

I went down and found the others in the kitchen, so I sat beside Toby and put my KitKat bars in the middle.

"We were trying to figure out what to do that doesn't involve leaving the house," Haylie explained.

"This is how Football Sundays were born," Jack shared before looking straight at Sarah. "You were napping so she couldn't come with us, but she didn't want to stay home and miss out, so she called and invited everyone over. We would play for hours, every single Sunday after that."

"We still play," I argued, but they looked at me like I didn't know what I was talking about. "Thanksgiving," I pointed out, since it was like the Sundays I remember from when I was little.

"We should play." Sarah got up from where she'd been resting her chin on her palm, leaning against the counter, suddenly alert. We looked at her, none of us in the mood to play. No one wanted to be happy without her. "Come on, when Ted died, we played. We came home from the funeral, all dressed in black and we played in his honor. If this was anyone else, she would have us playing by now," she insisted. She had a point. I wasn't sure she would play if it was one of us kids, but she did say it helped her cope when her dad died, and for Ted. She hadn't given up until she had each of us running across the backyard.

"This is ridiculous," Toby said with a smile before we all went outside.

WE MADE Uncle Jack and Matt the captains, as they were the oldest, so the teams were Uncle Jack, Haylie, Jared, Sarah and me against Matt, Toby, Peter, Katie and Kyle. My team was losing by a touchdown, which might have had something to do with Sarah and my inability to not give Katie the ball when she asked. I threw the ball to Jared when I saw her coming.

"Touchdown!" I called when he landed in the end zone.

"I thought you were professionals?" Haylie asked with a smile, as Matt, Toby and Kyle had been quarterbacks with scholarship offers and the whole nine yards.

"They also have me," Peter reminded her. By the time I met him, he was already a famous rock star, but he told us he was in band in high school, and avoided all team sports. Regardless of his skill, it was impressive how fast he could run in skin-tight jeans.

"And me!" Katie beamed at her dad, fully aware that she intercepted more passes than anyone else.

"It's always the cute ones." Sarah chased her daughter around the field as the tickle monster.

AFTER WASHING UP, we gathered in the kitchen for a pizza party, as my mom liked to call them. She got frustrated after constantly having to explain to the pizza parlor that we wanted half meat lovers, half vegetarian, a quarter no onions and so on. Her solution was for us to make our own pizzas, which turned out a million times better than anything we could have ordered.

We took out everything you could possibly imagine putting on a pizza and had pans ready with different kinds of crusts.

Over the years, we became more sophisticated and now boasted whole wheat, gluten-free, and this weird seaweed thing Kyle swore was delicious, in addition to the plain white crust. Our pizza parties were legit; a crucial part of every birthday party or celebration we have.

Toby's dream was to open an eatery of alternating fanciness, so he manned the oven. "Welcome to Toby's," he smiled when I handed him my pan. It was slightly experimental, with chicken, pears, spinach, lots of cheese and some crumpled up bacon.

We ate the pizzas as they came out, with people standing at the breakfast nook, sitting at the table, walking around with paper plates. We were everywhere, and it would have been like any other family supper, but the thrill of having everyone together was dampened by the empty chair at the head of the table. Just like none of the guests would be sleeping in mom's room, no one was eating in her chair.

"Is that a pizza or a salad?" I watched Toby make his own pizza while mine cooked. He had about a foot of spinach on the dollop of sauce he put on his whole wheat crust.

"Don't knock it until you've tried it," he warned. It used to drive mom crazy how I wouldn't try new foods if she spiced up a recipe, but I would eat almost anything Toby said was good.

"I love spinach, but that's more greens than pizza," I argued before he added pepperoni.

"Dude, there's meat in that," Haylie warned her brother, biting into her own pizza. She chose Kyle's green crust with pretty much only cheese on top.

"I'm hoping that's what pepperoni is made of," Toby agreed.

"Since when do you eat meat?" she was shocked.

"Since he moved in with me." Jared proudly showed her the meat lovers pizza he'd made himself. Bacon, prosciutto, sausage, pepperoni, ham...they were all there.

"He also quit smoking," I shared, since I had been nagging for him to quit ever since he started. He never smoked in high school, then he spent a year at a fancy cooking school in Paris and got hooked.

"You win some and you lose some," Toby shrugged.

"See babe, this is what happens when I go to Montreal with you instead of coming here," Haylie called to her fiancé, who rolled his eyes at her. Our Christmas lasted from the minute school let out for winter break, until the night before we had to go back. We had the traditional Christmas movies, baking and tree decorating, but Ted built us a skating rink in the backyard, and we had enough land for snowball fights, fort building, ice sculpting...everyone stopped by whenever they could, but you had to be there the whole two weeks if you wanted to see everyone and not miss anything. Alex always suggested we skip winter carnival at school to hang out in my backyard instead.

The memories that made me smile now had me biting my bottom lip. Christmas would never be the same. Nothing would.

I was lost in thought when Sarah came over. "Looks like it's someone's bedtime," she said of Katie, who was asleep in her father's lap.

"I'm not tired," she said when Matt stood to bring her downstairs.

"Of course you're not," he assured her, knowing she'd be out within minutes.

"Can Rachel read me a story?" she asked.

"Of course."

While Matt carried her to the room, I went upstairs to get The Lion, the Witch and the Wardrobe. I took the whole box down to the spare bedroom's cupboard of lost boxes, and found Katie all tucked in.

"Which one is this?" she asked of the new cover.

"This was my favorite book," I explained before diving in.

I was a page and a half in when she asked, "Is Alex with nana?"

"What?" she caught me off guard.

"Is that why he's not coming over, and you have his coat?" she asked, noticing it wasn't Kyle's which I think some of the others assumed.

I guess mom was the bigger loss, so none of us had told her about anyone else.

"Yeah, he's with nana." I tried to smile, like they were in a happy place now.

"That's okay, because he really likes her food," she decided. "But I miss him."

"I miss him too. A lot." I got under the covers with her and she cuddled into me.

"And I miss nana. Mommy was crying when daddy hugged her."

"There's going to be a lot of crying," I warned.

"But no one else is going to be with nana, right?" she asked.

"I hope not."

"Mommy said I couldn't go."

"We can't," I agreed.

"And you can't go see Alex?" she asked.

"Nope."

"Does his coat make you less sad?" she asked. "It's like a hug."

"Kind of," I agreed.

"He used to give me a hug, but then he'd put me over his shoulder and I would fly," she shared.

"I can do that if you want," I offered.

"No, I think it's only an Alex hug."

"That's fair." I remembered the teddy. "I think I have something Alex would want you to have."

"How do you know?" she asked.

"Because I know Alex." I went to the closet and got his teddy bear. It was better off with her than forgotten down here, and she was someone he definitely cared about.

"Enough reading, bedtime," Matt said as he came in, followed by Sarah.

"What's this?" My sister asked of the new teddy.

"Alex gave me his teddy, and his coat to Rachel because he

loves us," Katie said, which brought the waterworks, but also reminded me of what his mother had said this morning, how he loved me so much.

Matt wrapped an arm around me and kissed my forehead while Sarah got Katie tucked in again. We all kissed her, then went back to the others.

"This sucks," I said to them on the stairs.

"So much." Sarah put her hand on my shoulder when we reached the top.

EVERYONE WAS SITTING in the living room, so we joined in. I put myself between Uncle Jack and Toby, while Sarah and Matt shared the bean bag from the playroom.

"She's really gone, isn't she?" It was Kyle who said it after a few minutes of us sitting there. With the school closed and no one working, we hadn't been forced back to our normal lives yet. We were still in our bubble. Alex's funeral had made it real for me, but it was easier to try and pretend this was a horrible nightmare we could wake up from. No one else said it out loud, but it had crossed our mind that this could all be a strange, terrible mistake. I stared up at the picture mom had blown up and framed onto the wall, of all of us a few years ago at Thanksgiving. It was mom, Uncle Jack, Kyle, Jared, Sarah, Matt, Katie, Haylie, Toby and I, all smiling in the late fall colors after a football game. She chose it because no one was posing; the smiles were from having fun being with each other.

The silence went on forever after Kyle's statement until Sarah said, "Why's your hair so long Jared? You're beginning to look like Haylie." Mom used to say that to him, hoping it would convince him to get a haircut, especially the summer he wore it long enough for a ponytail. Jared and Haylie both have green eyes and wavy auburn hair, so you could confuse the two.

"That's okay Sarah, Jared can help me with supper," Kyle came to Jared's defense with our sister's non-existent cooking skills. She could actually ruin Kraft Dinner, which I thought was foolproof. Luckily, she was great at carving, which came in handy around the holidays.

"Kyle, sweetheart, that's not a hat, that's mommy's underwear," Uncle Jack joined in. Being the youngest, I had missed out on most of their embarrassing childhood moments, but I heard the stories and saw the videotapes. Kyle used to run around with these pink, flowered underwear on his head, which he insisted made him invisible.

"Knees together," Haylie reproached in the exact same tone mom used to when I was wearing a skirt. I used to be somewhat of a tomboy, but I always loved dresses, so I would sit with my legs wide open, for all to see. I blamed it on having two brothers, and a sister who only wore dresses at weddings.

"Was that for Rachel or for you?" Jared came to my rescue by accusing Haylie, causing everyone, especially my cousin and her fiancé, to give him shocked expressions. Only Peter's was real, because the rest of us knew mom had warned Uncle Jack to be weary of her constant study sessions. Mom apologized and ate her words when Haylie's study buddy turned out to be a twelve-year-old prodigy who didn't seem to realize sixteen-year-old Haylie was a girl, and a knockout at that.

"Freeze." I didn't say it loud, but everyone stopped laughing. Mom would practice her freeze on us, to keep it fierce and intimidating for actual perpetrators. Whether we were trying to sneak out, stealing cookies or attempting to leave a conversation when she wasn't done talking...it was her catchphrase.

"I swear, I nearly had a heart attack when she caught me smoking. I was a grown man, but it terrified me," Toby admitted, biting his nail, the nasty habit he picked up to replace the deadly one he quit. Mom had taken part of the credit, saying she put the fear of God and the Law in him.

"You might have technically been an adult, but you were never going to stop being her baby," Uncle Jack told his son, speaking from experience, and from mom insisting she had six kids, not four.

"Kevin told me that whenever she yelled it while they were working, pretty much anyone who heard it would stop. Even he did sometimes." Matt was on the basketball team with Kevin when they were in high school a million years ago. He had his fair share of freezes from sneaking Sarah in after curfew.

"I never thought I would miss the freeze," Kyle admitted.

"How could she do this to us?" Sarah blurted out before crying. No one answered, because we all knew mom. If there was a chance she could have helped, there's nothing that could have stopped her.

None of us wanted to disturb the silence that had settled until Kyle, who'd been looking around in the cupboard of the TV stand, took out a box of videos and put one into the VCR. When he pressed 'play', I felt the tears coming on again, but this time I let them. Everyone else turned to the screen as soon as they heard her voice. It was a home video of all of us at our grandparents' place in Lake Tahoe, and I was young enough to need Sarah's hands to help me walk. We all looked so happy, without a single care in the world. He was there, taking mom into his arms and kissing her, like they were still two teenagers who'd just fallen in love. I was transfixed, taking it all in, until the screen went black.

Without saying a word, Kyle put the tape back where he found it and Sarah turned the news on. I fell asleep on Toby a few minutes later, not interested in rewatching the footage from the shooting. I was vaguely aware of Jared carrying me up to my bedroom and kissing me goodnight.

❧ 7 ❧

THE FUNERAL

I woke up in my clothes and for a minute, I forgot. Or at least it took me a moment to figure out why my heart felt so heavy. I looked at the clock and saw it was only a quarter after five. I tried to bury my head back into the pillow, to go to a place where mom was still across the hall and Alex would be ringing my doorbell soon, but it didn't work. Other than football yesterday, I hadn't done much moving, whereas I usually jogged every morning.

I got dressed and tiptoed downstairs, careful not to disturb the quiet while everyone else was sleeping.

On a normal school day, and even most days this summer, I would walk out of my house just in time for Alex to jog around the corner. He'd make me roll my eyes by jogging on the spot while I locked the door and tied up my hair before joining him. This morning, everything was different, and I knew exactly why I hadn't felt an urge to go running since the shooting.

Alex and I would go around the block, stop at a park to stretch, then go back to my house after about forty-five minutes, where mom would have a cup of coffee for him and a tall glass of water for me. Today, since I had to outrun the pain and tears that kept trying to blur my vision, I got to the park and kept going, running until I could feel the blisters and it felt like my feet were on fire. Even then, I didn't go home. I looped back around to the park we stretch at and put my foot into one of the rungs of the ladder. I bent down to hold the stretch, but cried instead. I was grateful it was too early for kids to be there, because I definitely would have scared them away.

We'd chosen this park for the water fountains, so I went over and splashed my face, trying to erase the tracks of my tears, before running back home. It was nearly seven o'clock when I walked into the kitchen to find Kyle and Uncle Jack at the break-fast nook, drinking coffee.

"Morning," I tried to sound normal, but they knew I'd been crying. Uncle Jack poured me a cup of coffee and my brother handed me the vanilla milk that I poured in abundantly.

"What time do we have to be there at?" Kyle asked before Matt came in with Katie.

"Reverend Connors wants us there for eleven," I said while Katie climbed up into my lap.

Uncle Jack had just poured the last of the coffee into a mug for Matt when Sarah, Toby and Haylie came in the kitchen door, dressed like they had gone for a run as well. Kyle made a fresh pot while Uncle Jack got started on breakfast.

"We saw you at the promenade, but Toby couldn't keep up. We had to walk back," Haylie shared, so Toby gave her a half-hearted tap on the arm before getting them all waters.

WE HAD MOVED on to the dining room by the time Jared and Peter joined us. I realized our melancholic mood was affecting Katie when she kept cuddling into people without saying anything or smiling, so I went upstairs to get ready.

I knew we were a lot of people, so I took a quick shower, slightly on the cold side, then put on my second black dress in as many days. I usually went for bright colors when choosing summer clothes, but mom bought me the dress when I was her date to a formal event at the precinct. A lot of the cops she worked with were also divorced, so I wasn't the only daughter there that night. I pulled a bit of hair from either side into a pearl clip in the back, so my hair would be out of my face, but still mostly loose. Mom had kept her hair short, but she loved it when mine was long and down, which she said she would do all the time if she had beautiful curls like mine.

I was downstairs by nine. So was everyone else; sitting in the living room, showered and dressed in black. It was impressive, considering we were so many people with only three showers. I guess we were all concentrating so hard on the task at hand, to keep all other thoughts at bay, that we were efficient.

The minutes stretched on without us doing much, other than entertaining Katie. At ten, we realized it was almost time to leave and we weren't ready for what awaited us. Time slowed down, but everyone was also in a hurry. The house was clean and ready for the gathering afterward, but Jared suddenly felt the need to clean some gutters with Toby's help. Kyle noticed a pattern of grass that he'd missed. Katie wanted French braids. So, Haylie and I made cookies.

The others watched us running around like chickens with our heads cut off. They were exasperated and sympathetic, but didn't know how to help.

"DOES anyone else have anything they need to do?" Uncle Jack asked at 10:50, causing us to look around at each other, trying to find something, but drawing a blank. "Let's go then." He led us to Pete's escalade and his JEEP.

I rode with Jared, Kyle and Toby in Uncle Jack's JEEP and quickly saw we should have listened to Reverend Connors and come early. His idea had been that we'd greet everyone as they came in, which sounded horrible to me, but it looked like we wouldn't have to worry about that. The only reason we were able to park at all is that there were two spots reserved for us near the front. It looked like everyone I had ever met was gathered inside the church; my entire school, their parents, mom's precinct...

"There's so many people," Katie said when we got out of the cars. She took my hand to walk into the church, but Reverend Connors was waiting at the doors, so she let him take her up into his arms.

"We sent some people ahead to the cemetery. It would have been a fire hazard," he told us, taking me in for a hug. Kevin and Michelle were there as well, waiting for us to get in so they could guide us through the crowd. I gave Kevin a hug, but when we pulled apart he kept his arm around me until we got to the front pew, which they had roped off for us.

Kevin sat behind me with Michelle, who gave my shoulder a comforting squeeze. It was only when I sat down, took a deep breath and looked around that I saw *him*. The man at the end of the pew I thought was empty was someone I hadn't seen in almost ten years: my father.

He looked like he was going to come over to offer his condolences or say hi. I panicked, not ready to deal with this too, when someone behind me called, "Jack!"

It wasn't my name, but I turned because I recognized her voice. She crossed the aisle at record speed and took my uncle in her arms. After seeing Sarah the first few days before Matt came home, I understood that even the strong ones who hold everyone else up need someone to fall apart with. She was his person.

"Mackenzie." I gave her a sad smile as she held me close.

"I know it means nothing, but I am so sorry sweetie." She gave me another hug.

"But you being here means everything," I assured her, looking to my uncle before she made her way through the row and we all sat down.

. . .

REVEREND CONNORS WENT UP to the altar and spoke, the emotion overwhelming some of his words. With Jared's arm around my shoulders and Toby holding my hand, I was focusing on ignoring Christopher Glass and not listening to a word the Reverend said about my mother. So, I heard every word while stealing frequent glances at and continuously thinking about my father. Tears had welled up in my eyes, so he was slightly blurrier every time I looked over, but I could have sworn he was also crying. He looked absolutely devastated. I kept reminding myself he was an actor, so pretending to feel things he didn't was what he did for a living.

When the Reverend was done, he invited other people up to talk. I was about to stand, since we had written a few words, but at least eight other people were already lining up to talk.

The first person to reach the pulpit was Diana, the girl who'd run in front of our car, and the reason mom rushed into the school. Or, as I kept reminding myself whenever I tried to find ways I could have prevented her death, the reason mom knew what she was getting into when she went in without backup. The reason we knew to call Kevin and the ambulances that saved other people. Diana looked out at us, not a dry eye in the room, and shared her story.

"Most people don't know that I was close to Mrs. Glass, which is part of why I loved her so much. She would always chaperone school dances or activity days, and she would ask me how I was doing. Not in the way teachers do, but like she really cared. I was terrified she knew something was wrong, but she didn't press, she let me pretend. Or so I thought. The next time I saw her, I still told her I was fine, but she knew I was lying. I wasn't afraid of her finding out the truth anymore, I was hoping she would. For years, I'd been suffering in silence because no one else noticed, and my mom was so in love with him that I couldn't stand to break her heart. I had people ignore bruises, doctors pretend to believe I fell down the stairs, again...but Sierra Glass looked into my eyes and knew. When I told her, crying my eyes out and worried I'd done something wrong, she took me in her arms and promised me no one would ever hurt me like that again. I thought she would disappear after she arrested my step-father, but she brought me to her gym and took a self-defense class with me. We did something like that almost every month until I finally understood what she kept telling me. That I deserved more. That I shouldn't value someone else's happiness over my own well-being. I felt like I had to come up here and speak because Mrs. Glass wasn't a regular cop; she cared about people. When I ran into the street that night, I felt the same fear from years before. I was convinced I would never be safe again, but there she was. She found me. And even if she isn't here anymore, she did everything in her power to keep her promise. Thanks to her, no one will ever hurt me like he had. She not only saved my life, she showed me that I could have one." I had never talked to Diana before, but she would sometimes smile at me in the hallways, and now I knew why.

I was still processing Diana's story when a girl in crutches went up to thank mom for tackling the shooter whose stray bullet had reached her.

Kevin was up next. He had wiped all of his tears before walking up, so he could at least start off coherently, but he looked at her picture on the altar and tears ran down his face, which made them fall down mine. He talked about how she showed him the ropes when he was a rookie and how he became a part of our family. "As soon as I began working with her, she had me over for their family suppers and celebrations, open invitation. Michelle was invited too, but one week she was out of town, and I was playing pick-up basketball with Matt, who'd gone through a breakup, and I told him he had to come with me to this supper. It took some convincing, but he did, and I don't think he's left since. I'm not surprised he fell in love with Sarah, with that entire family, because if I hadn't already been married to Michelle, I would have done whatever I could to be a part of what they had going." He got us to smile through the tears before sharing work anecdotes to make us laugh.

Bridget's mom, Fay, went up after him. She was mom's best friend and usually had us all in stitches whenever she came over. I wasn't surprised when she turned her eulogy into a stand-up comedy routine mashup of their decades together. She cried through her laughter, but so did the rest of us.

Finally, it was time for Sarah and I to go up with Uncle Jack. He let us stand in front, with one hand on my shoulder and the other on hers.

"I had no idea how many people would have such wonderful things to say about my mother," I tried to will my voice into sounding less broken. "You would think that we wouldn't have anything left to say, but I could go on for days to tell you all the ways I had the best mother in the entire universe. How her heart is where our home is, and no one had more heart than her. I could tell you that everywhere she went, she turned strangers into best friends, lost souls into kindred spirits, and excelled at picking up your pieces to put you back together."

"We could tell you all that," Sarah continued, wiping a tear like it had no business being there. "But if you're here today, you already know how amazing she is. Was." She stopped, and I grabbed her hand, so she took a breath and went on. "If you met her, she made it a point to get to know you, and if you knew her, you couldn't help but love her. She loved and took care of us with a fierceness you don't often find, and she taught us to walk through the world with our heads held high, and to leave places at least a touch better than they were when we arrived."

"But if you saw her off-duty, you know she didn't teach us about fashion sense," I said as they played the montage of mom in her sweaters.

"But she did teach us to see the world through her eyes, which is so much more beautiful than we could have imagined." Sarah held tight to my hand, as Uncle Jack leaned forward.

"My sister was an angel here on earth, that we were blessed to spend time with, even if it would never have been enough. Keep your eyes on the sky, because it just got a whole lot brighter," he finished while the other pallbearers came up.

Reverend Connors said a few last words about the cemetery and the gathering at our house afterwards, then he walked with Sarah and I behind Uncle Jack, Kevin, Jared, Kyle, Toby and Matt, who carried her coffin to the hearse parked out front.

W E WALKED behind the hearse through the rows of tombstones until we got to the freshly dug grave that would be hers. Once there, I stayed back with Sarah, Haylie and Mackenzie, not wanting to be near her coffin. It was eerie how it was sunny, and the birds were singing, but everything inside me was black.

Mom's captain led the other officers into the twenty-one bells ceremony that we chose over the three-volley salute, because none of us needed to hear more gunshots right now. Kevin brought Sarah the folded up American flag, and she tried to stay strong, like mom had when she was the one receiving Ted's flag.

When the pallbearers came back, and they lowered her into the ground, I turned to look away and buried myself into Jared's chest. When I looked out, I was shocked to see Katie with *him*. She had always been good with strangers, but she had her arms around his neck and leaned into him like he was familiar and safe, two things he definitely should not be.

We each had white and red roses to put on top of the coffin. I couldn't imagine her actually being in the cold wooden box, but I knew she was. They were putting her into the ground and she would not be coming out. We watched as they shoveled some dirt on top of the coffin, then put a bouquet on top of the tombstone, that read:

Sierra Lee Glass (Harris)

1957–2003
Devoted Mother, Sister, Aunt, Neighbor and Friend.
She saved the world, one person at a time.

MRS. SIMS CAME over to me when it was over, with her husband standing uncomfortable behind her. "We're not going to come to the gathering. We don't want to take away from celebrating her," she told me, looking around at the people staring. Some were hiding it, but others were very obvious about their hatred of her son. "Sierra was a wonderful mother. I can tell because she raised you, and she was a second mom to my boy. She was the best person I have ever known." She smiled at me and I returned it, sadly, feeling so guilty because of the way they were treating her, and because of how many people were here today when it was only us yesterday.

WE GOT SCATTERED on our way to the parking lot, not bothering to find the cars we came in. Toby, Jared and I walked to the house together. Walking should have taken longer, but there were a lot of cars taking the same route to the same place, and some people stopped along the way. I forgot that walking would bring us past the high school, so Jared put his arm around me and we walked extra fast as soon as we spotted the yellow crime scene tape.

Our house was big enough for the four kids, the cousins, the uncle and anyone else who needed to stay over, but we would have needed at least two extra houses to accommodate all the people who wanted to tell us how sorry they were for our loss. I heard it about a thousand times before the food was gone and guests slowly trickled out.

By the end, it was only the family, Bridget and Fay, which only made it slightly easier to avoid the unwanted guest in my mother's house. He was helping out and talking to the others like he had every right to be there with us. I looked away whenever I felt he was going to look at me and switched rooms whenever he walked into one. I didn't know which would hurt more, if he managed to talk to me, or if he still had no interest in me.

🙦 8 🙤

THE SENTENCE

"Who has the address?" Jared asked once all the guests were gone.

"It's that old video rental place. They converted it into offices." I went with her once to drop papers off.

"Do we have to do this now? Can't it wait?" Kyle had tried to leave with Bridget.

"I'd rather get it over with," Jared shrugged, looking as exhausted as I felt.

"Exactly." Sarah looked around for her keys. We were all anxious for things to get back to normal, but it would never be the normal of last week. "Are you riding with us?" she asked me when I handed her the keys from the hook, since I was currently holding her child.

"If anybody wants to come with me..." With everyone else gone it was hard to avoid Christopher. As soon as I heard his voice, so close to me, I froze. I knew I wanted to run away, to be as far away from him as possible, but part of me wanted to see what he could say to make me want to listen to him. "Rachel?" he asked, a few inches behind me, but I refused to look at him, and couldn't find the words to speak.

85

"We're not interested," Kyle came to my rescue, putting himself between us.

"Kyle," Sarah said it in her warning tone, the equivalent of counting to three.

"It's okay," Our father assured her, looking crestfallen.

"No, it's not. You don't get to pretend to care now that it's convenient. You're here because they wanted to let you, but you better not talk to us, or come anywhere near my sister." A culmination of his anger and pain made Kyle speak up.

"Kyle!" Sarah skipped the other numbers and went straight to ten, looking shocked. She called after him, but he walked out and slammed the door.

"I'll wait in your car," I told Sarah, taking her keys and bringing Katie with me, while she followed Kyle.

I PUT Katie into her car seat and was walking to the other side when I heard someone walk up.

"It's me." Matt put his hands up, showing me he had no weapons, before putting them back in his pockets, trying to look way too casual. We could still hear them arguing in the yard. "Sarah told your dad he should take his rental car and meet us there."

"We weren't ready to see him back in the house." The last time I saw him there, he was my dad; a constant in my life, who kept me safe and happy. Having him walk around after a decade without contact, just as nothing felt safe or happy anymore...it was too much.

"She understands. We're all a bit on edge, and this isn't the time to push things."

"The sooner he flies back to his family, the better." I watched him get into his rental car and drive off alone, which I had to admit made me happy. Every time they got close to him, I couldn't help but feel betrayed, even if I knew they'd never want to hurt me.

"You're his family too," he pointed out, but I wasn't the one who needed to be reminded.

"He walked out on that a long time ago," I argued before Sarah showed up with Haylie and Peter. I let him take the seat beside Katie in the mini-van, and got in the back with Haylie, who put her arm around me and let me lean into her the whole ride.

WHEN WE GOT to the tiny law firm, they sent us to their 'large conference room'. Judging by the offices we passed to get there, we wouldn't have fit anywhere else. Once we took our seats, the lawyer called out each of our names to make sure everyone in the will was present. "Christopher Glass, Sarah Watson, Jared Glass, Kyle Glass, Rachel Glass, Katherine Glass, Haylie Harris, Tobias Harris and Kevin Nought."

We all said something to let him know we were there.

"I'm sure you're all anxious to find out who gets what, but the first issue when minors are involved is always custody," the lawyer explained, as if any of us cared about money at the moment. He was giving off a new and incompetent vibe. "How many are minors? Under eighteen?" he asked, glancing at his sheet, then back at us. "That would be Kyle, Rachel and..." he tried to figure out who Katie was.

"My daughter," Sarah explained.

"You can put your hand down," he told Katie before turning to me and Kyle. "The two of you are in the custody of your...of Christopher Glass until you reach the age of majority." He handed Chris some papers to sign, most likely his legal obligation to do what he should have been doing for the past nine years. I watched him sign my life away, but Kyle wasn't taking it.

As much as I had hoped I could stay with someone I liked and who loved me, like Sarah, I was pretty sure that legally, I would go to Christopher. I knew he wouldn't have the guts to refuse in public. I was still mad, especially when Jared said, "It's going to be okay," and put his arm around me. Of course it was okay for him, he was friends with the enemy.

"I'm in the Naval Reserves Officer Training Corps at Virginia Tech. I had parental consent and I don't need his permission to go." Kyle's anger was directed at our father and the lawyer, but the look he gave me was all guilt. "I enlisted. Unless he petitions the court to have mom's consent revoked, I have to go," he told me while they went over his paperwork, like he'd already done the research.

"You were going to leave me for college anyway," I assured him, with an overwhelming urge to enlist and defend my country as well.

"But not like this," he argued.

"You didn't go through hell week for nothing," I pretended I was okay, but my chest felt like I wasn't getting enough air.

"Rachel Glass will remain in the physical custody of Christopher Glass until her eighteenth birthday. Pretty straightforward." The lawyer didn't know our history, but Jared knew enough to pull me closer.

"Moving on, there are education funds for each of the minors, which they will have access to when they go to college," he simplified it. "The main residence, the Tahoe Lake House and the van go to her four children, to do with as they please. All other assets are to be split evenly, put in trusts for the minors. The contents of the black cage in the garage go to Kevin Nought, and I have one of these for each of you." He handed me a pile of envelopes, in her handwriting, that I passed to everyone. "That's the gist of it, although the actual document has some legal jargon and fine print," he added like we needn't bother ourselves with the rest of it.

"I'll take them." Haylie gave the lawyer a fake smile before we all walked out.

"Rachel, I..." Christopher came over to me, but Kyle immediately intercepted.

"I think you should go home," Kyle said it calmly, but he

made it clear it wasn't a suggestion. I had no idea what I would do once I was alone in a house with him.

"I'll call the house tomorrow." He walked out alone.

THE PARKING LOT was deserted by the time we said our good-byes to Kevin, who was going to make room in his garage before coming to get mom's weapons.

The ride home was silent, until we got to the kitchen and Uncle Jack asked how it went. He and Mackenzie had done all the cleanup while we were gone.

Mac gave me a hug when she found out I had to live with my dad, then we all sat around the dining room table and waited for Haylie to finish reading the full document. When she was done, we agreed to sell the van. The house was harder, because none of us wanted to lose the home we grew up in, but it wasn't like any of us would be able to live in it. It took us until ten o'clock to agree to sell it, because mom was what made it home. We unanimously decided to keep the summer house on Lake Tahoe, with everyone promising we would go back to spending our summers there.

Sarah, ever the organizer, made a list of what we had to do in the morning. We needed to start bright and early to pack up the entire house before everyone had to get back to their lives. Once she was done, we went to bed, exhausted.

IT WASN'T until I was in bed, under the covers, that I let myself cry. Not for all that I had lost, but because I didn't understand why mom would be so mean as to send me to the man who broke my heart and never cared enough to put it back together.

I didn't blame Kyle for sticking to his plan, that he fought with mom for weeks over, but it sucked that I would have to go into the lion's den alone.

9

TUCKING AWAY CLOTHES AND MEMORIES

I tossed and turned from all the thoughts running through my head and decided against going for a run. I put on my sweatpants and headed for the stairs, but froze when I reached mom's door. It was wide open.

"I was going to get a head start, so you guys wouldn't have to, but..." Sarah let the thought linger, so I put my arm around her and we went downstairs together.

OUR PLAN WAS to start packing at eight, so we could put in a full day's work, but still have time to decompress afterwards. Uncle Jack handed us each a steaming mug of coffee when we got to the kitchen, then opened the fridge to get me the vanilla milk.

"Who wants breakfast?" Toby offered when he got to the end of his cup. "We can't work on empty stomachs and a friend gave me a tweak for a recipe I need to test out."

"A girlfriend?" Katie asked.

Toby looked back at her, then at me, who was sitting beside him. Mom used to try to set him up with nice girls from the area, in the hopes that he wouldn't move away. Haylie and Sarah sent him on a million blind dates with all of their friends. It wasn't until we went to visit him and Jared in Los Angeles that mom understood why her plan never worked. How there was nothing wrong with the girls, except the fact that they were girls. When Toby came out to us, mom's biggest concern was that if she had known, she might have found him someone he could actually fall for, and prevented him from moving away.

"A friend from work, who is a girl," Toby agreed.

"Breakfast, but then we get to work," Sarah declared.

Katie and I helped Toby gather all the ingredients for his macadamia nut pancakes. She ate more white chocolate chunks than she put into the mix, but it was nice to see her smile.

Finally, after we ate all the pancakes we could stomach, we went up to mom's room and stood in front of the door. Uncle Jack went in first, so I took a deep breath and followed him inside. The room was exactly as we had left it before going down for supper that day, what now felt like lifetimes ago. The sheets were a mess and the bed was unmade since we'd spent the day watching movies in it. Her pajamas were still neatly folded at the foot of her bed, waiting for her to put them on.

We started with the closet, since it would be easier than her personal items, but it was harder than we expected. We'd brought up a garbage bag and a box for Goodwill and thought we were ready.

We made it through half the clothes in her closet before I shifted and grabbed shoes. Sarah kept most of them, saying I could borrow them when my feet grew, which wasn't likely. At 5 foot 4, I was a whole foot shorter than my brothers, and nearly half a foot away from my mom and Sarah, who were both 5'8". I apparently scored the recessive short gene.

"Come on Rache, pass the next hanger," Jared said once the shoes were done and I was taking out the empty shoe rack. We knew they had no interest in her clothes, but if we had to be there, then so did they.

"Here." I passed him her cop uniform, so he knew exactly

why I stalled. There were three in the closet and two more in the laundry room.

"Those can't go to Goodwill," Mackenzie stated the obvious.

"Can we give them to Kevin?" Kyle suggested.

"Her name is on them," Sarah pointed out, slightly choking up as she ran her fingers over the 'GLASS' stitched onto them. I didn't want to wear her uniform, but getting rid of them would be like losing a part of my childhood. Our mom was a cop and it had a huge impact on all of us.

In the end, Sarah and I each took one, and it was agreed that we would let Kevin take the rest of them with her guns.

"What's on the last one?" Toby pointed to the black garment bag. I'd only seen it in pictures, but I knew exactly what it was, and so did Sarah, Haylie and Mackenzie.

I unzipped the bag to show them the white splendor of mom's wedding dress.

"What do we do with it?" Jared asked, understanding that she must have kept it for a reason.

"She wanted you girls to wear it. Our mom rented her wedding dress and she was so sad," Uncle Jack shared.

"I didn't want it," Sarah said, looking guilty, but it was only in the past couple of years that she warmed up to Christopher. I wouldn't have wanted to wear the dress mom wore to marry a heartless monster who walked out and broke her heart either. Now though, it being hers was way more important than who she married in it.

"Can I have it?" Haylie asked timidly, feeling the same as me. Mom got married when she was younger than Haylie, so the dress was perfect for her and absolutely beautiful. "It'll be like she's there with me." Haylie had always been more of a daughter than a niece.

It was when I watched her carefully folding the dress back into the garment bag that it hit me: mom would never see me walk down the aisle. Or graduate high school. She would never even meet my future husband. Every memory I made from now on would be without her.

I already had tears running down my cheeks, so I went ahead and grabbed the sweater at the top of the pile in her closet. I put it on and wrapped my arms around myself, looking up to the others like I just couldn't. Their faces mirrored mine as they all came forward and chose one as well. Mom had a collection of sweaters that she wore year-round. The one I was wearing had a little girl with brown hair holding her mother's hand, with pompoms all over it to represent the balloons they were holding. Some of the sweaters were relatively normal, but we all went for the ones with weird pictures or sayings. We spent years teasing mom about them, but not a single sweater went unclaimed. We kept them for ourselves, for Katie...Mackenzie had been the only one to defend mom's sweaters, so she kept her favorite; blue like the sky with a plane stitched on the front.

"My flight leaves soon, if we wanted to take a break?" she suggested, since I was still sitting on the floor.

"Sounds good." I took her hand and stood up, getting a hug before we went downstairs.

"I'LL TELL the guys I can't make it yet. We can postpone the tour." Sarah and I pretended we weren't listening to the conversation between Haylie and Peter.

"Even I don't want to be here, babe. Run while you have the chance."

"I'm here because I don't want you to go through this alone, Hales. For all intents and purposes, Sierra was your mother," he completely understood. Unlike my dad, her mom sent cards for each of their birthdays and Christmas. There was always a check inside, but nothing else.

"I know," she swallowed. "I'm not alone. I have five siblings here with me."

"Call me if you need me and I'll be back in a heartbeat."

"I love you." They kissed before he went to put the bags in his car.

"He's definitely a keeper," I told Haylie when she sat between me and Sarah on the couch.

"Worth all the groupies and the paparazzi," she agreed before we got up to see them off.

"I can't believe you flew all the way here for less than twenty-four hours," I shook my head before hugging Mackenzie.

"This is five days of semi-unauthorized leave," she argued.

"You're crazy," Kyle told her.

"He'd never ask, but…"

"He needed me," Mac finished for Haylie.

"I'll see you at Christmas?" I asked.

She hesitated, aware that I would be living with a monster and everyone was scattered across the country.

"I promised her we would all spend it at my parents' old place in Tahoe," Uncle Jack came back from the escalade with Pete and filled her in.

"I don't break promises, so I will be there." She gave me one last hug and Peter assured me he'd figure out the concert thing, before we watched them drive away.

WE WENT UPSTAIRS to tackle mom's drawers, and Matt took Pete's job of occupying Katie. Bathing suits, socks and bras went straight to the garbage and Goodwill, but Sarah and I each kept a pair of boxer short pajama bottoms, hers plaid and mine with duckies. We each used to have a matching pair, and I remember how special I felt when I was her twin.

"Garbage?" I figured when I opened her underwear drawer.

"I wouldn't dump that," Uncle Jack warned.

"I don't think any of us want her underwear," I pointed out.

"As the brother who used to read her diary as a kid, I would go through it," he argued.

"Okay, then everyone out while Haylie and I go through it."

Sarah exchanged a look with Uncle Jack, who put his hand on my shoulder and guided me out the room.

"What's that about?" I asked him on the stairs. I could tell something was going on, but I didn't want to go through her private stuff either.

"I didn't want to see her panties," he said, like it was a valid explanation, before we made lunch. We received a plethora of casseroles and salads yesterday, so I took out everything we didn't need to heat and finished setting the table as Sarah and Haylie came down.

"Was he right?" I asked them.

"Nope, nothing much," Sarah shrugged without looking at me.

"Nothing?" I pressed.

"Something battery operated we think belonged in the garbage anyway," Haylie told me in a whisper, a plausible story I wouldn't want to question. I wasn't sure I wanted to know the truth, so I pretended I believed them.

KATIE NAPPED AFTER LUNCH, so Matt came up to help us. There was something about us all wearing the silly sweaters that made me feel like we would be okay, even though we were done with the clothes and moving on to the memories.

WE DID the night tables first. On one side there was the phone, her little black book of phone numbers, an unloaded gun (which we all stood back to let Uncle Jack take care of), a pad of paper, pens, and the reading glasses she'd had to buy a few weeks ago. On the other side, there was the book she was in the middle of reading and would never finish, some crossword puzzles she would never solve, and her diary. It was no secret that mom kept one, and I always knew it was in her bedside table, but I'd never felt the urge to come looking. If I had wanted to know what mom was thinking, I would have asked her. My siblings felt the same, and even Uncle Jack stood there, none of us wanting to see the entry it was open to.

"I have an idea," I said, going to my room and emptying the spare sheets from the chest at the foot of my bed. We put the uniforms and the diary inside, as well as anything else we found and wanted to keep, like photo albums, scrapbooks and random trinkets. Sarah promised she would keep it safe at her house for me.

At long last we got to her jewelry box. "Certificate of Authenticity," Jared read from the box on top. Inside was a beautiful diamond necklace with emeralds.

"Can I have these?" I asked, reaching for these small, purple button earrings mom had made for Halloween when she was a teenager.

"If I can have this." Sarah grabbed the charm bracelet that made mom even more of a baby whisperer. The bells on it jingled and mesmerized even the fussiest of babies.

"Oh my God!" Haylie picked up the seashell ring mom lost at least once every time we were at the Lake House.

"Nobody wants the expensive thing in a velvet box but you're fighting over dollar store costume jewelry?" Uncle Jack thought we were being ridiculous.

"She wore these," I said simply. Sarah did keep the expensive thing, that we could all take whenever we wanted, but the other less expensive but well-worn pieces took a lot of bargaining. Even Kyle took what was most likely a cracker jacks ring to give to Bridget someday.

BY EIGHT O'CLOCK, we were done with mom's room, so Uncle Jack and Toby took the boxes to Goodwill while we heated up some casseroles.

. . .

THAT NIGHT, when I went to bed, I wore one of mom's shirts along with the ducky boxers. Even though they came from her drawers, they still smelt like my mom, which made me feel close to her, and the void a tiny bit smaller. For the first night in what felt like forever, I didn't toss or turn.

10

MOVING ON

It was amazing how much stuff each of us had in the house. At first, everyone thought they'd be helping me and Kyle move out, since we were the only ones who still lived there, but everyone had at least one box of stuff, and most had three or four. Or ten. It wasn't only me and Kyle moving out, it was packing up every memory from over twenty-five years inside the house. Even with the extra help, it took us the entire weekend, packing up the final boxes into the U-hauls on Monday afternoon.

"I could climb into the back and he would have no idea," I said wistfully of the middle-aged, balding man getting into the truck that would bring my stuff to L.A.

"You would rather spend days in a box driven by a stranger than to fly there first class with dad?" Sarah asked like I was being ridiculous. She was wearing the snowman sweater mom had been looking for, which we found with the Christmas decorations. Sarah insisted it wasn't her, and that if it was, it was because mom wore it out of season, but here she was doing the same.

"Definitely," I didn't even hesitate.

"What do we do now?" Kyle asked. Tomorrow morning was

the decided time for everyone to get acquainted with their new normal. Except for Matt, who'd gone back to work this morning.

"A Farewell supper," Sarah suggested.

"You said See You Soon," Katie corrected, wiggling so she could get out of her mom's arms and come take my hand. It was breaking my heart to look at her, knowing I was moving half the world away from her after being there nearly every single day since she was born.

"A See You Soon Supper sounds good," Jared assured her.

"Bridget can come," Sarah told Kyle, who'd been sneaking her into his room, or going off to see her pretty much every day.

"We broke up...again," he admitted, adding the last part when Sarah opened her mouth to remind him they'd done that already.

"Because you're leaving tomorrow?" I asked.

"She isn't a fan of long distance, or my career choice at the moment. It might be for good this time."

"I'm not a fan either." He came over and put his arms around me, knowing I wasn't mad, just jealous. And not into all these changes.

"Tortellini then? To ease his heartbreak?" Sarah suggested. It was Kyle's favorite meal, but pasta was pretty up there for all of us.

"You're not cooking." Kyle looked horrified.

"You know I'm married and I have a child? I can boil water and make simple meals...." she became less sure of herself as she went on, which got us to laugh.

"Rachel and I have this," Toby assured her and Kyle. The others would have made a delicious sauce from a jar, but we were making ours the way mom did; from scratch, without a recipe.

We were leaving all of the pots and pans for the new owners, and had already packed the furniture we wanted, so the rest would be sold with the house. Still having so much of our stuff lying around made it feel less permanent, but I knew it was a trick.

. . .

"A teensy bit more mushrooms please." Sarah watched us from the breakfast nook, sipping wine with Haylie.

"Yes, chief." Toby did a military salute to her, nodding for me to cut some more.

"Do you need mom's box? I haven't brought it home yet." She was taking a lot of the kitchen stuff, which was hilarious given how she never cooked, but we all let her have mom's recipe box. It was ancient, with pink ribbons drawn onto the faded green box, and not mom's style at all. She used it mostly to find out how long to cook things, or for the special family recipes that had been passed on for generations. The rest of us knew our favorites by heart, which was good, because the best recipes were smudged and covered in grease stains, barely legible at this point.

"We're good," Toby and I assured her with complicit smiles.

"God, I am going to miss this." Haylie was already on her second glass. Otherwise, she would have been more careful about saying things that made it worse.

"Having other people cook for you?" Uncle Jack came into the kitchen to grab beers for the guys who were cleaning the now empty rooms while we cooked.

"Sarah gets this 24/7," Toby teased my sister.

"I mean the 'us being together' this. Aunt Sierra was the one who brought us all together for Christmas and Thanksgiving. She even called when she knew I had a Monday off to convince me to come home." No one corrected her, because mom spent all of our lives making sure we knew this was our home, as opposed to wherever we settled once we moved out. Or in Haylie and Toby's case, where they actually lived.

"Home is where the heart is," Toby told her. Mom used to say that to him and Jared when they'd say they had to go home after a visit.

"What happens when your heart is broken into a million little pieces?" I asked quietly, but they felt the same.

"Then you have a million places that can be home. It doesn't matter if we all come here or to LA or to the Lake House, as long as we're together," Toby reminded us. He was right, but mom wouldn't be at any of those places.

"Why don't we play a game where tonight we act like nothing changed? Like this isn't the end of everything, it's the in-between days at Christmas, where everyone will be here tomorrow," Sarah suggested.

"I like games," Haylie agreed.

I THOUGHT it would be impossible, but for one night, we pretended everything was okay. We ate the pasta in the dining room, with conversations spreading, and real laughter filling the space for the first time in what felt like forever. After supper, Kyle had the worst idea ever for our full stomachs, but we all agreed to play football in the backyard with him. One last game to say goodbye to the hundreds, maybe thousands that had been played on that grass. When Uncle Jack drove Jared and Toby to the airport for their red eye flight to make it to work on time in the morning, we said goodbye like they'd be back in a few weeks. While they were gone, we watched an old romantic comedy in the basement, then came up for hot cocoa with cinnamon and marshmallows when he returned. It was nice to escape reality for a while, even if it didn't last long enough by anyone's standards.

WHEN IT WAS GETTING LATE and Katie fell asleep for the second time, we called it a night. I went to my room after hugging everyone, with Sarah promising to bring Katie to sleep in my room once she brushed her teeth. It was her idea, but I was definitely going to treasure one last night in my own house with my little cuddle bug.

"You haven't opened it?" Kyle surprised me by standing in the doorway, watching me like mom would. I had the envelope from her in my hands, debating for the hundredth time whether I should open it, or save it.

"I know the others did and they all smiled and cried, and maybe this letter has all the answers and I should read it so I can understand, but..." I voiced the debate going on in my head.

"But once you read it, that's it. She'll never be able to tell you anything new, ever again," he understood, taking a seat on my bed. "I haven't opened mine either."

"I want to, so badly, because I miss hearing her voice, even if it's only in my head, but then I'll never have anything to look forward to." I sat beside him.

"You have a million things to look forward to, Rachel," he argued, laughing at me as he pulled me close.

"You know what I mean. It won't be the same."

"It'll never be the same," he agreed. "But we're all going to be okay."

"How can you say that? You're training to eventually go to war and I'll be living with..."

"I know," he cut me off before I could find an appropriate word to describe the man I had to live with. "But it's like Diana said in her eulogy. We're all going to be okay, because mom raised us that way. She didn't want to leave us and would have done anything in her power to stay with us forever, but she also made sure we were all strong, caring, decent human beings who would make it in the world."

"And be incredible," I recited. You only had to get that speech once after a bad report card to never want to disappoint her again.

"You're going to go to Los Angeles and you're going to be incredible, in spite of living with him," he told me.

"And you're going to stay alive and come visit. Lots. Maybe kidnap me sometimes?" I knew he was technically in school, not on active duty, but I heard about the stop-losses and didn't think their pool of college students was that much of a stretch.

"Of course," he assured me.

"Are you staying for the sleepover too?" Katie rushed to Kyle, so he could lift her onto the bed.

"No, but I will see you both in the morning." He kissed us each on the forehead before we went to bed.

THE NEXT MORNING, Katie woke up unreasonably early and went to wake her parents, so I went for one last jog around town. I lingered in front of Alex's house, that now had a 'For Sale' sign in front of it, although it had never been a part of our route. Every landmark I passed felt like something I was going to miss, even if I had never paid attention to it before. I caught sight of Mrs. Sims in a window, and realized I had been staring at the house, but she waved with a smile that didn't reach her eyes. I did the same before running home. It occurred to me then that I would probably never see her again either.

After I showered and got dressed, I packed up a few final items that I didn't trust the U-Haul to bring. They all fit in my backpack, so I carefully slipped mom's letter into Alex's book and put it in the side compartment, opting to wear the jacket, even if it sometimes made it hard to breathe.

We didn't have time for a long breakfast, but Matt made us bacon and scrambled eggs before we left. All I could do was stare back at him and the house, until they disappeared from view.

"WHEN ARE YOU GOING BACK?" I asked Uncle Jack while he took our luggage out of the back of the van. I had Katie in my arms, her head resting on my chest in a way that convinced me I wouldn't be able to give her back to Sarah without breaking my own heart.

"As soon as I can't see you through the doors anymore." He finished and brought me my backpack.

"Those things you told mom about Kyle, you meant them, right? They weren't just to make her feel better?" Our world was upside down now, which was the only reason we weren't making a huge deal of Kyle going off to ROTC. Mom would have thrown a huge pizza party for him.

"Every word," he assured me. "And I've got a lot of friends who will make sure he gets the best training and education possible before he gets to active duty. I can also have him court-martialed if he doesn't write home to our liking," he added when Kyle came over.

"I'll shoot you a text every couple of months." Sarah shot him a death stare that had us all laughing, even my sister. "Kidding," he assured her.

"I'm only a call away. Always." Uncle Jack came and gave me a hug, his look telling me these were the final goodbyes.

"I might hold you to that," I warned while Katie wiggled her arms out, so she could be a part of the hug instead of crushed by it.

"Your mom was more vocal about her six kids, but there isn't a thing I wouldn't do for you either." He gave me a kiss on the head before going to Sarah, while Kyle came to me.

"Don't cry," my brother told me.

"You don't cry," I countered, totally childish, but also on point.

"I love you," he made a point of each word, so it wasn't the casual 'love you's we said all the time.

"I love you too." I went in for a hug and he held me tight, so I could hardly breathe, but I didn't ever want him to let go.

"And remember..." he got serious.

"I'll be incredible," I promised.

"I'll stay alive," he did the same.

"You need to be incredible too," I laughed through the tears.

"Now you're asking a bit much," he warned.

"You're good for it." When I finally got out of the hug, I found Sarah in front of me with a red, leather-bound book in her hands.

"My sketchbook!" I exclaimed. When I couldn't find it this

morning, I assumed someone accidentally put it in the truck yesterday.

"Bottom of a soccer bag in my trunk," she agreed with a slight nod to her daughter, who buried her head deeper in my chest.

"Why would it be there?" I tried to get Katie to look at me.

"It might have something to do with how you don't usually leave the house without it."

"So I wouldn't dare leave for good without it," I understood.

"She's smart." Haylie hugged my sister. She was used to only seeing us on holidays, but I was not ready for this.

"Takes after her mom," Uncle Jack smiled.

"Katie Bear?" I tried. She still wouldn't look at me.

"No." She refused to come out.

"I don't want to go either," I whispered.

"I can show you my spot." I smiled at the image of me trying to fit under the seat, where she hid when she didn't want to go places.

"That won't work this time."

"But who will walk me home from school? And do the braids when mommy's at work and I have a soccer game?" she made good points.

"Your dad is awesome, so I'm sure he can learn. Or your mom can do them before she leaves. And you can go to daycare with Abby," I smiled and made my eyes big, overselling it.

"I don't like Abby," she argued.

"She's your best friend," Kyle called her on the lie.

"But she isn't you."

"This means it'll be even more special when we do see each other. You can come visit me in California, and I can come see you." I hoped I wasn't lying, for both our sakes.

"But they have to go now." Sarah came and took me in her arms, a trick to get her daughter back, but I held her just as close, if not closer than Katie was holding me. The only reason I wasn't throwing a fit was because I didn't want to upset Katie more than she already was.

Sarah had to pry Katie's hands off me, then transferred her to her right arm so she could continue hugging me with her left. I took a deep breath, but bit my lip instead of speaking. I didn't trust myself to not cry.

"You've got this Rache, and I am there for you every step of the way," she told me.

"God, I wish I could stay here." I bit down harder, not that it helped, and prayed she'd say I could.

"I wish you could too," she told me. "But you should give him the chance to get to know you like I do."

"I'm going to pretend you didn't say that." I wiped the tears.

"I thought you might." She shook her head. "I love you. And I'm too old and I know better, but I would hold on to you like Katie did if I could."

"I know. I love you too." Haylie and I waved goodbye with an attempt at happy faces before making our way through the airport.

"And then there were two." She took my hand like I was a lost child and I was grateful. I spent the week moving from the arms of one person I loved to another, so as I got closer to leaving them all, I felt utterly alone. I was losing everything. We wouldn't be getting together for Sunday night suppers anymore, Kyle was off to school, mom was gone...I pulled Alex's jacket tighter around myself and nervously ran my thumb over the leather of the sketchbook in my other hand.

"There's still time to come to California instead," I suggested while we walked to my gate.

"If I miss any more school I won't make it to the Lake House this summer," she argued. "And delaying this won't make it go away."

"You're abandoning me?" I tried the guilt angle.

"Make it through the flight, go home with him, then starting tomorrow, you can call Jared and Toby whenever you need rein-forcements," she suggested.

I was about to remind her that Jared was Team Evil in this situation, but I spotted Christopher, already garnering the attention of tourists asking for pictures. I hadn't seen him since the lawyer's office and would be fine if I never saw him again.

"I'll try to come visit and come up with a scheme to rescue you sometimes," she offered as a bribe before they called first class passengers. Christopher was still catering to his fans, who kept asking if he was the one flying the plane today, so I decided not to wait.

"I love you munchkin," she said while she hugged me.

"I love you too peanut," I replied, closing my eyes to take her in, before we both took a breath and pulled apart.

"I'll see you at Thanksgiving," she said as I handed my passport to the woman at the gate.

I nodded, then waved back to her as I made my way to the plane, making it clear that it was me against the world from now on. I boarded the plane, took my seat and immediately put my headphones in. Then I took out my C.S. Lewis. Hopefully Christopher would get the message.

"Sorry, it was a bit crazy out there," he said when he got to me, under the impression it was the crowd I'd rushed away from. I knew I'd eventually have to talk to him, but I was good with putting it off for a very long time. He lingered in the aisle, waiting for a reaction, but I had the headphones in and didn't look up, so he eventually had to take his seat beside me. I tried to ignore the look in his eyes when I glanced over, but he looked hurt. I didn't feel bad, because I knew he deserved it, but at the same time, I kind of did. Mom would have said, "You hate him for the person he is, but you feel bad because of the person you are." Right now, I wished I could be more like him and not care.

· · ·

ALL THINGS CONSIDERED, the flight wasn't bad. I had the window seat and was able to read until the movie came on. Once we were allowed to deplane, I hurried off without making sure he was following, but assuming he would. I only had my backpack, so I went pee while he waited for his luggage, then followed him to the parking lot. I sat in the back, behind the driver's seat, while he put his bags in the trunk and made a call.

He looked surprised to see the empty passenger seat, but had to know I wouldn't want to be alone up front with him, especially in LA traffic for hours. My iPod died before takeoff, but I kept my headphones in for the drive and stared out at the city and scenery around me. I was jealous of the rest of my family, who were still struggling to get back to some kind of normalcy, but at least they weren't being thrown into a horrible unknown. Even Kyle got to choose the struggle he was going to. We were the two who still hated him, yet we were the ones mom wanted to force to live with him. I didn't understand why mom couldn't have let me choose where I wanted to live, or sent me to Sarah or Jared or Uncle Jack, who were all adults and perfectly capable. Most importantly, they actually knew and loved me.

11

HOME, BITTERSWEET HOME

We got to Los Feliz around six o'clock. His house was in a gated community called Laughlin Park, which didn't surprise me. I saw his wife, Tracy, as soon as we pulled into the driveway. She walked over like she'd been sitting on the steps, waiting for us. I only recognized her from pictures in magazines, so I didn't know if Kyle even knew that he remarried and replaced us. Kyle had waited a few months to see if our dad would come back, then eventually wrote him off as dead. I was stuck in the waiting to see if he'd come back stage.

I gave Tracy the littlest bit of credit for not coming to mom's funeral with him. She was about mom's height, but with red hair instead of blonde, that went past her shoulders. The most obvious difference was Tracy's five-month pregnant belly, which wasn't in any of the magazines I read. She looked nice enough, standing there on her own in a summer dress, but as soon as he went over and kissed her, I remembered that she married *him*, so she couldn't be that great. They turned to me, waiting, so I reluctantly got out of the car, keeping my backpack in front of me, like a barrier between us. My goal was to lock myself in my room as soon as possible and only emerge when absolutely necessary.

"Trace, I'd like you to meet Rachel," he said proudly, as if he had anything to do with who I was. His arm was wrapped around her, like he used to do with mom.

She actually extended her hand when she said, "Hi, I'm Tracy." As if she expected me to shake it and be friendly.

I did my research before coming, or you know, kept track of him, so I knew they met less than five years ago, on set, and she had nothing to do with him leaving us. I gave her a little hand wave thing, motioning to the backpack I was holding with both hands as an excuse. She nodded like it was fine, but I would have dropped whatever I was holding and rushed into their arms if it was anyone from my family standing there.

"Come on, your stuff's already in your room. But feel free to rearrange everything, or we have a spare room if you want to change, or…anything you want," she told me nervously, a little too eager to please. "Do you want the grand tour?" she asked with a smile.

"I'm tired."

"Of course," she waved it off. I followed them inside and pretended to not be impressed by the five bedrooms, media screening theater, zen pond and so on. Tracy reminded me of Sarah, how she talked a lot when she was nervous, and I wasn't helping. There was a lot of fancy décor, but there were also boxes everywhere.

"With this new baby, we thought we could use a little more space, which turned out perfect now that you're staying with us," she explained them. She was either insensitive, or didn't realize there was nothing perfect about my mom dying so I could be sent to live with them. "That's our room, and Owen's, but he won't be here until tomorrow," she said when we got to the top of the stairs. She didn't feel the need to explain, but in addition to the baby they were expecting, my dad and his new wife had a one-year old son named Owen. The 'happy family' was photographed on the beach once in People and I have hated Tracy and Owen ever since. I knew it was childish of me, hating them because he stayed with them when he left us, but I was well aware that my rationality took the back seat when it came to anything related to my father. "I started dinner, so it should be ready in an hour or so. I'll let you get settled and come get you when it's done."

I knew I was going to hate everything about this house, this town and this family, but my room and its view were breathtaking. My computer desk was already set up, as was my TV stand, with a new TV where I used to keep my books. I didn't have to worry about finding a new place for them, because there was a bookshelf on either side of the bay window. It was a reader's paradise, with a bench and a view. I put my backpack down and took out the picture of me with Alex, as well as one from my room with my whole family, and put them up on the bookshelves, right at eye level. The bed was the kind I had dreamed about ever since I saw A Little Princes; a four-poster with curtains hanging around it. Sarah had told me the nets were actually to keep bugs out, but I didn't care. I wanted to be mad at them for thinking something I wanted as a six-year-old would still be something I wanted now, but I was also kind of excited.

The closet was so big that I didn't even have enough clothes to fill half of it. I would call it a live-in more than a walk-in. The ensuite bathroom was cool, because it meant I wouldn't have to potentially face them every time I had to use it.

The property was bigger and more beautiful than I could have imagined, but it didn't make up for what brought me there. I would give every single one of his bribes back, everything I've ever owned, to be back in the house I grew up in with mom.

There was also a box with a card I didn't bother to read. Inside was a cell phone, house keys, a laptop and a credit card 'for emergencies'. I shuddered at the thought of how spoiled and obnoxious we would be if we had actually grown up like this. Then again, mom wouldn't have let that happen. Her parents were wealthy, so we probably could have had this life, but she chose to spend time with us instead of throwing money at us. I didn't know if he was trying to relieve his guilt, but I knew what he did, and a decade worth of Christmas and birthday presents was not going to change that.

I opened a few boxes and put my clothes in the closet, then some DVDs on the TV stand. I added the last Z movie to the shelf as Tracy walked in.

"Dinner's ready." She lingered in the doorway, reminding me I should shut the door next time. I didn't look at her, I just bent down to take the DVD box apart. "Listen Rachel, I know you hate your dad, and you hate me because I married him. You must hate me even more because you think I'm trying to replace your mom, but I'm not. She was an incredible woman from what I hear, and I wouldn't dream of ever trying to fill her shoes. I know this is the last thing you want to hear, because I felt like strangling my stepmother when she said it to me, but if you want a friend, I'm here." I wanted to trust her, but I couldn't. Not when she was married to the monster who abandoned me without a second thought.

I FOLLOWED her to the dining room, not venturing on my own because I didn't want to get lost. I sat as far as I could from them at the dining room table, that had turkey, stuffings, gravy, mashed potatoes, meat pie, cranberry sauce and everything to make you think of a family dinner. Without knowing if Tracy could cook, I concluded they had a chef, so the food was as fake as the family.

"How do you like your room? Is anything missing?" he asked.

I shook my head since my mouth was full, but I also hadn't spoken to him since the phone call.

"And Rachel, if you still like horses, we have a ranch in Santa Ynez. I can take you tomorrow if you want?" He waited for an answer I didn't give. "Or I can write the address down and you can go with Jared some time." The hardest thing about what he did was that as far as I could tell from my early childhood memories, he'd been my favorite person in the world. Not my mom or any of my siblings. All of my memories from before he left were with him. I had absolutely loved horses, and would get him to pretend to be a horse and bring me around the living room on his back when I couldn't wait for us to actually go horseback riding on the weekends. Mom brought us a couple of times after he left, but it had always been our thing, so she stopped. I can't even remember the last time I saw a real horse. I looked down at my plate and ate, doing my best not to acknowledge him, so he wouldn't see that these weren't happy memories for me, they hurt.

WE ATE QUICKLY and there was no more talking after that. As soon as I was done I brought my plate to the kitchen, then sought refuge in my room. I unpacked my pictures, souvenirs and trinkets, then finished with the bookshelves. I kept mom's last letter in Alex's book and put it in its place on the shelf, figuring that would be the safest place until I resigned myself to reading it.

I spent a few minutes programming numbers into the cell phone, but he'd already put his and Tracy's. I texted Sarah and Jared goodnight, then put mom's PJs on and went to bed.

12

NOT ALL BAD

I was still mostly asleep, so it took a minute for me to figure out I was in my new room, and the voices were Christopher and Tracy outside my curtains. I was pretty sure I shut the door, so I either didn't hear them knock, or they needed to learn some boundaries.

"We're going grocery shopping and we were wondering if there was anything special you like to eat, a favorite cereal…" Tracy asked after his good morning went unanswered.

I was asleep when they came in, so I didn't see a reason to let them know that changed. I rolled over and buried my head into the pillow, ignoring them.

"I'll ask Sarah," he told her before they gave up.

I felt bad, because mom raised me to be polite, and she would cringe if she saw me treating someone like this, but I had to assume she would make an exception for him. And feeling guilty made me hate them more, so I tried to get back to sleep, exasperated and wanting to stay in bed forever.

AROUND TEN O'CLOCK, incessant pounding on the front door and a doorbell in the distance woke me up for good. I got out of bed, tied up my hair and hoped I didn't have a trail of drool on my face as I made my way to the front door.

When I opened it, there was a guy in his late twenties with shades on, his brown hair styled in a faux-hawk. Ryan Brooks, the newest addition to Chris' TV show and my celebrity crush, was standing on the doorstep, holding a baby bag and who I assumed was Owen.

"Hi, you must be Rachel." He put out his hand. "I'm Ryan," he added like I wouldn't know. Before he joined Flight, he was in so many box office hits and cool indie films. Starring in a Nicholas Sparks movie launched his career to superstardom, but Sarah and I had gone to the movie theater in town for every single one of his movies. She was going to freak when I told her I met him while wearing Duckie boxers, an oversized t-shirt and morning breath.

"And Owen?" I pointed to the kid.

"Yeah, he's your half-brother?" he answered with a question. "Here." He put Owen in my arms. "Your dad called and said they'd be home any minute, but I'll be late for practice if I don't leave now, so...would you mind?" Sarah and I had spent an evening downloading all of his music off LimeWire. It was a little too 'growly' for our taste, but we still listened to all of it.

"No, I guess not." I loved kids, but I was determined to be immune to Owen's cute smile and gazing eyes. The fact that he smiled as soon as I took him was making that harder.

"Thanks, I'll owe you one," Ryan smiled. "And I'm sorry about your mom. I know you just got here, so if ever you want to talk or hang out, or if ever you need a tour guide, you can call me. My number's on the fridge," he offered.

"Thanks." I watched him leave, completely flustered. I put Owen on my hip, locked the door and went to the kitchen, taking the time to check it out. There was a pad with numbers on the fridge, like Ryan said. There was an actor or two from the cast, some that I think lived in the neighborhood, but there was a tightness in my chest when I saw Sarah and Jared's numbers. I knew they talked to him, but seeing them on the list meant he might call them, when he never called me.

I got myself an apple from the fruit drawer, since it was something easy to eat while holding Owen, then went to his room, which was between mine and theirs. I had yet to explore most of the house, but that would be for another day, when they weren't on their way home.

Walking into Owen's room was like entering Toyland; teddy bears and toys everywhere, neatly placed on shelves and chairs. I went over to the crib, thinking I would put him there and listen closely until they got back, but then I saw the mobile and felt a pang in my chest. It caught my attention because it had a necklace on it, nothing special; macaroni noodles on a string. It didn't fit with the fancy décor, but it stopped me in my tracks because I was pretty sure I was the one who made it. I remembered bringing one home from school on the day he left us, so proud to show it to him because I used his favorite colors. He wore it for the rest of the day. I wondered if he knew he was leaving when I gave it to him, or if it was a spur of the moment decision he made in the middle of the night.

I kept Owen in my arms a little longer, knowing I wouldn't cry with him there. I walked around and examined the toys and pictures on his bureaus. Some were of Owen, smiling at different milestones, and others were of his picture-perfect family. I wasn't surprised to see pictures of Owen with my siblings, or one with Katie, even if it hurt. What shocked me was the old picture of Christopher with my siblings and I, right next to the Christmas card we made last year.

"Do you know who I am?" I asked Owen. Maybe he smiled when I took him because he recognized me.

"Ball," was all I got as a reply. Instead of leaving him for them to find, I found myself taking the ball and sitting on a pile of pillows to play with him. It wasn't like anyone could see me being nice to him, and his language skills weren't advanced enough to rat me out yet.

"I'm not going to like you, okay?" I warned him a while later, letting him hold on to my fingers and slowly stumble around the room. He smiled like it was the most fun activity in the world. "I can see you're cute and cuddly, and I love babies, which makes this really hard, but you also have everything I want and don't have. You have a dad who loves you and doesn't seem to be planning on leaving you. I wouldn't be good at seeing it coming if he was, and I'm here so he might want to. You even have my siblings who visit you and love you. But the thing I'm most jealous of is how your mommy's still here. You'll see yours any minute now, but mine left and she isn't coming back, and it hurts."

I was taking advantage of the fact that he couldn't talk yet to pour my heart out to him. As long as I said it with a smile and spoke softly, he didn't know anything was wrong and just smiled back. "I knew she was going to die someday, everyone does, but I never expected it would be so soon." I paused for a second to bring my smile back. "I have so many things I wish I could say to her, so many questions to ask, but I can't. And I need her right now. To tell me everything is going to be okay. That my dad isn't as horrible as I think and that she trusts him to take care of me... but I can't trust him. I hate myself for saying this, but I wish it had been him instead of her. She could have helped me through Alex's death and she would have known exactly what to say and do. Even if I could have Alex now, he would be someone I can lean on and rely on, who understands, but he's gone too, and I feel so alone." I stopped walking and brought Owen back to the pillows and the ball. He smiled like nothing could ever be wrong in the world, and I was so jealous of that innocence.

After I got tired of the ball, that he could have kept playing with for hours, I read him some old school children's books from the shelf. When I finished a Winnie the Pooh and picked up the Bernstein Bears, I realized it was getting late. I worried a teensy bit that they weren't back yet, even if I didn't care either way. I shifted my now sleeping half-brother into a better position in my arms, so I could get up and see what was going on. As soon as I stood, I saw Christopher watching me from the doorway. I hadn't bothered to close it because I didn't think I would stay.

"How long have you been here?" I asked, the anger rising. This was a complete invasion of privacy, especially if he was there long enough to hear everything I confided in the baby that was not meant for adult ears.

"Not long. We heard you in here with him when we got home so we left you alone, but I came again around when Pooh got his head stuck in a jar of honey," he admitted. "We didn't want to bother you."

"What changed?"

"I came to tell you dinner is ready, but seeing how you are with him, it reminds me of way back when, how Sarah would carry Kyle around in her arms like a doll and..."

"Here," I cut off his memories and handed him his son. My tone was meaner than I'd intended, but he had no right to talk about the past like it was the good old days. I felt terrible that my roughness woke Owen and made him cry, but I had to get out of there.

I walked straight to the dining room without caring if he followed. I knew the main reason I was upset wasn't because Chris knew I didn't hate Owen. That wasn't a big deal. But he stood there and watched me read to Owen. Like she would. I don't know how many times I would be reading a story to Katie, only to look up and catch mom listening in the doorway with the same smile he had.

"I hope you like salmon. Sarah said yes, but no capers?" Tracy put a plate in front of me.

"It's fine," I said without looking up.

"Look who just woke up!" Chris walked in holding Owen, who was no longer crying. Tracy rushed over to get her son and held him close, which made me realize that she made the conscious decision to let me stay in the room and be with the son she hadn't seen in over twenty-four hours.

They tried to have a normal dinner conversation, asking me what I liked to do, my favorite meals...but I mostly shrugged. I ate as quickly as I could, then went back up to my room.

I DEBATED CALLING Sarah or Jared, but they wouldn't understand.

"I don't know if I can stay here and hate them for three more years," I told Toby when he picked up.

"You don't have to hate them." He knew exactly who I was talking about.

"But I do. I hate him for what he did and I hate her because he loves her and he hasn't left her. I want to hate them forever, because I can't let them in and get close to them, but I hate how I feel when I'm mean to them," I admitted.

"Then don't. Just be quiet," he suggested.

"That's just as hard sometimes," I pointed out.

"Being nice and polite is good, but there's nothing wrong with not being friends with everyone."

"Whenever I feel bad, like I'm being mean and mom would shudder if she saw me, I remember every birthday, every recital, every big moment he wasn't there for, and I don't feel so guilty."

"Do you feel better?" he asked.

"No," I admitted. "It just hurts."

He had a catering gig to get to, and another one tomorrow, but he promised he would see me soon. "You're stronger than you think," he reminded me before hanging up.

13

ONE LAST TRY

The next morning, I woke up to my new phone buzzing, then nothing, then buzzing again. I saw I had five new text messages from Toby.

"Come outside."

"But bring your shoes."

"And comfy clothes."

"Running shoes."

"Whatever you jog in."

It was 8 a.m., but I wasn't going to complain. I texted to say I was coming, then got dressed with my running shoes. I crept through the house as quietly as I could, hoping they didn't have an alarm. When I got to the gate, I couldn't see a button to open it, so I grabbed a hold and climbed over.

"You know there's a latch, right?" Jared came from where I was supposed to come out; the pedestrian exit.

I didn't even respond to his comment, I ran straight into his arms. It was less than two days, but it felt like years.

"She's quite the daredevil," Toby talked about me instead of to me, then got his hug as well.

"Here to rescue me?" I asked.

"We have a few hours before we need to get to work, so we're entertaining you," Jared corrected.

"I will take it," I smiled, wishing I wouldn't have to come back.

"Last one to the pier is a rotten egg." Toby took off on a sprint.

"I don't know where that is!" I called after him.

"He doesn't either," Jared assured me.

It turned out that the Santa Monica Pier was way too far for us to jog to, at least not in the time they had. Instead, we saw a whole lot of big houses in gorgeous neighborhoods. In different circumstances, this would have been new and exciting. I could add taking the enjoyment out of this to the reasons I hated *him*.

We stopped and got a bite to eat, then saw an ice cream shop on our way home. We each ordered sugar cones; Jared got bubble gum, which was a very unnatural pink, Toby opted for chocolate, and I ordered cookie dough before I even saw their options.

"How is it going so far?" Jared asked. We had enough time that we could walk home and enjoy the cones, but they would have to head to work afterwards.

"Horrible," I said automatically, but he raised his eyebrow at me. "I mostly try to avoid them."

"And how's that working for you?"

"Like how successful am I or how does it make me feel?"

"Oh, I know you can do whatever you put your mind to." He smiled, but I didn't smile back.

"Can I stay at your place while you go to work?"

"Nope." He didn't even consider it. Toby looked like he would have said yes.

He changed topics, and they both gave me their lists of favorite places, but it wasn't like I wanted to go to them on my own.

"How old do you have to be to become a firefighter?" I asked when we got to the gate.

"You're too young," Jared sighed. In his defense, he wasn't

enjoying my pain. He just wasn't making it better. "Next time we'll take Ferndell all the way up," he promised, pointing to a trail in the trees.

I held them extra close for the goodbye hugs, then stopped in front of the gate.

"Shoot, I forgot my key." I never bothered to take it out of the box.

"Here." Jared handed me his key ring. "Throw it back over the gate," he told me, since it closed automatically before I reached the front door.

I was glad I didn't have to ring the doorbell and have them let me in, but Jared having their key on his ring gave me another pang. Another reminder that they had a relationship, while he never came for me until mom died and made him.

I watched them drive off, then went up to my room, managing to avoid everyone. I grabbed a book and a towel, then went out to the pool in my bathing suit. I tanned for a bit and swam a lot, but was ready to get out and go upstairs if ever they came out.

Tracy and Christopher were both in the kitchen when I went back in, so I went straight up the stairs.

I changed and put on a DVD, but I could hear Owen laughing across the way. They were making what smelt like fajitas downstairs, so I went over to check on him. My heart melted when he looked up at me with that big smile, so I picked him up and brought him over to the pillows.

I took out the Bernstein Bears book from yesterday and read it in a whisper, hoping the baby monitor by the crib wouldn't pick me up.

When the book was done and the house smelt like chicken and spices, I went back to my room, with none the wiser.

Less than five minutes later, Tracy came up to get Owen and tell me dinner was ready. I knew they wouldn't make me starve if I didn't go down and eat with them. I could easily make myself something, or order in, but I was brought up in a house where everyone ate together, and it was a hard habit to break.

TRACY TRIED a few conversation openers once we sat down, before understanding that I had no interest in being friends. She was under the impression that all I needed was time. He, on the other hand, looked so hurt when I ignored him that he stopped saying anything to me unless it was necessary. The only person making noise was Owen, who was playing with his chicken more than eating them. Tracy kept picking up the pieces he would throw on the floor, while Chris looked like he was debating whether he should say something. I only had one bite left on my plate, so I tried to finish it as quickly as I could, but he made up his mind to speak just as I pulled my chair out.

"Mrs. Williamson, the headmistress at the high school, she called today to see when you might be ready to go back to school. She wondered if tomorrow would be okay?" It sounded like a speech he'd rehearsed many times.

I knew that I had to go back to school, but I had expected someone to realize this was wrong and send me back to New York before that happened.

"I would never want you to go before you're ready, but it might be nice for you to get out and interact with people, even if it is to get away from me."

I had to admit I was surprised at how observant he was admitting to being. Another wave of guilt hit me before I could remind myself that he was the bad guy and he hurt me long before I did anything to deserve it. It took me a little longer this time. He was genuinely trying and the annoying part of me I usually loved, the one that was my mother's daughter, it was thinking that he deserved a second chance.

"Sure," I said, sounding way more pissed off than I actually was.

"I'll call Mrs. Williamson," he said before the silence resumed and I went up to my room.

GOING to school would be better than trying to avoid them here, and classes started today back home. That should have clued me in, but as long as I wasn't in school, I wasn't officially living here. I had never been the new kid before. I always started the first day with my teachers wondering if I would be good at math like Kyle, excel at biology and chemistry like Sarah, or kill it on the court like Jared. I remember hating how everyone compared me to Sarah and told me how much we looked like twins, but I would love to go back to that now.

I went to my closet and tried to find an outfit. I wouldn't tell anyone about mom, or Alex, unless I wanted to end a conversation quickly, because what else could a normal person say to that? I could tell every person I met a different backstory to see if anyone noticed.

I finally laid three outfits out, so I could decide on one in the morning. I set my alarm, dreading what tomorrow would bring. I had always loved school, but it had a lot to do with having Alex there. All of my siblings made friends everywhere they went, but I had always been happy with my family and Alex. I didn't need any before, but now I had none.

I put some things in my backpack and saw my sketchbook, which I used to use to sketch my family and Alex all the time. I was working on sketching nature too, but I was a lot better at people. I tried to open it to the last page, so I could draw out some of my fears without the shock I would get from seeing my mom or Alex smiling up at me, but instead I found "I Love You" in Katie's unmistakable handwriting. She must have stolen the book a few days before I left, because there were notes from everyone in it, even Peter and Mackenzie. There were pages of sweet and encouraging things that would hopefully get me through tomorrow.

❧ 14 ❧

FIRST DAY ON A NEW PLANET

I woke up unnecessarily early, showered, and got dressed after trying on everything I owned and settling on one of the outfits I laid out last night. Then I went downstairs for breakfast. I found cereal in the pantry, every kind imaginable, and debated between Honeycombs and Honey Nut Cheerios. I settled on Honeycombs and went to grab a bowl when they walked in.

"This is nice, having breakfast as a family," Tracy said happily, putting Owen in his high chair. She realized it was the worst thing she could have said and froze, waiting for my reaction.

"I'm actually done," I lied, leaving the bowl where it was and putting the unopened cereal box away.

"That's too bad. I'll wake up early and make French toast tomorrow," Chris offered, but he knew I wouldn't be there, just like they knew I was lying about breakfast.

I wanted to rush out, but Tracy looked so guilty that I at least gave a noncommittal response. "Maybe."

"I can drive you to school if you want. It's on the way to the studio." Chris looked hopeful, but the idea made me shudder.

"The bus is there." I grabbed my backpack and a jacket and went outside, using the pedestrian gate to get to the street.

I had at least a half an hour before the bus would show up, so I walked towards the ice cream parlor we'd stopped at and got myself a bagel and a coffee from the place next door. They didn't have vanilla so it was bitter, but I deserved it.

THE BUS WAS PRETTY empty when it came, and everyone who got on was way younger than me. I sat in the back and listened to Pete's CD on my iPod.

"Mrs. Williamson?" I waited in the doorway of the head-mistress' office.

"You must be Mr. Glass' daughter," she said warmly, but sounded fake. It might be because we were in LA and I was prej-udiced, or because she associated me with him, but I didn't like it.

"Rachel," I agreed.

"I hope you're enjoying the new town?"

"I didn't come here by choice," I said with a sigh, then caught myself. "It's beautiful," I told her.

"Here's your schedule, your locker information, and anything else you might need to know. Your first class is right around the corner with Mr. Smith." She smiled as the bell rang.

"Thank you," I tried to match her sunny disposition before going in the direction she indicated.

MY FIRST CLASS WAS ENGLISH, where the students were already divided into groups of four. I went to the teacher and showed him my papers.

"Welcome to my class, Miss Glass. You can take a seat over there." He pointed to a table with three girls at it before going back to his papers.

"Hi, I'm Rachel," I introduced myself right before the second bell rang.

"Jessica." She had a friendly smile and I finally let out a

breath I didn't know I was holding. Her hair was a million times curlier than mine and she was tall enough that she could probably drop the ball right into the basket if she ever played basketball.

"Carmen." The girl in front of me smiled before turning to the girl beside her, who was staring at her nails.

"Clarice." She sounded bored and unimpressed.

The teacher told us to continue the work he assigned last class, so Jessica filled me in.

"Where are you from?" she asked once we were both working on the assignment.

"New York," I said loosely, hoping none of them watched the news too carefully.

"Like Broadway?" Clarice perked up.

"No, like New York State...Lake George," I specified, trying not to sound as nervous as I felt.

"Oh, I went to the Great Escape last summer. It was so much fun!" Carmen told me.

"My brother used to work there when he was in high school. He was a lifeguard and now he's a firefighter, so he's been pretty consistent in saving people," I shared.

"I love firefighters," Jessica smiled. "I've never met a real one, but they had a special on the ones from 9/11, who rushed into the towers when everyone else was running out..."

I knew she didn't mean to, but my heart got tight in my chest and I froze. I was barely listening while Carmen told her about the time firemen came to her house and they were all fat, short or balding.

"Ew, is your brother like that?" Clarice asked me, so I shook off the images of Ted's plane crashing into the second tower, and mom's guttural scream when she understood what happened.

"Um, no. He's...I guess you would consider him hot." To me, he was just Jared, but the girls had gone crazy for him in high school.

"You'll have to bring him by sometime," Jessica said before I finally got the chance to read the teacher's question. They asked about me every so often, or talked amongst themselves, so I got to know the girls.

"We're going for coffee. Wanna join?" Carmen offered when the bell rang.

"Won't we be late for history?" We had established that we were all in the same history class, that would start in fifteen minutes.

"History is a joke. Mr. Adams is waiting for his big break, which isn't coming," Clarice explained.

"I think I'll try it out, since it is my first day and all. But next time," I turned them down after weighing the academics against the potential friendships. I did need friends, but I didn't need to settle on the first people I met. I had succeeded at reinventing myself though, because the people who skipped class would never have invited me to tag along. They would have asked Alex, and he would have invited me if he ever took them up on it. What saved us from growing apart in high school, when he joined the football team and I began tutoring, was that we both loved learning. It didn't help our cool factor, but we never cared.

I FOUND my locker during the break and unloaded the few things I had brought to put inside it, as well as the books I wouldn't need. I put a magnetic mirror on the door with a picture of my entire family, that we took before Toby went to school in Paris.

WHEN I GOT to history class, there was only one other student there, a boy with short brown hair, who smiled at me before I took my seat in front of him. I was trying to figure out if it would be weird for me to turn around and introduce myself when the teacher walked in.

"You must be Rachel," he said when he saw me. "I heard I

had a new student, so I brought you the textbook. We're covering World War II, so I'm starting with Pearl Harbor to make it interesting," he shared, placing a book called 'World History' on my desk.

"Thank you," I told him.

"Oh, I'm Mr. Adams," he added as the bell rang and more people came in.

After ten minutes, I knew exactly what they meant. His teaching was possibly the worst I had seen, academically speaking. I wasn't sure I would have learnt much if I didn't already know about the topics he was covering, but it was worth it. He made it fun. Not the whole class, but I couldn't take my eyes off him when he did the FDR, post-Pearl Harbor speech as a monologue. I had never seen it done with such enthusiasm.

I DIDN'T BRING A LUNCH, so I went to the cafeteria and got myself a salad with grilled chicken and avocado, something Toby turned me on to, then found a table outside in the quad. I took a bite before the guy from history came and sat in front of me.

"Hey, you're Toby's cousin, right?" he asked.

"Toby Harris?" I realized how crazy a coincidence it would be if he meant a different Toby. Still, I had no clue how he would know who I was.

"Yeah, you're Rachel?" he went up at the end, but it wasn't a question. He heard Mr. Adams.

"Have we met?" I tried to smile and come off as friendly, rather than my first instinct.

"Not yet. I'm Nick Carver. Toby did the catering on Legends in the Dark, and your picture was in our craft trailer," he explained how he recognized me.

"We didn't want him to forget what we look like when he went to school in Europe, so it became a thing we do every year." Mom orchestrated them, and often used costumes, like superheroes, Disney characters, those olden day photos at the Great

Escape...everyone got a copy, but they were mainly for the people who moved away.

"I thought you lived on the East Coast?" he asked while I wondered which of our themed photos he saw.

"We moved," I shrugged. "Too cold over there." They must have talked a lot if he not only knew my name, but also where I was from.

"Very true, but nothing beats a White Christmas." He smiled easy and got me to smile as well. I could vaguely remember Toby mentioning an actor on set that he got along with. Toby thought he might replace my crush on Ryan Brooks, but it was before everything happened, which made it seem like a completely different life.

"I'm guessing you're not from here either?"

"Denver, Colorado," he admitted. "I used to be out snowboarding or skiing every single day from the first snowfall until it all melted away." I was going to ask what made him move here, but that would give him permission to ask me, and I didn't want to lie, or for this conversation to end.

"My sister would try to get us to go skiing all the time. We would go once a year, to make her happy, but I'm more of the hang-out-in-the-cabin-and-read-a-book-while-wrapped-up-in-a-warm-blanket-by-the-fire type of girl."

"You're one of those, huh?" he pretended to be disappointed. "I don't think I've hit the slopes since Sundance. My mom moved us out here when she married my stepdad, who was a 'director'." He used air quotations to imply he didn't agree with the title. "He won't be winning awards any time soon, but he makes my mom really happy and she has dated a lot worse." He gave me a look that said I didn't want to know what kind of crazies she'd encountered.

I wanted to ask about his father, but I knew this was where I should share my story, and I wasn't ready, so I switched topics. "Were you acting in Denver, or did that happen here?"

"If you ask my parents, they'll tell you I've been acting my way out of timeouts since I was a toddler, but I didn't do it professionally until a couple of years ago. It was completely by accident, but I fell in love with it." The girls had been nice this morning, but Nick felt like my first LA friend. "What about you? Do you dream of being discovered?" he teased.

"I'm not a big fan of actors," I teased, but there was some truth to it. "I'm not sure what I want to do."

"What do you love?" he asked.

"My family," was what I wanted to answer, but instead I said, "I love learning. If I could be a student forever and get paid for it, I'd do that."

"Just learning?" he raised an eyebrow.

"I guess I love to paint. But that's not a career."

"Of course it is," he argued before pointing his finger at me like he had me pegged. "I knew you were an artist. Anyone who makes her own Clogsworth and Lumiere costumes has to love art. Or Beauty and the Beast."

"That's the one you saw?" I asked, going a bit red. When we did Beauty and the Beast, Haylie was Belle, Sarah was Mrs. Potts, Katie was Chip, Mom was Madame Garde-Robe and I was Featherduster.

"There were like ten pictures of you guys on the walls. You were the truck mascots."

"You've seen them all." I went through them in my head, some more embarrassing than others.

"Don't worry, it was cute. He shows them to everyone who goes in." He had a big smile, so I couldn't tell if he was serious or not.

WE TALKED about the other pictures, about school, Los Angeles, all kinds of things. He could tell there was something I wasn't saying, since I would change topics whenever we got close to talking about mom, or Chris, but he knew enough not to ask about it.

"Same time tomorrow?" he asked when the bell rang.

"I'll see you then." I was surprised how comfortable he made me feel.

THE REST of the school day went by without much excitement. I went through the traditional new girl questions, but no one asked me any awkward ones I couldn't worm my way out of. The shooting had made national news, but the killers were caught and the grieving families didn't make it onto the screen.

I took the bus home, but when it stopped in front of the house, I didn't feel like going in. I knew they were expecting me for supper, but I was expecting him nine years ago and he never came.

I took the path Jared had pointed out, that took me through the forest and along a small creek. I followed it to a little shop selling sandwiches and stuff, the Trails café. I guess the phone signal on the actual trail wasn't great, because when I sat to eat my food and watch the sunset, a bunch of phone calls and text messages came in.

"I'm having supper somewhere else. Don't worry, I'll be back." I considered adding "Unlike you" at the end of my text message, but it might have been a bit much, and I didn't want to get grounded. I packed up and finished my sandwich on the way down.

"WHERE WERE YOU?" Chris was waiting in the entrance when I came in.

"I went for a walk." It was the truth, but he definitely thought I was lying.

"Next time, if you could please consider calling before we're at the dinner table, waiting for you to show up..."

Part of me wanted to go to my room and shut the door, to let it go, but a bigger part needed to face him. I stopped in the middle of the staircase and turned to him. "Welcome to the club," I caught him off guard. "I've been waiting for almost ten years. And even though I have to live here, I'm not a part of your happy family, so pretending that I am, it's...it's exhausting, and it hurts."

I left him standing there in the middle of the stairs and went to bed. I wore my mom's PJs and was in the comfiest bed I had ever slept in, but for the life of me, I couldn't fall asleep. I kept seeing the look on his face when I said it. I was beginning to think that making him feel as bad as he made me feel wasn't the best way to go.

15

BEHIND THE SCENES

I was just beginning to like the new school, and make friends, when our social studies teacher gave us an assignment masquerading as a day off. I had to go to work with one of my parents, so I could write a report on what their job entailed.

"It's a twenty-minute drive, but it will feel a lot longer if you stare out the window and pretend I don't exist." Christopher pointed out when he got in the car and I failed to respond to his greeting. I'd been waiting for him for five minutes, in the passenger seat, which I thought was enough of a concession. I wanted to get it over with.

"I can stay home if you prefer," I offered. I'd called Jared as soon as I knew about the assignment, but there was apparently some kind of safety issue with following a firefighter around all day.

"You can go to work with Tracy if you—" She had mostly been on maternity leave, but she was going to a photoshoot as a favor for a friend today.

"Let's go back to not talking," I cut him off. I had been acting like this whole thing was ridiculous, but I kept remembering how much fun it was last year when Alex and I went to work with my mom. We spent the day driving around with her and Kevin, went to the precinct's shooting range, watched an interrogation through a two-way mirror...Alex had decided he wanted to be a cop afterwards. He researched all the requirements and even asked my mom for her old textbooks. He also wanted to be a lawyer and an astronaut and own an arcade, but it planted a seed. It was hard to go from an amazing day with my favorite people to a day on a television set with Christopher. Plus, it turned out my school was in the complete opposite direction from the studio, not at all on the way.

"RACHEL!" I was barely out of the car when Ryan spotted me and came over.

"Hey," I blushed, not expecting him to take me in for a hug.

"Here to start your acting career?" he teased.

"I'm a terrible actress," I turned him down, but I actually had no idea. I avoided every drama class or school play because I didn't want anyone to compare me to Christopher. "It's a school project," I explained while Chris was brought to hair and makeup.

"My dad was a janitor," Ryan let me know he understood and had done this once upon a time as well. "Come on, I'll introduce you to everyone."

I followed him to one of the sound stages. I knew he was only taking me around because I made it clear I didn't like my dad, but still, I appreciated it.

They were fixing the lighting for a scene in the conference room, so the stand-ins were on set while the actors were sitting in their cast chairs close by. They were all talking to each other or the director, drinking coffee, reading a book...normal things. They were super sweet when Ryan introduced me, which was expected. What surprised me was how telling them I was Chris' daughter seemed to make them like me even more. I knew from watching the show that they were all great actors, but these were the people who worked long hours with him, almost every day, for years, and they still loved him. I didn't think they could all be wrong about him, but I also couldn't see how someone nice would leave their family without calling or checking in on their kids. Jared was the one who moved here and managed to track him down, long after he was done growing up without a father. Ryan noticed how I cringed every time he told someone, and how uncomfortable I got when they pointed out our similarities, but he didn't stop them. He waited until they were done to whisk me away.

"I SEE you haven't warmed up to him yet," Ryan pointed out when we got outside. He wasn't reproachful, be he did like my dad a lot more than I did.

"He doesn't deserve that." I didn't want to get into it.

"It looks to me like he's trying," he argued.

"Maybe. If I had never met him before and he just found out he was my father, then I'm sure I would be thrilled by the attention, but..."

"You can't forgive him?" he finished for me.

"How much did he tell you?"

"Enough." He smiled, knowing that wasn't a real answer. "He doesn't talk about it much, but you're not the first of your siblings to drop by."

"And Sarah talks when she's nervous," I understood. She probably told him the entire story.

"I'm not judging, because I get why you hate him, but I think you'll be miserable until..."

"He hasn't even apologized," I blurted out. "He tucked me in and said he'd see me in the morning, then he disappeared without an explanation or a goodbye. He only took me in now because the court ordered him to, and that doesn't count for much in my books."

"Want a ride in my plane?" he changed the subject for me.

"You know you're not a real pilot?" I teased, grateful for the escape.

"I do, unfortunately, but while it's grounded you can sit in the cockpit and pretend," he offered.

"Sure," I agreed.

AFTER THE PLANE, he brought me behind the monitors in Video Village so I could watch them film a scene with Chris. I would never admit this, because I hate the guy who plays him, but I love Lieutenant Eric Danvers. Chris' character on the show was everything the dad from my memories would be like. He was honest, brave, kind, vulnerable and he almost always did the right thing in the end. Even when he made mistakes, he did it in a way that you forgave him, because you saw him struggling with it and knew he would never do it if there was any other way. Watching the scene was exciting for that reason, but at the same time, seeing him become someone else so seamlessly was undeniable proof that I could never trust him.

UNFORTUNATELY, after they turned around and covered all the actors in that scene, Chris was wrapped for the day. Which meant Ryan was off babysitting duty and my father could finish the tour.

"I think I'd rather go home." I hated the look of disappointment when I turned down his offer, letting him know it was him I wasn't into, not the set.

"Sure." He pretended he didn't mind.

. . .

IT WASN'T until we were about halfway home that he broke the silence. "They gave me a short day when I told them you were coming, so I'd be able to spend time on set with you. I asked Ryan to show you around before his scenes because I knew you wouldn't want me to," he admitted. I considered arguing, but we would both know I was lying. "And it's okay. I'm glad you had a good time. I wish you would talk to me or at least not hate me so much, but I'm not going to push you. I'm going to be here, waiting for you to decide to give me a chance. Because I might not be the terrible person you think I am."

I looked at him when he said the last part, but he also looked at me, so I turned back to the window. He'd said what he wanted to say, so he stayed quiet the rest of the way, without expecting an answer. He also didn't acknowledge the couple of tears that slid down my cheek when he said it.

As soon as he parked in the driveway, I grabbed my bag and rushed into the house, grateful he took his time and didn't follow. Once inside my room, I shut the door and went to my desk. More than anything, I wanted to call my mom, to tell her I didn't understand the guy she married at all. I wanted to beg her to come get me, to bring me home where everything was easier and I was happy. Jared and Sarah wouldn't understand, because they were on his side, but Kyle might. He didn't have to deal with him like I did, but he hated him just as much.

I wrote him a letter on the fancy stationary Haylie got me when she moved to Boston for school. I'd written her a letter or two before we decided calling would be easier, but Kyle was in a stricter program, didn't have a cell phone, and would never call here in case they picked up. I poured my heart out to him, using half my stack of paper. I tried to explain how horrible it was to live here with the guy who broke my heart long before another boy ever could. I told him about this guilt, that I hated, because I knew he didn't deserve me being nice to him, but he was so good at acting like he cared. I told him how the worst part wasn't his being mean to me, because he wasn't. It was him being nice

that broke my heart and made me feel guilty on top of everything else. I also asked how he was doing and told him how
much I loved and missed him, before putting my letter in one of
the envelopes and tucking it away in my school bag.

I put on one of mom's oversized sweaters, then got in bed on
top of the covers, curled into a ball, and let my tears lull me to
sleep.

16

ALL ABOUT LASAGNA

I was in line for the bus, staring out into the parking lot, when I saw someone older than all the other students, wearing jeans and an FDLA t-shirt.

"Jared?" I asked, rushing over to him. "What are you doing here?"

"I had the evening off and thought it might be nice to have supper with my favorite little sister." He put me down after the customary twirl.

"I haven't seen you before." Clarice came over with Carmen and Jessica. We still sat together in English, and were friendly in the hallways, but we didn't hang out.

"This is the brother I was talking about. Jared, this is Clarice, Carmen and Jessica," I introduced them.

"The firefighter?" Clarice bit her bottom lip, but for a very different reason than I usually did, and twirled her hair around her finger.

"I am," he agreed.

"We saw you waiting and wanted to offer you a ride, but I guess you have it covered," Jess explained.

"I should be good," I smiled, appreciating it.

"And you're right. He is hot," Carmen giggled before they went off to Jessica's car and Jared looked at me, confused.

"New friends?" he asked.

"Kind of. We have English together. Carmen thought all firefighters were fat and bald in real life, so I told her you aren't."

"And did you tell her I was hot?" he asked.

"I said they would think you are. Which isn't the same thing," I defended.

"Of course not," he agreed, unlocking the doors when we got close to his car.

"I always knew you'd come and save me." I smiled, but didn't want him to know how relieved I was. He was going to bring me back, but any excuse to avoid a 'family dinner' was more than welcome.

"More like keep you company. Tracy and Chris invited me over." I appreciated him saying Chris instead of dad, for my benefit, but this wasn't cool.

"You used to be nicer," I told him, getting into the passenger's seat while he laughed at me.

"Are you giving him a chance? Or do you still hate him and avoid all interactions?"

"You know the answer." I was torn between feeling guilty for being mean, and being mad at him for forgiving Chris so easily.

"I promise I will make tonight as painless as possible."

THEY WEREN'T HOME YET, so I used my key and we went to the backyard to play basketball. We heard their car pull up not long after he beat me in the first game of HORSE. Jared thankfully read the situation and knew me enough to let us hang out there until Tracy called us in.

"You'll stay miserable until you give them a chance," he warned before wrapping an arm around me as we walked into the house.

· · ·

ONCE WE WERE WASHED UP, we went to the dining room. I took my seat as Tracy brought out the lasagna. Every year on our birthday, we get to choose what we want to have for the meal. Sarah always chose some new and exotic dish, which was sometimes delicious, but often ended with us ordering pizza, or filling up on cake and bread. Jared, on the other hand, always wanted lasagna. I was more of a stuffed pasta kind of girl, but Jared liked the layers. And not just any kind, as Elena Mitchell discovered when she tried to get to his heart through his stomach in the tenth grade. Mom had this old, battered recipe from an ancient relative that we all knew by heart, which was good, because it was probably the most faded of all the recipes in her box.

I was expecting the generic spaghetti sauce, noodles, pepperoni and cheese, but the piece Jared put on my plate looked way too familiar. I used my fork to explore a little more, even tasted a little piece, but it was definitely mom's. I don't know why it bothered me so much, but all of a sudden, I was overwhelmed with a feeling of betrayal, that they stole her recipe, or that Jared gave it to them. Either way, she would never be able to make her famous lasagna again, so they had no right to be making it instead of her.

"You stole her recipe?" I asked, beyond upset.

"What?" Tracy was confused. She looked like she felt bad, not because she did anything wrong, but she was sorry something upset me. Which made me even more mad.

"Nobody else puts spinach and alfredo sauce in their lasagna. And people don't slice tomatoes like this, they mush them. This is mom's recipe and you had no right to make it." I glared at Chris, because this was his fault. Tracy didn't know any better.

"Rachel," Jared tried to calm me down, but I was tired of being the bad guy for not forgiving him.

"No, Jared, stop defending him. I don't know why you think what he did is okay now, but he left his wife and his kids and made it so we all grew up without a father. Taking me in now doesn't change what happened, and stealing mom's recipes to win us over isn't going to—"

"Rachel."

It was Chris who spoke in a calm, apologetic tone that shocked me as much as the fact that it wasn't Jared who said my name. I glared at him, looking for a way to explain to him how badly he hurt me, and why this wasn't okay, but he spoke before I could. "The green and white recipe box, with the pink ribbons and bows and all those handwritten recipes, it was my grandmother's. She gave it to my mom and when I married Sierra, my mother gave it to her. I didn't take it with me, but I know a lot of the recipes by heart."

"I'm sorry." The anger was still boiling inside of me, but it was over way more than a recipe from the box he left behind, like he did to us. It wasn't like I could keep yelling at him for making lasagna the way his grandmother taught him.

"If it will make you feel better, we can stop using her—"

"You don't have to do that," Jared interrupted Chris' offer. "Rachel will—"

"I'll go back to not talking. Sorry." With that, I went upstairs to my room, ignoring the lot of them.

ONCE I WAS ALONE, a multitude of emotions rushed over me. I was embarrassed by my outburst, but also wished I said more. Pushed the dagger in deeper so he would understand why I wasn't willing to give him a chance. Why I hated everything he did, no matter how meaningless or innocent. I hated the way Jared loved him and felt the need to defend him and apologize for me.

I was debating if I should reach out to Toby or take a chance on Nick, who had lunch with me every day now, when there was a knock on the door.

"What do you want?" I had no interest in talking to him.

"It's me," Jared said with caution, making me feel worse. "Can I come in?"

"It's not like I have a lock."

He waited for me to open the door to come in. "Do you want to talk about it?" He brought me to sit on the bed.

"Not particularly." I cuddled into him.

"Are you okay?" he sounded concerned.

"If I say no, will you let me live with you or Sarah?" I asked. "Or even Uncle Jack. I would rather be anywhere else than here with him."

"Rache, it's not up to me."

"Why would she do this?" I asked what was bothering me.

"Who?" he asked, then realized I meant our mother.

"Why would she send me to him, instead of one of you guys, someone she knew would love me and take care of me?"

"Maybe she wanted you to get to know him?" he suggested.

"I don't know why she would want us to do that. I think I've been so mad and angry lately because as much as I want to blame him for everything...he did his wrong years ago. It was mom who decided I had to come here. She sent me to him, and I don't think she wanted me to suffer more than losing her would do, but I can't see why else she would want me to come here, to this torture."

"Torture?" He pulled me closer.

"You have no idea how hard and complicated it is in my head right now." I got a pity laugh from my big brother.

"Why don't I make a deal with you? Stay here for the school year, try your best to actually give dad a chance, and if you're still miserable come June, we will petition the courts and I will convince them to let you live with whoever you want."

"Really?" I failed to mask my excitement at the prospect.

"Cross my heart and hope to die. But you need to give him a chance."

"I'll try."

"And until you see things the way I do, I promise to come around more often, or to kidnap you on occasion."

"I would appreciate that." I genuinely smiled before he pulled me close and kissed the top of my head.

"I have a very early shift tomorrow, so I will see you next week." He got up and headed for the door.

"I love you." I got up and hugged him one more time.

"I know you hate it, but when it comes down to it, I am still on your side. Always."

ONCE HE WAS GONE, I took out my agenda and did a countdown to the last day of classes. I knew he offered it with the assumption that things would get better, but no matter how civil I became, I doubted I would ever want to live here instead of back home with Sarah and Katie. If I missed the friends I made, like Nick, I would just have to visit Jared and Toby more often.

I put a DVD on and went to bed, optimistic for the first time since the funeral.

17

HAPPY BIRTHDAY, RIGHT?

I couldn't sleep, so I went up the path, making it to Dante's View as the sun came out. I was finding myself up there at sunrise more often than not. I decided against a coffee and was going to head back down when I saw a discarded newspaper by the trail. I brought it to the recycling bin and saw the article on the corner of the front page: "One Month Since the Lake George High School Shooting: What Is Being Done to Prevent These Tragedies?" It was Wednesday's paper, so my mom died over a month ago, yet it felt like centuries since she last took me in her arms. Absolutely nothing was the same as it once was.

I made it through the path, back to our neighborhood, before it hit me. That meant today was October 4th. I immediately took out my phone and dialed Toby's number.

"Are you okay?" were the first words out of his mouth.

"I'm fine, I—"

"What are you doing awake? It's seven o'clock on a Saturday," he pointed out.

"You should wake up at the same time every day, even on weekends," I stalled. "I have an important question I need your opinion on."

"No, you should not become a popstar. We encouraged you

because we love you, but singing is not actually your strong suit," he mumbled as if trying to get back to sleep.

"You already crushed my dreams of becoming the next Spice Girl. This is about *him*."

"What did he do?" he woke up a bit.

"I just realized it's October 4th." I waited for the same light to go off in his head as it did in mine. Mom always made a big deal of birthdays, and Toby would have been there for more than ten of his. "Today's his birthday. And I know I hate him and I was initially going to avoid him when this day came, but now that I promised Jared I would try, I'm wondering if I should pretend I didn't know, which would be completely understandable, or actually wish him a happy birthday, as proof to Jared that I tried?"

"I think you should do whatever you feel okay with." He was serious now. "No one would expect you to remember, so I think you can wait and see if it comes up. But at the same time, you were a child when he left, so if you still remember his birthday after all this time and what he put you through, then maybe you should say it and see how it goes."

"I could have looked it up online," I argued.

"But you didn't. You remember from back when he was your favorite person in the entire world." No one had brought that up before. It was a given that I was Team Mom and hated him now, but even the ones trying to convince me to give him a chance didn't remind me that I was a daddy's girl until I no longer had one.

"Part of me thinks I should, to make Jared happy and show him I'm trying, but at the same time, it might make him feel horrible to see how I remember his birthday when he forgot most of mine," I admitted.

"Be careful," he warned.

"To not hurt him?" I wondered if Jared was getting to him.

"To not get hurt in the process."

I let him go back to sleep and rushed to the house under the rain that was building. I decided I would go up to my room and spend the day doing homework, as planned, but if I saw him on my way, I would say it. Otherwise I would just go about my day.

I made it to the stairs and was on the top step when he walked out of the nursery with Owen in his arms.

"Morning." He wasn't expecting an answer.

"Happy birthday," I said quietly when he was about to go into his room. He still heard, because he stopped immediately and turned to make sure he hadn't imagined it. For a second, we stood there, staring at each other, before I turned and went to my room.

"Can I come in?" Tracy knocked on my door while I brushed my hair after a shower.

"What is it?"

She waited for me to come to the door and open it, which was definitely progress. "We're going to see a movie at the Grove since it's raining. We wondered if you wanted to join us? By we, I mean Chris told me not to bother you, because he knows how you feel, but I know you love movies, and even if you say no, I still think we should invite you."

"I have a lot of homework." It was partially an excuse, but I would actually be writing an essay while they were gone.

"I wouldn't want to interfere with your schoolwork," she assured me. "He never makes a big deal of his birthday, so there won't be a party, but I invited a few people over for dinner, and I would love it if you could come." She worried I might avoid a gathering in his honor.

"If I'm done my homework." The look on her face told me she saw the fear in mine, and knew exactly why I wouldn't want to come.

Once she was gone, I went to my desk to work on the essay for English class. I stared at the instructions for five minutes without reading them before I called Jared.

"Do you work today or are you coming to the birthday bash?" I asked when he picked up.

"I work, which is why they had me over the other night."

"How come you didn't mention it was for his birthday, or that it was coming up?" I felt even guiltier now for ruining his birthday lasagna.

"Because although I think you should give him a chance and get to know him, I don't think pushing you to be nice to him for his birthday would get us anywhere."

"I wished him happy birthday this morning," I confessed. I'm pretty sure I would have said it even if there was no deal with Jared.

"Because you're trying?" he asked.

"Mostly."

"And the other reason is..." he sighed, knowing he wasn't going to like it.

"Because I want him to understand I shouldn't feel guilty for avoiding him whenever I can. I want him to know it's not because I'm a terrible person, it's because of what he did."

"You wanted to show him the reason you stay away is because he hurt you and you can't trust him and let him hurt you again, because it took a long time to get over the last time, and to be honest, you're not sure you have. Wishing him a happy birthday was your way of showing him that even after everything he's done, even when you're horrible to him, you still remember his birthday, and that's what kills you."

"Since when are you this observant?" I asked instead of agreeing with his spot-on analysis.

"I went through the same thing when I moved here. I didn't just forgive him and let him back into my life."

"What changed?"

"I gave him a chance and he showed me he deserved it."

"What did he say when you found him? Did he explain why he never came home?"

"Give him a chance, Rachel. I hate seeing you sad and I think you can be happy there."

"Okay," I reluctantly agreed before letting him get ready for work.

WE HAD to write a paper titled "My Biggest Regret" with no other guidelines. I was always way better at pouring my heart out onto a canvas, and was definitely taking advantage of the supplies at this school. Still, while it might not have been the most elegantly structured essay, I had pages to say.

My first sentences took a while, because my biggest regret was also a secret I wanted to keep, not something I wanted anyone reading. But as soon as I got going, I couldn't stop until I was fifteen pages in.

I WAS PRETTY okay with the essay by the time there was a knock on my door.

"I'll be there in a minute," I told Tracy, saving my file. I was wearing an orange dress I got for our Fourth of July Party last summer. I didn't know if the people downstairs were dressed up, and I didn't need another reason to feel out of place.

"I would love to accompany you to the dining room." I heard Ryan's voice instead of Tracy's.

"They have you babysitting again?" I was nervous and relieved when I opened the door for him. It was nice to have an ally.

"I volunteered," he corrected, so I raised my eyebrow.

"Are there a lot of people?"

"I think we'll be ten of us, including your brother." It took me a second to realize he meant Owen.

"Can I ask you a question?" I tried to gauge how much I could trust him.

"Anything," he smiled, letting me know I could ask, but he

might not answer.

"How did you get close to Christopher? You joined the show less than a year ago and you already babysit Owen, you're at his birthday party..."

"Right, they never introduced you to me, so I'm just an actor."

"Do you have another profession?"

"No." He only kind of laughed at me. "But Tracy is my sister."

"Since when?" I wasn't expecting that.

"Well, since I was born, and my parents already had her."

"I meant how come no one ever told me," I rephrased, but he understood the first time.

"I would say it's because we were never properly introduced, but I think they thought you would like me more if you didn't know I was related to her. I mean, if we're being honest, you like me a little less now, don't you?" he smiled.

"Do my siblings know?"

"Jared and Sarah do," he shared. "I haven't met Kyle yet."

"Have you been telling your sister everything I tell you?" I was definitely taking advantage of how nice he was being, and sharing a lot of feelings.

"No. And they want you to keep liking me, so they haven't asked. Not that I would tell them if they did. I wasn't sent here to spy on you."

"That means you knew him before Jared moved here?" I asked, knowing Tracy would already have been pregnant when Jared found him.

"I did," he agreed.

"Did you know that I existed?" It was silly, but I needed to know.

"I did," he admitted. "Tracy told our dad she was seeing a guy who already had four kids he never sees."

"And that wasn't a red flag?" I could forgive her more if she was fooled into falling for him, rather than chose to marry him with the full knowledge of what he did.

"You won't know this, because she doesn't tell people, and she's gotten a lot better, but Trace had terrible taste in men." I was looking at him like this wasn't a surprise to me, given who she married. "You don't get it. Yes, we were concerned when she told us about the kids he doesn't see, and we wanted to protect her, but once we met your dad..."

"He's an actor," I reminded him.

"She married her first husband straight out of high school. I'm pretty sure she became a makeup artist because it taught her the best ways to cover up the bruises." Luckily, his anger was directed at the asshole who hurt his sister, not at me for being a spoiled, oblivious child.

"Very bad taste in men," I said quietly.

"He nearly put her in a coma before she left him, and even then, she almost went back. The guys that came after him weren't any better, but she didn't think she deserved a nice guy. She believed everything those jerks told her."

"I didn't know. I've seen some abused women and she doesn't —" I was thinking of the women mom sometimes brought home for a night or two, who didn't trust the shelters and looked lost and broken.

"That was your dad," he cut me off. "After meeting him...we would have been happy as long as he wasn't hurting her, but he actually put her back together, piece by piece. She smiles now and she sings and that might seem normal to you, but I was thirteen the last time I saw her as anything other than scared, quiet, and a shadow of my big sister."

"You forgive him for his past because he fixed her," I understood.

"I don't know what happened to make your dad leave, or why he stayed away, and I am sorry he did that to you. But even if he had no reason for it and he was just being an asshole, the guy downstairs is trying, and whether you believe it or not, he truly cares about you."

"I guess we should go down." I tried not to show how heart-broken it made me to lose my ally.

"This doesn't change anything. We can still go off and avoid them as soon as the meal is over, if you want."

"I don't want to say you're the enemy now, but…"

"Hey, Uncle Ryan's got your back," he smiled.

I laughed at him before smiling back.

RYAN GOT a call during dessert and had to go take care of something for his band, so I offered to bring Owen up to bed instead of following the guests to the backyard. I was watching him sleep, about to go back to my room, when I heard someone in the doorway.

"March 8th," Christopher said, taking a step into the room while I stood by the crib without looking at him. "You were born on March 8th at 4:15 in the morning, after the longest and hardest of your mom's labors."

"So?" I knew my eyes were watering, but if I didn't look at him, maybe he wouldn't.

"I wanted you to know that I never forgot. That even if I wasn't there with you, even if you didn't get anything from me, that doesn't mean I wasn't thinking of you. On that day and every day of my life, I think of all of you, and I miss you, and I love you. The day you were born is one of the five happiest days of my life, and I could never forget it. You can be mad at me and hate me, but I don't want you to ever doubt that I love you." He lingered for a minute in the doorway and said, "Thank you for being there tonight. It meant the world to me," before going back to his guests.

I was glad he left, because I had to clench my fists to avoid saying words I knew I would hate myself for, but that I felt he deserved. Because thinking of doing something didn't matter if you never actually did it, and if he loved us so much, he would have been there.

18

HONEYBEE'S HALLOWEEN

"You can be a witch?" Nick suggested when I turned down every one of his elaborate costume ideas.

"I can also give out candy," I argued. "Or sit in my room and eat candy while working on our history project." Part of our presentation was about the civilian casualties of Pearl Harbor, and the off-duty lieutenant who rushed in to help on his day off, but was killed for looking Asian. I was using it as an opportunity to research gun laws, and what is actually being done to prevent things like Columbine and what happened to my mom from happening again. I still got weird looks from the librarian, but less than if she knew it was something I was doing on my own time, unrelated to school.

"How can I live vicariously through you if that's all you give me?" he shook his head before taking a sip of his pumpkin spice latte. They were popping up at coffee shops, but so far none even came close to the ones mom would make.

"You'll be dressed up, isn't that enough?" I teasingly countered.

"I'll be on set. Which isn't the same thing. And the elf costume doesn't count because it's a Christmas movie, which isn't at all like Halloween."

"You can pretend you're in a live version of the Nightmare Before Christmas." I tried not to laugh at the image of him with pointy ears in an elf suit.

"Bah humbug." He shook his head at me.

"That's for people who hate Christmas, not for high school students who are too old to dress up and go trick or treating."

"It's actually someone who behaves in a deceptive or dishonest way, and I feel this qualifies as being deceived."

"You happen to know the actual definition?" I asked.

"It's one of my lines," he explained. "And the point remains that someone who dresses up in the most elaborate costumes for a photoshoot every year should have a killer Halloween costume. Especially when there's a kid involved," he brought up Owen.

"I'm not into it this year," I tried not to show that I was upset, because it had nothing to do with him. There was something about Katie telling me she hates me for refusing to come home and make her costume like I promised that made me not want to participate, especially not with a different kid.

"Next year, I'll put a clause in my contract that I can't work on Halloween, and we'll all go out," he decided.

"Are you like this every holiday, or..." He nodded so I laughed and shook my head before the bell rang and we went to history.

WHEN THE BUS dropped me off that afternoon, the house was empty. I had at least an hour until Chris would be home, and Tracy usually stayed at the park with Owen until five, so I went to the kitchen and found all the ingredients to make mom's pumpkin spice steamed milk. We weren't Halloween people, but mom loved getting the costumes together for the picture, and I loved designing Katie's costume with her, then bringing it to life. Autumn was my favorite season. All of my Fall memories were of everyone playing football in the backyard, sipping pumpkin spiced hot beverages at Kyle's games, trick or treating with Katie, cuddling under big blankets on the lawn chairs in the backyard, playing in the leaves...it felt warm and like family.

"Something smells amazing." I heard Tracy as I poured my drink into a big mug.

"It's pumpkin spice—"

"Those are my favorite," she said longingly, cutting me off in her excitement before looking down at her stomach. "I don't mind not having my morning coffee, but come PSL time..." she tried to get Owen to stop squirming when he reached for me.

"It's actually just milk and the spices. I only pretend to be a coffee drinker," I admitted.

"I never even thought of that. Would you mind sharing the recipe..." she stopped, probably remembering the lasagna incident. "You don't have to, obviously..."

"There isn't one." I felt terrible that she expected a meltdown from me. "But I made too much. I'm not used to doing it for one person, so...do you want some?"

"You would be my favorite person in the world," was her answer, so I took out another mug and poured what was left of the flavored milk into it. When I handed it to her I took Owen, which I didn't often do when they were watching. I acted like it was so she wouldn't spill the drink, but it was impossible to resist him when he reached out for me.

"It's delicious. Heavenly. Thank you," she said after her first sip.

"My mom came up with it. It's not a recipe so much as a list of ingredients that go by taste for quantities," I explained why I couldn't give her a recipe.

"She didn't like measuring, did she? When we were dating, Chris told me pasta was his favorite meal, but every time I made it, even if he said it was delicious, I could tell it didn't compare to the memory he had in his head. I scoured recipe books, asked your siblings when I met them, tried to figure out how to make the pasta he loved, but I couldn't. Because it was her recipe he wanted, and she never used one." I couldn't tell if she told me more than she meant to, or if she was intentionally letting me know that my dad still loved my mom. Or at least her cooking.

"She cooked like she lived her life. I don't think she had a choice but to learn how to take things as they came and roll with the punches after she found herself raising four children on her own." I handed Owen back to her and took my mug to go to my room.

"Rachel," she called, but whether it was to yell at me or apologize, I didn't go back.

THERE WAS a package for me on the floor in front of my door, so I brought it into my room and shut the door.

The handwriting and Virginia postmark told me it was from Kyle, probably a very late response to the letter I sent him. I tore it open and found a T-shirt, as well as a small white envelope.

"Rache,

I'm sorry it took me so long to write back, but things are crazy here. I'm completely exhausted from the moment I wake up to the second I fall asleep. Still, it's way better than the thoughts that come whenever I'm not busy.

To answer your question, no, I do not think that you should enlist. Or run away. Or join a circus. Although these are all very realistic options for you, I think Sarah is your best bet. She must be missing you as much as I am, so combined with Katie, who is usually very vocal about the things she wants, I think she'll cave. Or you can live in my closet once I turn eighteen, if no one else will take you.

I'm sorry I bailed on you. When I signed up for this, I thought I would be the one calling you because I was homesick. That you would be the one telling me everything would be okay, and I'd be home soon. As it is, I don't think I can provide much comfort, as I have no idea where home is anymore. I keep remembering that sign from the living room, "Home is Where the Heart Is." That might be why it hurts so much, because our hearts are scattered across the country instead of in the one place everyone couldn't wait to come home to.

If I were you, I would spend all my time at Jared and Toby's, accidentally falling asleep and stuff until you're basically living there, so it makes sense to officially move in. It worked for Haylie that Summer Uncle Jack was working in Maryland.

Other than that, just stay strong. Be awesome. Be you. And as soon as I can, I'll kidnap you. Promise.

Xoxo

Kyle"

THE T-SHIRT WAS DARK BLUE, with MARINE written in white across the chest.

TRACY DIDN'T TELL Chris about my outburst, because dinner went on as normal. I ate quickly, excused myself and spent the rest of the night in my room.

THE NEXT MORNING when I went down for breakfast, there was a big pile of black and yellow material on the table. I moved closer to inspect it before Tracy came in with Owen.

"Oh, those are our Halloween costumes," she beamed. "We're bees."

"Was it your idea?" I asked, trying to push the anger back inside.

"Owen's." She looked worried and confused. "I brought him to the costume store and he wouldn't let go of this one. I was thrilled because it hides my bump...what's wrong?" She looked so sincere, like upsetting me was the last thing she wanted to do.

I debated if I wanted to tell her, then took a breath and went for it. "Did you listen to the rest of the call when I..."

"I did," she admitted, answering so I wouldn't have to remind her which call I was referring to.

"Do you remember what he called me?"

"Honeybee," she said as it hit her. "I completely forgot about that, I didn't think...is this one of those things..."

Seeing how accommodating she was trying to be made me realize that it must be hell to live with me; getting upset about all kinds of things she couldn't predict or understand.

"It's fine," I assured her.

"But it is something," she understood.

"Only if it came from him," I argued. "I'm sorry for being difficult." And at least to her, I meant it.

"I know it's nothing like what you're going through, but my dad cheated on my mom. When he remarried, I was horrible to his new wife. I hated her, so I get it."

"I don't hate you," I reluctantly admitted. "You didn't know." I was reminding myself as much as I was reassuring her.

"I would like to. Know you, that is," she tried.

"I was a bee for the first few Halloweens of my life. I don't know how it started, but I know I was the one who chose it the fourth time, and I got upset whenever anyone called me a bumble bee. In my head, there were bumble bees that sting you, and honey bees that make honey. Two entirely separate entities."

"You wanted to be a honeybee."

"My mom would hand out candy while my dad took us trick or treating, so he made it a point to call me honeybee when we walked up to every single house, so they would know what I was. After that, it was his nickname for me, until..."

"I don't think I've heard you call him that," she said quietly instead of finishing the thought for me.

"I'm not talking about your husband when I say that. This was the dad I had when I was little, who died in a tragic accident, because he loved me so much that he would not have left me otherwise," I explained, trying not to let on how much it hurt, because I knew they were the same person. He didn't love me all that much, because he left.

"Would you like to come trick or treating with us? To make sure everyone knows he's a honeybee?" she offered, looking down at Owen. I could tell she wanted me to come, but wasn't the least bit surprised when I turned her down.

"I have a lot of homework," I told her. "But thank you."

WITH NICK ON SET, I spent my lunch in the library, doing homework and more research on my pet project. I waited until 12:45 to call Sarah, knowing she would be home with Katie by then.

"Aren't you in class?" she asked.

"They still let students eat, even in California," I told her.

"She wrote you an apology. It's in the mail," she said of her daughter.

"You didn't have to do that. I deserved it."

"It was all her. She felt bad and wanted you to know she loves you."

"I love her too. So much." I wiped at the tears I was having trouble controlling. "And I miss her. Both of you."

"God, I wish I could go get you and bring you home."

"You can," I said hopefully, remembering Kyle's letter.

"No, I can't. And you promised Jared you would give him the year," she reminded me.

"School year," I corrected.

"Were you calling to make me cry?" she asked.

"No, I wanted to talk to her, since I can't be there tonight."

"Coming right up," she assured me. I saw Carmen and Jess heading off to the parking lot, meaning they wouldn't be in class this afternoon either. I returned their wave as Katie came on the line.

"Rachel!" she said excitedly.

"Hey Katie Bear." I smiled at the sound of her voice.

"I didn't mean it. I don't hate you. I love you," she said quickly.

"Don't worry about it. I completely understand how you feel. You know how much I love you, even if I don't see you that much anymore, right?"

"To the moon and back," she answered.

"And even farther."

She told me all about her costume, which was partly made from previous costumes I'd done for her, so she insisted it was like I was there with her. When the bell rang and I told her I had to go, she asked me to call again tomorrow, so we could compare our loots, and she could maybe convince Sarah to bring her here next year if they gave better candy.

"ON SET AGAIN?" Mr. Adams asked when I walked into class without Nick. He was dressed like Captain Jack Sparrow, and not the cheap costume store kind.

"Playing an elf," I agreed.

"We'll have to make it extra fun, so he knows he missed out," he said before getting into character for everyone else who came in. He was completely undeterred by his abysmal attendance rate, with most of the students only ever showing up for exams.

WHEN I GOT HOME, Tracy was in the main entrance, taking pictures of Owen in his bee costume. I went into the kitchen to get some grapes as a snack before dinner, but when I got back to the stairs, Tracy was on the phone, with Owen on her hip.

"That's too late for him, he'll be asleep...no, of course... I've got the pictures, but he won't remember if we actually went or not...are you sure? Okay then, I'll show you the pictures when you get home...I love you too," she said before hanging up and seeing me there.

"That was Chris?" I asked.

"They're running late on set, so he won't make it back in time to go trick or treating," she said, looking like she was debating something. "I know you have homework, but..."

We both knew the reason I said no this morning was him. She was far from being my favorite person, but she had been making it hard to not like her lately. "I guess if it's only for a couple of hours..." I relented, since I promised Katie I'd check out the loot, and I couldn't if they didn't go.

"There's an extra bee costume upstairs if—"

"That's okay, I've got something," I assured her before going to my room. I wished I had brought my mom's uniform, so I could bring her with me, but that would definitely make me cry, and would probably make Tracy feel bad. Instead, I got the Marine T-shirt Kyle sent me with some blue cargo pants. When I put my hair in a tucked French braid, the costume worked.

Tracy drove us to another neighborhood, where there was less of a distance between house. I carried Owen, since he was getting heavy, and she brought the honey pot candy bag. We didn't talk much to each other, because I made it a point to mostly talk to Owen, but by the time we pulled back into the driveway, I knew she understood a lot more than she let on, and I should be nicer to her.

19

TOO GOOD TO BE TRUE

"It was like ten seconds."

"More like two. And that's being generous," Jared argued as he drove me to school. We'd been surfing almost every week, and this morning I caught my first wave.

"I'm surprised I have any confidence at all."

"Two seconds is still awesome. A lot of people don't get to standing, even after—" I didn't get to hear the rest of his statement, because the song on the radio ended and the show host got our full attention.

"New evidence was found on the Lake George High School shooting back in September. At first, no one knew what drove three students to take down their fellow classmates and teachers, but a letter was found that details their troubled reasoning." Jared tensed up as I did, and moved his hand to hold mine. "Philip Sims left the letter for his girlfriend, Alice Yung, before heading out on that fateful day. Apparently, the shooters compiled a list of forty-eight people from the community that they felt deserved to die. They always planned on taking their own lives at the end, because they knew what they were doing was wrong, but they didn't see any other way."

"How did they come up with this list?" her co-host asked.

"Were they bullies? Did a teacher give them a bad grade?" he mocked, making light of the murders.

"The list has some pretty hefty accusations, everything from child abuse to rape, drug dealing, hit and runs, murder..."

"Is anyone looking into these accusations?"

"They'll have to, now that the letter has been made public. This is most likely the misguided rantings of troubled teenagers, but all claims will need to be taken seriously," she said before introducing the next song, so I turned the radio off.

"Are you okay?" Jared asked me.

"Are you?" I countered.

"They didn't mention mom. Or Alex." His hand that held mine was shaking.

"They lumped them all together," I agreed.

"We can ditch and go..." He couldn't think of anywhere we could go to feel better.

"It's okay. You work, I need to give Nick my notes from his time on set, and mom always said it was better to face it."

"If you change your mind, let me know. We can drive home if it helps." He meant Lake George, and I loved him for it.

I GOT out of the car and went to find Nick in the quad.

"Are you okay?" he asked as soon as he saw me.

"I'm fine," I shrugged it off and sat in front of him.

"This is about that thing you're not telling me that I pretend I don't notice, isn't it?" he asked.

"I don't want to talk about it," I tried not to snap, because I knew he was trying to help.

"Rachel," he pressed, but I wasn't in the mood.

"Alex, I said no," I snapped, running my hand through my hair, trying to calm myself.

"Nick," he corrected.

"What?"

"I'm Nick," he repeated, making me realize what I said. Maybe I should have gone with Jared.

"I'm sorry, I...my mind is somewhere else. Here are my notes." I handed him the papers.

"You don't need to tell me, but you don't look okay, Rachel. Maybe you should call Jared or Toby or—"

"I'll be fine. See you at lunch?" I tried to smile.

"I'll be there," he agreed. I could feel his eyes on me the whole time I walked to art class.

I GOT INTO THE STUDIO, ready to let my emotions out onto the canvas. The school had excellent supplies, more like the ones my mom would get me for my birthday than the ones at my old school. My last painting was gone, which happened when Mrs. Markham graded them, so I went to get a new canvas from the supply room. I was mixing my paints to get the perfect shade of blue when Mrs. Markham came in.

"Rachel." She paused. "First bell doesn't ring for another five minutes."

"I know. I wanted to get started early. I hope that's okay?" I asked, but I knew that Daisy, who had the easel beside mine, did it all the time.

"Of course. I'll be back by the bell," she said before leaving.

I HAD the beginnings of my deep blue background by the time Mrs. Markham came back with our Headmistress and the school's security guard.

"Miss Glass, would you mind coming with us please?" Mrs. Williamson asked politely, but I could tell I didn't have a choice.

"What's wrong?" I asked, following them, immediately terrified that I'd lost someone else.

"We need to ask you a few questions." This made no sense with my initial theory, which was a relief, but also confusing.

"About what?" I asked.

"Come with us please." The security guard carefully led me to a small room close to her office.

THEY LEFT ME THERE, alone, for what felt like hours, until they finally opened the door and brought me to the Headmistress' office, where Chris was waiting.

"What happened?" he asked as soon as I came in. He moved close as if to hug me, then pulled back when he thought better of it.

"I have no idea. They brought me from art class," I shared.

"What's going on?" he asked Mrs. Williamson as I took my seat.

"Mr. Glass, we called you here because Rachel has been exhibiting some aggression in class, and we're afraid she may want to harm other students. With what has been going on around the country these past few years, we have to take every potential threat very seriously," she explained, grouping me with Phil and the Columbine shooters.

"Are you sure you're talking about my Rachel? Rachel Glass?" he pointed to me.

"Multiple teachers have voiced concern," she agreed. "Mrs. Markham, Mr. Smith, our librarian…"

"Excuse me, Mrs. Williamson?" Mr. Adams poked his head into the office.

"Yes?" She was just as unimpressed with him as the students.

"I teach Rachel history, and she's a great student. One of the only ones who actually shows up and participates. She hands in her assignments on time, and she's a relatively happy student," he defended me. Hopefully, he heard about this through a teacher grapevine and not the student gossip mill.

"She's always happy?" Mrs. Williamson latched on to it, implying that would cause concern as well.

"We've been covering World War II and genocide, so no, not

always happy." He smiled before seeing his humor was not appreciated here. "She's a normal teenager. A few things upset her, but everyone has triggers. And I say upset as in sad, not dangerous."

"You think she might hurt others because she gets sad sometimes?" Chris was upset.

"What are her triggers?" The headmistress ignored Chris' question and looked like she was about to prove a point.

"Guns, 9/11, Columbine…things that normally upset people," Mr. Adams filled her in. I guess being the only student who paid attention meant the teacher noticed when you stopped.

"Her English teacher gave us an essay where she confesses to murdering a student, she has been painting dead people, taking out books on guns from the library, and her locker has newspaper clippings—"

"You went in my locker?" My paintings were behind her desk, and she was rummaging through the newspaper articles I couldn't bring myself to add to the scrapbook mom had of every single time one of us was in the paper.

"Lockers are school property," she pointed out.

"Would the newspaper clippings be about the shooting at Lake George High School?" Chris asked like he'd figured it all out.

"Yes, and—"

"And the student she confesses to murdering, his name is Alex?" he cut her off. I knew he was defending me, but he had no right to say Alex's name so casually, like this was all some misunderstanding that didn't matter. I never told him about Alex, and he never met him, so he had no idea.

"She was kicked out of her old school, and we don't accept this type of behavior either." The headmistress was upset Chris knew I was troubled and hadn't bothered to get me the appropriate help, far away from her students.

"I wasn't kicked out of my old school." I had no idea where she came up with that one.

"On her first day of school, I asked about her transfer and

she said she didn't have a choice," she said to Chris, who raised his shoulders at me, wishing I hadn't told everyone how miserable I was.

"Did you bother telling her anything before I showed up?" I put it on him.

"I didn't know you were going to be painting dead people," he defended himself, which was a valid point, but I would have warned Katie's teachers if she was sent across the country to a new school after her mom died in a school shooting.

"Maybe that's because you don't know me," I shot back before he turned to the headmistress.

"Rachel was forced to come and live with me because she lost her mother, who was a police officer, in the Lake George High School shooting. Her best friend also died that night, because he tried to protect her mother, which is why she feels responsible for his death. And those paintings are without a doubt of her mother and the other victims. She isn't aggressive, and she isn't going to hurt any of your students. She's just sad and needed an outlet to deal with her feelings," he summed me up in a perfect little bow, and although most of it was on point, he didn't get any of it from me.

"Your mother was the cop," she connected the dots.

"Yes," I agreed, wanting to get out of there more than anything.

"You still can't go around putting death and murder into paintings and poems and essays," she warned me.

"Rachel understands. There will be no more of that," he assured her.

"I won't put a suspension on her record, but I would like her to take the rest of the day off and find a better outlet for her feelings," she said like I was the one in the wrong here.

"She will." Chris thanked her as he shook her hand, then we left the office.

. . .

"You're not going to walk home, are you?" Chris asked when I walked down the halls, away from the parking lot and way ahead of him.

"I'm going to call Jared." I didn't slow down.

"You can't make your brother leave work because you don't want to hang out with me. I can drop you off at—"

"This has nothing to do with you. Jared offered to—" I needed to get away from him as badly as I'd needed to leave that room.

"I came here from set so I could convince your headmistress not to expel you, yet you're mad at me?" he was exasperated.

"I'm sorry I ruined your work day. I'll try to not have feelings anymore."

"Rachel, I am not complaining. I know you don't want to talk to me, but I think you should talk to someone if—"

"If I'm having trouble dealing with how I was sent to live with strangers because my mom and my best friend were shot while I waited outside in the car?" I stopped and turned to face him.

"I know this is hard."

"No, you don't. You don't know anything about me. You can get Sarah and Jared to tell you, but you still won't know me. And you didn't know Alex, so you can't pretend you know what he meant to me, and you can't act like you knew what my paintings were about, because you lost the right to care about my mother when you abandoned her," I emphasized the last two words, so he would know what he did. This wasn't only about him hurting me, it was all those years she had to switch the channel when his show came on, because seeing him still made her sad.

"I am still your father. And your legal guardian. Will you please come home with me before they try to expel you again?"

I knew Jared was working, and the halls would be flooded with students by the time he got here, so I reluctantly followed Chris to his car and sat in the passenger's seat, staring out the window.

He tried to stay home with me at first, but I stayed in my room with the door shut, so he came to let me know he was going back to work. I didn't care either way. I stayed in my room and left the TV on CNN. I didn't like the pictures and videos they played, but any bit of information that could possibly explain why my life fell apart was worth it. I took the notebook where I'd written the names of the victims, to try and see if I could figure out their supposed crimes, and added all the names to make the forty-eight person list. Alice was right that they would twist it, because the news stations were finding a way to make the shooters seem like delusional people while also making some of the victims seem like they deserved it. I was starting to see the picture they were painting. I still thought they were in the wrong, and Phil should have gone to my mother, or found a better way to bring them to justice, but I was slowly able to see why each of them was willing to play along. What crimes they would kill for.

Alice had rewritten the list of forty-eight names, which made some newscasters question her, and the authenticity of the list. The only difference was that the guys had been more specific, whereas she only gave in the names and the crimes. Which I understood. When Alice and Phil were best friends, not dating yet, Alice went to Junior prom with Drake Johnson. She went out to eat with him after, while Phil drove us home, but his pager went off and he left us without an explanation. The next week, Phil and Alice were dating, and she avoided any room Drake happened to be in.

The one time I went to a high school party, Jason Smoak won one of those contests where you drink a keg of beer while doing a handstand, then drove home. The next morning, Mrs. Avery died as the result of a hit and run, two streets away from the party. Everyone was questioned, Jason was the only one who left drunk, but he was released after fifteen minutes and everything was dropped.

Charlie Morris was the guy who would hang out behind the

bleachers and deal drugs. Corbin's twin sister had a serious crush on him, and they started going places together before she died of an overdose last June. Mom said it looked like she'd been with other people, but she drowned on her own vomit because they panicked and ran away instead of turning her over.

Daniel Stewart was the guy I told Uncle Jack about at Alex's funeral. A high-priced lawyer that mom did not go with for her will, even though he was more qualified and she had the money. His daughter always wore long sleeves, even when it was super hot outside. She said it was because she had sensitive skin, but mom never bought it. Michael was his son, that he sent to a school for troubled boys, a type of boot camp for his drug addiction, but I think there was another reason his dad wanted him out of the house.

Drake Johnson, Jason Smoak, Charlie Morris and Daniel Stewart were all on the list, with rape, hit and run, murder and domestic abuse as their crimes. I still hated Phil and his friends for what they did, and how badly they messed it up, but I understood a little better.

I GOT to school the next morning knowing I would have a terrible day. First, Jess' text let me know that everyone knew my mom was one of the victims of the Lake George shooting, and I was now known as 'the weird kid who paints dead people'. She did let me know that she, Clarice and Carmen were still cool to sit with me in English, so at least there was that. Second, every news station was talking about Phil's confession letter, with only three of them bothering to explain that two of the victims were not on the list. Even then, they rarely specified that it was mom and Alex. Third, the picture they used every time they mentioned Phil or Alice was one of the two of them with me and Alex. I knew why his parents gave that one, because he looked sweet and innocent in it, but I did not need the extra attention it would bring.

The bell rang before I even reached my locker, since I had been avoiding the crowds. I made it to math class as the bell was ringing and tried to ignore the fact that all eyes in the classroom were on me. Even the teacher was surprised to see me in class, rather than waiting it out at home. The stares continued intermittently throughout the hour and a half.

As soon as the bell rang, I rushed out into the quickly filling hallways. It wasn't to get away from the students, who were everywhere now, but to find Nick.

I always loved school, especially now that it offered me a chance to escape Chris, both when I was there and when I was doing homework, but my favorite part about this school was Nick. I wasn't sure if he would understand why I had those weird painting instincts, or what he would make of me calling him Alex yesterday. Before this new mess with me being suspended and on the news, Nick knew nothing except what I shared with him. He knew something had happened, but instead of asking me about it, he would let me pretend there was nothing to talk about. For a few hours with him at lunch and between classes, I didn't feel like an orphan forced to live with a man who didn't care about her, I felt like a regular girl, who could go home to the one of her memories once the bell rang. He made me feel like I wasn't broken and falling apart, so all I could think of last night while trying to fall asleep was that I might have lost him along with everyone else in this place.

I went straight to his locker, trying to think of what I could say to explain it to him, but he wasn't there. He also wasn't in the quad, where we normally hung out between classes. I went back to my locker, so I could get the books for my next class and continue looking for him, but he was there, leaning against my locker and waiting.

"I was looking for you," I said when I got close.

"I was hiding in plain sight," he said with a smile.

"I'm sorry I left like that yesterday."

"I heard. You're a rebel who got suspended. Very exciting

stuff." He was acting like yesterday was any other day, which I would normally appreciate, but I felt like I owed him an explanation.

"I'm guessing you saw it on the news or heard about it around school. I appreciate you pretending it doesn't matter, but I think I need to explain myself, because I'm not..." I tried to find a way to explain what everyone must think I am, but I couldn't. I had no idea what people thought of me at this point.

"You did absolutely nothing wrong, Rache. If you want to talk to me and explain why you called me Alex, I'm all ears, but if you want to keep pretending nothing happened, I have a multitude of conversation topics that have nothing to do with what you don't want to talk about."

"You're taking this really well. You did hear what I was suspended for, right?"

"I know you love to paint, so it makes sense that you would try to let out whatever is haunting you, and the teacher can't be upset at what you write when they ask for 'My Biggest Regret' as the title."

"You don't need me to tell you because you already know," I realized.

"About your mom and the shooting? Yes, I know," he said delicately.

"For how long?" I was pretty sure it was before the rest of the school found out yesterday.

"I knew when I saw your mom's face on the news, the day after it happened. I recognized her from the pictures, then word on the set was that Toby left because of a death in the family."

"And you didn't say anything?" I didn't blame him. I hadn't wanted him to.

"You were carefully avoiding any mention of why you moved, and didn't seem to want to talk about your parents, so I let you."

"And you don't think I'm weird? Or a freak?"

"I saw your picture on the news last night, which explains as much as it brings new questions for me, but no, I don't think you're a freak. I think you're my favorite person at this school, and I'm very glad you weren't expelled."

"You saw the picture of me with Phil?" I asked.

"And Alex," he agreed.

"Alex concerns you more than the mass murderer?" It felt wrong referring to Phil like that, but it was what everyone else was calling him.

"I'm fairly confident you didn't know what he would eventually do, and you're way too sweet for me to worry about you becoming one. But I think Alex is the bigger story I might not be ready to hear."

"I only called you that because it was such a him thing to do; calling me on not being okay when I was trying to pretend I was." I knew that nothing about Alex would ever be that simple again. I still wore his jacket whenever the weather was cool.

"But he meant a lot to you." He tried not to ask, but still wanted to know.

"Alex was...from the time I met him when I was seven, he was my best friend. And I'm sure this will surprise you, but I didn't have many of those. It was always either me and my family or me and Alex. Well, actually, Alex kind of unofficially became a part of the family. Losing him would have been like losing a part of myself, but losing him and my mom at the same time was like...it was like I couldn't breathe. Like I didn't understand how I was still dealing with things and going places because I felt utterly dead inside. I mean, some of those paintings I did, they're not all victims of the shooting. Some of them are me," I admitted for the first time. It felt good to get it off my chest, but I was also terrified this would make him run in the opposite direction.

The bell rang, telling us we had to get to our next class. I figured this saved him from having to respond, and went to grab the books from my locker, but he held my arm and made me look at him. "I think you're kind of amazing, Rachel, and I am happy you are dealing with things and going places. Your paintings don't make you a freak, they make you human. I'll see you at lunch."

He said the whole thing looking straight into my eyes, then went off to his locker as if that wasn't the most intense moment we'd shared. I went to class, still feeling the eyes on me, but I felt okay. Maybe the majority of the student body thought I had issues, but I had Nick, and he thought I was kind of amazing.

20

SKIPPING

"A little old for high school, aren't you?" Nick said when we were walking to history. I turned and saw Toby, which had me rushing into his arms.

"I'm sorry I haven't been around lately, they've been doing overnight shoots."

"Jared and all of your messages said the same thing," I assured him while he and Nick did that guy handshake thing.

"You know school doesn't let out for another five and a half hours, right?" I asked.

"I do know that," he agreed. "That's why we're skipping."

"What do you mean?"

"I mean that I am kidnapping you because I'm working nights and weekends now and it's a shame you haven't been sightseeing yet."

"We did all that when you guys moved here two years ago," I reminded him.

"Those were tourist places. I'm taking you hiking and all over the underground scenes."

"Really?" I looked at him in a way that implied I thought he was crazy.

"Yes, and since it's a kidnapping, you don't have a choice."

"The school will call him," I warned.

"Who do you think I am?" he pretended to be offended. "I have it all figured out. And Nick can cover for you, pick up your homework, all that stuff. He's a very good liar."

"A very good actor," Nick corrected.

"Same thing," Toby shrugged before taking my hand and leading me to his car.

"Have fun!" Nick called after us.

"YOU GOT HER TO COME?" Jared was waiting in the driver's seat.

"He didn't think I could. I told him I would throw you over my shoulder and carry you if I had to," Toby told me.

"You're basically a parental figure...you could qualify as my legal guardian," I got Toby to laugh.

"She has never skipped school. No even once, unless mom said it was okay, which isn't skipping," Jared stated.

"But we're talking about the school that suspended me because I did as I was told." Neither of them was surprised that I got suspended, so word got around, but they weren't convinced with my why, so I elaborated. "In an unconventional way, yes, but I would have gotten As for them back home. I was being honest."

"Speaking of school," Toby started.

"Are you trying to bring up how you sent a spy to look after me, then report to you?" I finished for him.

"I didn't send him," he argued. "And he's not a spy. We just talk occasionally."

"About her," Jared amended.

"Sometimes," he agreed. "But honestly, I didn't tell him what school you were going to or even that you were here. I just talked about you on set, because I always do. I never thought you were going to meet each other, until he called."

"He called you? About what?" I asked.

"Nothing," Toby lied.

"He came to me the first day I was at school and asked if I was your cousin," I shared.

"He did mention that," Toby agreed. "He was worried he blew it."

"What was the reasoning behind the call?" I wondered if he wanted details on me, to make sure I wasn't crazy, asked if I was seeing anyone...

"He wanted to know if I told you anything about him. If you knew that he knew about your mom. He got the feeling you didn't want to talk about it, so he didn't. He wasn't sure if he should tell you he knew, so you wouldn't have to mention it again if you didn't want to, or if he should wait for you to tell him."

"And you told him to wait," I guessed.

"I though you could use someone you thought didn't know," Toby explained.

"I told him everything. It was nice having someone who didn't know I was broken, but then it was all over the news. Now it's nice to have someone who knows all my darkest secrets and family history and still wants to hang out with me."

"A guy called you for advice on befriending my sister, and you told him to lie to her?" Jared reproached.

"Yes, but it was a lie with her best interests in mind," Toby defended. "Now tell me, my favorite Gremlin, how is school? Who do you hang out with? Gal pals? Bosom friends?"

"Rachel doesn't make girlfriends," Jared answered for me.

"Why not?" Toby was confused, and so was I. Was I socially awkward and no one ever told me?

"Her closest friend has always been a guy. First Alex, now Nick."

"Why?" Toby asked again, but I had an idea.

"Because mom was her best friend. She never needed another one."

All the happiness was sucked out of the car until I said, "Who needs the rest when you already have the best," which got sad smiles, before they told me our itinerary.

. . .

OUR FIRST STOP was the Santa Monica Pier, where we walked around, eating junk food and trying a few of the rides. Jared took me on the Ferris wheel, but when I tried to go on the roller coaster with Toby, he insisted the fun part was hanging out under the Pier. Not to do drugs or smoke, which some people did, but to watch the waves crash, or the sunset, without the crowds.

Next, Jared took us through the path by the house, Ferndell Trail, but we actually hiked up to the observatory. It wasn't the best idea after corn dogs and funnel cake at the pier, but we worked up an appetite.

Jared had to work, so his plan had been to leave me at home, but Toby and I were starving. We went to drop Jared off at the fire house, then Toby brought me to the restaurant he worked at when he first moved here. We had a delicious supper, with the owner bringing us free dessert.

WHEN TOBY finally drove me home, it was after nine o'clock. I stayed in the car and hesitated with my hand on the door handle.

"You okay?" he asked.

"If he's mad, I'm blaming you," I decided, opening the door.

"I'll do you one better. I will come in and tell him it was my fault and you are not to be penalized." He got out as well.

"You don't have to," I assured him.

"I'll miss you too much if I don't," he teased.

"Ray-ray." Owen was crawling down the hallway, away from Tracy when we came in, so he came to me instead of back to her.

"Are you being a bad boy?" I got him to giggle when I picked him up.

Tracy nodded to say he definitely was being a little devil way past his bedtime, before Chris came out from behind her.

I froze, convinced he would be upset that I skipped school, which would cause more drama.

"Tobias," he said, surprised, but in a happy way.

"Mr. Glass," Toby went formal as well.

"Did you have a good time not in school today?" Chris only showed the tiniest hint of sadness at Toby's greeting, before offering me a half-hearted smile.

"They brought me sightseeing. And hiking." I was trying to gauge the situation.

"No roller coasters, I guess?" Chris smiled sadly, so I turned to Toby.

"No, I still don't trust heights," he agreed. "Happens when you're let down too many times."

And just like that, it came back to me. How Haylie told me that Toby was terrified of heights because he fell off a roof when his mom was watching him and not paying attention. He wasn't badly hurt, but he never liked heights after that. Not long before my dad left, Uncle Jack got sent to Afghanistan, so Haylie and Toby stayed with us. Chris was trying to help Toby get over his fears by slowly bringing him higher in safe environments. I remember watching my dad carry Toby down from the tree house we used to have back then, promising he would always be there to catch him.

"You better not let her fall," Toby warned Chris before giving me a hug and a kiss goodbye.

"He really loves you," Chris said once Toby was gone and Tracy brought Owen back upstairs to bed.

"We're family. That's what we do," I explained, because it might be a foreign concept to him.

"Jared has spent the past year trying to get Tobias to come over for dinner with him and he won't. He also completely ignores me when they make him cater my show, but he usually avoids it. He denies we're related if we're at an event and it ever comes up."

"You're not," I reminded him.

"Blood and marriage—" he sounded like he was going to lecture me.

"No, you can't go there. Because I know Mackenzie is more of an aunt to me than Toby's mom ever was, and even Kevin... they're family. Without blood ties or being married to someone. What they have in common is how they're always there for us. Right now, if I called either of them and said I needed them here as soon as possible, they would come, no matter what, with minimal questions asked." I didn't want to reproach him or be mean, just to explain why Toby had no reason to warm up to him.

"I get it, that from your side of things, I completely checked out and didn't care, but that wasn't the case. I missed you so much, all of you. Anyone I met when I first got here, I told them all about my kids, as if you were coming as soon as school was done. Tracy has known about you, every detail, since our second date."

"But not all the details. Just the ones you knew from before. You think that how you say you felt for us internally counts for something, but it doesn't. You can't expect to go back to the way it was. You have to earn him back, not from scratch, but like you did something horrible to break his trust and his heart and now you have to make up for it."

"We're talking from experience," he said gently, hopefully understanding.

"Maybe," I agreed, trying to stop the emotions. "We don't owe you anything. You have to earn it."

"Then I'll do my best," he said after a moment to digest my advice.

"Okay." I felt like we were getting somewhere.

"And Rachel?" he called when I was on the stairs. "I won't let you fall," he promised. I gave him a sad, but hopeful smile before going to my room.

21

MEET THE PARENTS

"Should we make salad, pasta or rice on the side?" Tracy asked while I helped her wrap the pieces of salmon with lemon and caper inside tin foil.

"Salad," I said, but she could tell it was only because that was the healthiest option.

"What if we put strawberries and apples on top of the salmon instead of hollandaise, then we can have a little bit of pasta as a side?" she offered a compromise.

"I like the way you think," I smiled.

I had just put the salmon in the oven when the doorbell rang. She was chopping up strawberries, with her hands all wet and red, so I told her, "I got it," before heading to the front of the house. I opened the door to find Nick.

"Hey," I looked at him curiously. "What are you doing here? I thought you were in New York for an audition?" He hadn't been in school today or yesterday, and explained that it was a huge process with producers and networks and chemistry reads that could take weeks.

"Nailed the audition and didn't even need a callback," he explained.

"You got the part?" We ran lines for hours before he left.

"Signed on the dotted line this morning. Although I also signed an NDA, so maybe don't advertise it to anyone."

"That's the thing where they kill you if you give any spoilers?" I asked.

"It's a non-disclosure agreement. They won't kill me, but legally, they can fire me and sue me if they find out I told you."

"Then I guess I'm honored?" I wasn't sure what the appropriate response should be.

"You should be. I must really like you," he pointed out, gesturing to the empty driveway.

"I figured as much when you decided to be my new best friend." I didn't get what he was trying to show me.

"I took a bus. For probably the first time since I moved to California. Except for in movies. I don't even take the school bus, and this was city." It was my understanding that the city bus only came about half the time.

"Haven't you also spent most of that time being tutored on set, not in school?"

"Exactly. And I did this for you. My mom was exhausted after all the travel, so I could either take the bus or wait until school tomorrow."

"And you just had to see me?" I raised an eyebrow, but he looked at me in a way that made me nervous, before shrugging it off.

"I wanted to let you know what was going on, and I'm going to be filming that horror things for a few weeks, so..." he didn't say it, but he was going to miss me.

"Rachel, who was at the door?" Tracy came into the hallway with Owen.

"It's for me," I assured her. "Do you want to come inside?" I asked Nick, the polite thing to do. I didn't mind him being here now, but Chris would be home soon, and I would die if he took his side over mine.

"What do you mean it's...oh." Tracy came to the door and stopped when she saw Nick come inside.

"Tracy, this is my friend, Nick. Nick, this is Tracy and my little brother, Owen," I made the introductions. I wasn't ready to call her my stepmother, but I would have felt mean calling Owen her son, or my half-brother.

"It's a pleasure to meet you." Tracy didn't lie and say she'd heard all about him, because I hadn't mentioned him at all. I was slowly trusting her, but I assumed everything I said would be reported back to Chris.

"Likewise."

"Would you like to stay for supper, Nick? We're having salmon and I always make extra."

I tried to make signs for Nick to say no, but I had never been good at charades. "That's really nice of you Mrs. Glass, I would love to." That was one thing I wasn't used to yet. Tracy married him, and it was his name that my mom kept, but Mrs. Glass had always been for my mother. I couldn't remember meeting my grandmother, and Sarah was always Miss Glass, like me, until she married Matt and became Mrs. Watson.

"Call me Tracy. You can catch up in the living room or play in the backyard while I finish cooking." She let me know I was not to bring a boy to my bedroom.

"I was trying to tell you it wasn't a good idea," I said once she was gone.

"I know," he smiled, knowing he did something wrong and not caring.

"Then why did you say yes?" I was already leading him to the backyard.

"Because you like having buffers at family dinners," he reminded me.

"I'm not sure if I want you to like him or not." I tried to figure out which worried me more.

"My loyalties are very flexible depending on how you want me to feel," he assured me. "I take it we've warmed up to Tracy?"

"Her brother made me see things a little differently. And she doesn't expect anything from me."

"Sometimes it's nice to have someone pushing you." He caught the basketball I threw at him.

"I don't mean like that. But relationship-wise. She isn't trying to be my mother, she doesn't want to be my best friend and confidante...she's there for me if I need her. Which I don't, but sometimes it's nice to have an adult on your side."

"I'm glad. It would have been hard to be mean to a pregnant lady. She seems nice." We weren't playing an organized game, but he'd make a throw for the basket, I would get it on the rebound and try, then over and over again.

"She is. Which was annoying at the beginning, but we're okay now."

"And your dad?" he asked. "Or are we still calling him Chris?"

"It's fine to say my dad when I'm talking about him, but I'm a long way from calling him daddy," I answered. "And I don't know, it's weird."

"Weird how?" he waited until he made the basket to ask.

"I was pretending to make an effort for Jared, but then...I don't know. I don't think I want you to love him like everyone else does, because he's still the bad guy in my story, but we've been civil lately."

"Nothing sounds more warm and fuzzy than a civil father-daughter relationship," he teased.

"It's better than frigid," I pointed out. "And it's hard to trust someone..."

"When he's the one who gave you trust issues in the first place," he finished for me.

"I don't have trust issues," I argued.

"Want to do trust falls?" he asked as if it proved his point.

"That's not the same thing."

"It comes from the same place," he countered.

"It's hard to get close to someone when your brain wants you to run away before he can be the one to leave you again."

"That sounds more emotional than logical," he argued.

"It's actually the sensible thing to do."

"I'm glad your degree in psychology recommends it," he laughed at me.

"I'm sure Sarah agrees. Probably not from her medical degree, but she is excellent at using avoidance." I saw Chris' car pull into the driveway. It was my turn to throw the ball, but I stood there, watching. Nick was about to be the first person I'd ever introduced to my father.

"Earth to Rachel." Nick was waiting for me to throw.

"How about I show you the rest of the grounds?" I offered, hopefully giving Tracy the time to fill Chris in on how he better not blow this for me. I hadn't told her about Nick, but I think she understood.

"I'll follow wherever you lead."

I brought him to the pond, where all the ducks live, and apparently a swan I've never seen. "We have one of those in our yard, but mom calls it her Zen garden or tranquility zone or something that means we're not supposed to bother her when she's there," he shared as we walked to the fire pit. It had comfy lounge chairs, but also a few log seats.

"I haven't come out here yet," I said while he tested the logs. "I used to love campfires."

"What happened?"

"I still love them, I guess. I just haven't had one in...forever."

"They do a bonfire on the beach every year to celebrate the end of the school year. We can go if you want," he offered.

"That could be fun," I agreed, but it was months away and I would hopefully not be here anymore come summer. "I remember roasting marshmallows on the fire and making s'mores. Toby had this little guitar and tried to get us to sing campfire songs. They stopped when I sang the same lyrics as everyone else."

"How old were you?" he looked at me like he could picture it.

"Maybe three or four?" It was long before Chris left. "I might be making it up, but that's what I see when someone mentions camping. And we didn't even have tents. We were at the Lake House, but there was a huge fire pit."

"Did they get rid of it? I thought you still go there every summer?"

"We do, but we stopped the fires for Sarah. I can't blame her, because she accidentally caught her hair on fire while roasting the perfect marshmallow."

"Was it worth it?" He could joke about it because he knew my sister wasn't hurt or disfigured by it.

"She blamed the fire and forgave the marshmallow," I shared. "Mom barely had time to register what was going on and panic before Jared grabbed one of the super soakers we had lying around and sprayed her with it. He walked around like a hero for weeks, and the firefighter dream was born."

"It's a wonder you all made it out alive," he teased before I saw Tracy in the distance.

"It's time," I told him.

"Are you ready?" he asked.

"Not at all," I said before leading him to the house.

WHEN WE GOT to the dining room, I saw Tracy had put out the plates we used for Chris's birthday dinner rather than the ones I'd set the table with.

"Hi, you must be Nick." Chris came over to shake his hand. "I'm Chris."

"Nice to meet you," Nick said before taking his seat.

"Do you play any sports?" Chris asked.

"I used to be on the football team." Nick hadn't been expecting that question.

"What happened?" Tracy asked, serving herself some of the salad she put in the middle of the table to go with the salmon and fettuccini alfredo.

"Nothing, I got busy," he shrugged.

"Do you still play?" I asked. I wore Alex's jacket at least once a week and talked about Kyle all the time, but he never mentioned being on a team.

"Sometimes we play in between scenes on set, or at lunch, but we have to be careful. They freaked out when another elf almost sprained an ankle," Nick shared.

I was about to tell him how we used to play, how he should come when my siblings visit for Thanksgiving, but Chris spoke. "My brother and I were on our high school team, and I loved it, but I was never going to make it past varsity. Jeff, on the other hand, got recruited straight out of high school, full scholarship. I would have loved to be able to play football and call it a job. Although I guess we do get paid to pretend."

"I hated giving it up, but I was getting pummeled out there. I used to go to auditions with my arms and legs covered in bruises, a couple of black eyes..."

"Ryan tried rugby for a month or so in junior high, which nearly gave me and my parents heart attacks every weekend. I prefer flag football," Tracy joined the conversation. "Do you play?" she asked me.

"Not for real. We used to play at home, some Sundays and every holiday," I said it dismissively instead of excited as I had planned when I was going to invite Nick to join.

"Are you any good?" Nick asked with a smile.

"I'm decent? I'm a girl and the baby, so most people won't tackle me, but I have no problem jumping on their backs and tackling them to the ground," I answered with a smile, knowing that as long as I was playing with family, I was really good.

"She's selling herself short. If she is anything like she used to be, she was my secret weapon," Chris cut in, surprising me.

"How so?" Tracy knew I was young when he left.

"No matter what team they put her on, she was always secretly on mine. The ball was nearly as big as she was, but she could throw it. Not far, but she was cute as a button and she loved to play, so everyone would give her the ball when she asked for it, and she threw it to me. Every time."

"And nobody noticed?" Tracy asked while I digested this information.

"Eventually. And Sierra always knew, but Rachel would give this innocent smile and say she missed and nobody was going to stop her from playing."

"Basically, you cheated," Nick pointed out.

"Kyle tried to do the same thing with Sierra, he just wasn't as good at the innocent smile. No one believed he missed his throw," Chris explained.

"If you're in town on Thanksgiving, you should come over. Chris has been going on and on about how he wants to have everyone over for a game like they used to," Tracy invited Nick. As much as I hated the idea of Chris trying to do Thanksgiving the way mom always did, I really wanted to see everyone and play like we usually did. Maybe having to have Chris there would be worth it to have everyone else.

"We were talking about actually going home for Thanksgiving this year, which would be nice, but if we don't, I would love to come here," Nick answered, looking to me.

"Where is home?" Chris asked him.

"Colorado. There were less people in my entire town than there will be on set next week," Nick said like he loved his hometown for it.

"You've gotta love small towns." I didn't know if Chris was talking about the town he and mom grew up in, or where they raised us once upon a time ago. Either way, he missed it.

"Knowing everyone in a town isn't always a good thing," Tracy argued, probably referencing her abusive first husband. "I think it's time for dessert."

"I'll help you," I said, before realizing this would put Nick alone with my dad. He didn't know me, so he wouldn't have embarrassing stories, but I could see this was what it would have been like to bring a guy home if I'd had a father. I'd never experienced it before, and it made me nervous.

"Dinner seems to be going well," Tracy said once we were in the kitchen.

"It is." I was surprised.

"You didn't know about the football?" she asked, taking out an apple pie. I used to run off as soon as the meal was done, but I was discovering that she always had a dessert, just in case.

"I know I've been playing forever, but I didn't know that specific story." I grabbed forks and plates.

"He has a million of them. Stories. There were so many after Owen was born. There wasn't a single thing he could do that one of you hadn't done before," she shared.

"And you wanted him to say that your son is the most handsome, smartest baby he has ever seen." I let her know I understood.

"See, you get me," she smiled before we brought dessert to the dining room. The guys went quiet as soon as they saw us. I figured they were talking about me, but Nick smiled like everything was okay. "Pie?" Tracy offered, handing out slices.

"Do you ever have fires at that pit in the backyard?" Nick asked once we were done with pie and coffee. We'd been talking about Mr. Adams' latest historical performance.

"We do, occasionally. Not as often as I'd like." Tracy looked to Chris.

"Would you like me to make you a fire?" he offered, and she nodded. "Nick, would you like to stay for a fire? I'm pretty sure we have marshmallows and graham crackers."

"That sounds great," Nick told Chris, but he smiled at me.

"It's like you don't want to leave," I teased when Nick and I went to grab the s'mores ingredients. Chris went to start the fire, and Tracy was putting Owen to bed with the baby monitor.

"Are you not having a good time?" He reached to grab the graham crackers from the top shelf when I couldn't reach.

"I am." It surprised and worried me.

"Then stop waiting for the other shoe to drop and enjoy it." I followed him out to the backyard.

"This was a brilliant idea. I love campfires," Tracy told Nick once we got to them. The fire was roaring, and Tracy was sitting in a lounge chair.

"Rachel loves them too." Nick pulled up a log to sit on, so I took one and sat beside him.

"Do I love the fire, or do I love the s'mores?" I asked.

"What are you doing?" Nick looked down as I tried to stick a square of chocolate inside my marshmallow.

"I like my chocolate melted," I explained, putting my contraption on top of the flames. I occasionally had to move the square of chocolate so it stayed at the top and didn't drip, until it fused with the marshmallow. "Can you hand me two graham crackers?" I asked Nick, then let him put one on top and one underneath my blob. I pulled the stick out while he pressed the crackers together. "And voila!" I was the only one who opted for s'mores instead of a marshmallow. "Try that and tell me it isn't the best s'more you've ever had." I let him keep it and worked on one for me.

"Yep, definitely worth melting the chocolate," Nick said, his mouth full.

I saw the look on Tracy's face, so I gave her the next one, which she shared with Chris. I finally got to enjoy the third one I made.

"We used to spread peanut butter on the graham crackers. It was an absolute mess," Tracy smiled.

"Peanut butter does make everything better," Chris and I said at pretty much the same time, which made him smile, but I shuddered out of habit. I always hated being like him or having things in common with him.

"They weren't exactly s'mores, but if you put a marshmallow in the microwave for about ten seconds, then put it between two Reese's peanut butter cups, you save the mess and it's pretty delicious." Nick moved the conversation along, so I gave him a grateful smile.

"Next time you come over for supper we can have that for dessert," Tracy decided, taking it for granted he'd be back.

"That sounds...delicious," Nick assured her.

I HAD EXPECTED the entire evening to be awkward before Nick would rush home and I would go hide in my room. Instead, we had the best dinner together since I moved in, and I actually stayed with them after supper, and enjoyed it. We stayed out until the lights came on, which gave the place an air of fairytales and magic. Chris had us believing he knew the names to all the stars, until Nick realized he was saying a line from a movie he'd done last year. "I actually have no idea where any of them are, but those are the names," he conceded.

AFTER PUTTING OUT THE FIRE, Chris and Tracy went upstairs to check on Owen, trusting me to walk Nick out.

"How are you going to get home now?" I asked. He had told Chris he didn't need a ride.

"Stepdad was working late," he said as a red Cadillac pulled up.

"You were delaying leaving so you could have a ride home," I called him on it.

"Or I enjoy spending time with you. I have no idea why, because you're completely boring," he teased, getting a playful tap on the arm.

"Me too," I admitted.

"And next time, you can come to my place and meet my crazy family."

"Are you saying mine was crazy or that yours will be?" I teased, knowing this had been an awkward family situation to observe.

"I'm going to plead the fifth and see you tomorrow at school," was his answer.

"Excellent idea."

"Dinner at my place when I get back from filming. And I'll try to find out about that bonfire," he said while he walked to the car.

"I'll be here," I assured him, waving as he got in. His stepfather smiled and gave me a wave as well, before driving away. I stayed out until I couldn't see them anymore, then headed for my room to watch Bowling for Columbine.

✤ 22 ✤

THANKSGIVING

"Tﾠhere should be a bag with the organs, and you take that out."

"The organs?" Tracy asked me, taking a step away from the turkey. Chris had gone to the airport to pick up Sarah, Matt and Katie, leaving Tracy and I to figure out Thanksgiving dinner. I asked about the first night I was here, and she explained that Chris was the turkey guy. She usually made chicken, or bought it rotisserie, and I usually made sides while someone else did the gross part.

"Some people put it in the stuffings," I explained.

"That's what...I thought it was just a name, like pig's tongues or—"

"I put breakfast sausage in ours, don't worry," I cut her off, figuring the truth about pig's tongues could wait for another day.

It took us about another fifteen minutes of basting, tin foil covering and removing insides without looking to get the turkey into the oven. Once that was done, we got to work on cranberry sauce, a green bean casserole, pumpkin pie, meat pie...getting everything ready for later.

Owen supervised us from his playpen, and Tracy walked me

through a secret family recipe when she took a break from all the standing.

"We never really had sweet potato in our repertoire," I explained my cluelessness.

"You'll see, it's delicious. Most people make it a dessert with marshmallows, but we keep it more dinner. My grandmother taught me when I was like, six years old," she shared, rubbing her stomach with a humongous smile at the memory.

"Peanut butter though?" I asked, mushing them together as she'd instructed.

"You were the one who said peanut butter makes everything better," she reminded me.

"It's the yams running the peanut butter that worries me."

She rolled her eyes before giving me more directions, like adding cinnamon and raisins and chopped cashews. She was very precise with her measurements, but I was my mother's daughter and may have added an extra shake of cinnamon and a few more raisins than she intended.

"And now you know how to make the Brooks Family Yam Casserole," she smiled. It was the last thing on our list to do before the guests arrived.

I heard Owen before I heard the door, but as soon as it was open, a three-and-a-half-foot ball of energy threw herself into my arms, holding onto my neck so tight I could hardly breathe, but I made no effort to get her off.

"I haven't seen you in forever," she told me, trying to bury her head deeper into me.

"Two and a half months," I argued, but I looked to Sarah like this was unacceptable, because I completely agreed with my niece.

"Let's make sure it never goes longer." Sarah came over and wrapped both of us in her hug. With Katie starting school, me being in high school and them having jobs, the best we could hope for was Summer, Thanksgiving, Christmas, Easter and March Break. Unless I chose her in June, which I most probably would. Except for Nick, who might complicate things. He left for Colorado yesterday, but texted this morning to give me a safe word in case something went wrong. If at any point I texted 'cantaloupe', he would create a diversion so I could escape. The logistics were lacking, but the thought was there.

"What about me?" Matt tickled Katie, so she'd loosen her grip, then joined in. I had no room and barely enough air, but I closed my eyes and took it all in. I was even crying happy tears.

"Is this where the Turkey Bowl is happening?" Ryan walked in the open front door, dressed head to toe like a football player.

"Ryan, hey." Sarah let go, trying to wipe her eyes and look presentable. Her face was crimson.

"Still?" I asked.

"Every time," Matt told me, picking up their bags and heading to the guest room.

"We just got here from the airport, so we were saying hi. Or, you know, suffocating her. She probably wishes she was wearing all your gear. You know we're not professionals? Sweatpants and a t-shirt would have been fine."

"It's nice to see you again." He came over and hugged her, unfazed by her nervous talking. "My sister said you play every year, and most weekends, and that you cheat, so I thought I would come prepared," he explained.

"Did we go pro?" Jared came in and shut the door.

"I haven't played since junior high. I was in band," Ryan reminded us, getting Sarah to giggle before Katie decided Jared was worth leaving me for. I waited until he picked her up to go over and get my hug.

"Still no?" I asked.

"Tomorrow," he assured me. We invited Toby, and everyone else who usually came to mom's, but this was it. Kyle said he had a training thing and couldn't leave town once he found out Sarah was flying here, and Toby said he'd find a soup kitchen to volunteer at, until Uncle Jack decided to make the trip. Since they would see everyone tomorrow, when Toby was making us dinner, they declined Chris' offer. I wasn't sure if I was more sad that they weren't here, or that I wasn't there. It would have been better if we'd all gone to the Lake House, because Kyle would have come, but I would have felt bad for Chris and Tracy. Not bad enough to not go, or to try and change our plans, but I said I'd try, and this was me trying.

"How is everybody?" I asked Sarah when the others went to get ready.

"Slowly rebuilding. Everyone asks about you, wonders where you are, if you're okay." She rubbed my shoulder, making sure I was.

"And Alex's parents?" I asked cautiously.

"They moved as soon as someone bought the house. They sent me a postcard with their new address in case you need anything."

"And how's Katie?" This was the only time I ever wished my niece loved me less than I thought she did, so she could miss me a little less than I missed her.

"She has a box full of drawings and bookmarks and art pieces she wanted to send to you, but decided she wanted to give you in person instead," she shared before Katie came back from the spare bedroom, where she'd been searching through her Barbie rolling suitcase.

"I didn't want them to get broked in the mail." She opened the box and put things in my lap. "This is a drawing I made of all of us. My teacher said we had to draw where our family lives, and I put us all on top of the planet, because we don't live together anymore, and she didn't understand until another teacher told her about nana and how you moved away, so then she said it was okay." I got descriptions like this for a bookmark painted purple and pink, my favorite colors, a paper plate she cut into a heart shape and glued colored macaroni noodles to, and a picture frame with a picture of the two of us that she had decorated with paint, coloring crayons, glitter and stickers.

"This one is my favorite." I brought it to my chest to show her how much I meant it.

"Are you going to put it in your room?" she asked.

"Right beside my bed," I agreed.

"I don't even know what your room looks like," she told me.

"Wanna see?" I asked. She nodded, so we went up and I showed her my room, my reading nook and my view.

"IS OWEN PLAYING TOO? He can be on my team and I'll teach him how to play," Katie offered when we came back downstairs, where I braided her hair.

"He's a little too young, sweetie. In a couple of years," I told her.

She nodded, then tried to turn and face me, which made the braiding a little difficult.

"What's up?" I asked, knowing she wanted to ask me a question.

"Do you love him more than you love me?" she asked in a whisper, like she was afraid he would hear.

"Of course not," I said like the question was preposterous.

"But you see him every day, and he's little too."

"Katie Bear, you are my heart. Seeing you every day or every few months doesn't change that." I shrugged off the dirty feeling that I was using his excuse. I didn't abandon her, I was forced to move away. I still call her every day on the bus ride home, before she goes to bed.

"Can I be on your team?" she asked me.

"Why don't you be captain and I'll be on your team?" I offered.

"I can be captain?" Her eyes got big at the possibilities.

"Of course," I assured her, the smile spreading on my face.

. . .

I slightly regretted it when she chose me, Jared and Chris as her teammates, but as long as she was happy, it was more than worth it.

"Come on sweetie, pass it to mommy," Sarah tried every time Katie ran past her with the ball.

"Nope." Katie shook her head and held the ball tighter until she got to me. Sarah was running after her, so she switched to me. Matt and Jared were pretty close, but I thought I could get it to Jared anyway.

"Dad was wide open," he told me after Matt's interception.

"I didn't see him," I argued. And it was true, I hadn't. But I also hadn't been looking for him.

Our team eventually won, which was expected when Katie always got the ball, and Sarah got nervous whenever Ryan was anywhere near her.

"It doesn't bother you?" I asked Matt, drinking some of the lemonade Tracy brought out for us.

"It's like if I was spending the day with Tom Brady. I'm not jealous of him, so I think it's cute." He shook his head at his wife, who missed her mouth a bit.

"She's hilarious like this," I agreed. Sarah had boyfriends in high school, and a lot of guys asked her out, but they all seemed like something she was doing because it was expected of her. Until Kevin brought Matt over and she giggled like a school girl. Mom thought that it was funny too, until Matt became the one who calmed her when she got stressed out, who stayed at the foot of her bed the entire time she was in the hospital for appendicitis...that was when we knew he was the one.

We let Sarah and Matt be the captains of the second game, so we ended up me, Sarah, and Chris against Matt, Jared, Ryan and Katie. I wasn't impressed with her decision, but I did get the reasoning from a tactical standpoint.

Sarah guessed, mostly correctly, that Katie would pass me the ball even if we weren't on the same team, and she played a lot better when she wasn't distracted by her teammate.

"Time out!" Sarah called halfway through the game, which technically she could do, but we never did. "What's wrong with you?" she asked me in a two-person huddle, having said no when Chris tried to come over.

"Nothing, what's wrong with you?" I asked, but I knew she meant how I was pretending I was on a two-person team.

"Why aren't you passing him the ball? I thought things were going well?"

"They're okay," I agreed.

"So..."

"I don't want to be like six-year-old me. I don't want to be his secret weapon, who only throws the ball to him and had his back and—"

"I get it, Rache," she assured me. "But this isn't like that. We're a player short to start with, and you're acting like it's just you and me. It's not playing favorites if he's on your team."

I wanted to remind her I wasn't entirely sure that he was, but he was trying. I was also trying, and I didn't want to ruin Thanksgiving. "You're right. I'm sorry," I apologized.

WE RAN a few more plays where the ball was stolen, or rather requested, by Katie before I had to make good on the promise. We only had a few seconds left on the clock when I asked and Katie, who was not on my team, giggled and gave me the ball. Sarah was completely blocked by Matt and Jared, who knew I would throw the ball to her. Ryan was loosely covering Chris, in a way that still left him wide open. I sighed before going for it, throwing the ball to Chris, who easily ran it into the end zone, winning us the game. Katie tackled me after I threw it, so I fell to the ground and tickled her, very aware of all the eyes on me.

"Sarah?" Tracy called her over once the teams shook hands.

"Mommy can't cook." Katie shook her head with worry.

"But she can carve," I reminded her, a benefit of choosing surgery as her specialty.

We all went to get washed up, then Sarah carved, and I helped with the final steps of getting everything on the table.

Mom often did this game where we would write down what we were grateful for and put it in a jar. Sometimes we saved them for a day we had to be reminded, but most of the time we passed the jar around the table and read them out, guessing who wrote what. It was hard, because most of us were grateful for the same things.

This year, we opted against that, because Family was always the top thing on our list, and it felt like a lie to write it with mom gone. Luckily, conversation was easy, and there were so many going on that I didn't have to talk to Chris if I didn't want to. Plus, Tracy was right about the yam casserole being the best dish ever.

"Can I have the recipe?" Sarah asked her.

"By that she means can you please give me the recipe, so I can make it for her," Matt corrected.

After dessert, I went for a walk around the neighborhood with Jared to digest some of the food.

"I'm proud of you kid," my brother told me.

"For all the food I ate?" I teased.

"You're trying," he smiled, not wanting to make a big deal of it, but I shrugged.

When we came in, the guys went to watch the football game we'd recorded, leaving me to go make the pumpkin spice drinks.

"I couldn't say it, because I wish that she was still here and it hadn't happened, more than anything, but if we could have found a way…what I'm grateful for tonight is having you here. My girls and Jared…it's the closest my heart has come to being whole since—"

"Pumpkin spice?" I asked, cutting Chris off as I walked in, not needing to hear how broken he had been since he abandoned us. It was a lot easier to be nice to him when I wasn't reminded of what he did.

"Yes please." Sarah came and wrapped her arms around me.

"You got good, Rachel. Really good," Chris told me.

"Practice makes perfect," I gathered the ingredients.

"We'll have to play more often." I could hear the smile in his voice, but I didn't turn around.

"You need people to play, but Owen will be older and—"

"And Nick can come," Chris reminded me, but I wasn't sure I was ready for that level of closeness.

"I heard about that." Sarah came and grilled me for every detail of the evening, so Chris slipped out.

"That's it?" Sarah asked when my story and the drinks were done.

"That's huge," I argued. "It's the longest I've spent with him without storming off in tears."

"For you and dad it's amazing, and introducing someone to him, you're right…but no kiss? No letting him know you think he's amazing too?"

"He knows he's awesome. He's in a superhero movie. He has fans," I reminded her.

"Yes, but it's not the same as knowing that you think he's awesome." She walked out after she said it, so I followed her to the living room, where we drank our drinks and watched football. Katie fell asleep on me and it felt like at least half of my heart was back together.

. . .

THE NEXT DAY, SARAH BORROWED CHRIS' car and we went to Jared and Toby's apartment for Thanksgiving Number Two. I was suffocated by hugs from Uncle Jack, but didn't mind one bit.

Toby and I cooked while the others drank and set the table. "How come you never told me he hurt you too?" I asked while chopping mushrooms.

"He was an uncle, but even after he left, I still had a dad."

"But he still hurt you."

"He did," he agreed. "But if it was just me I would agree to disagree and suck it up."

WHEN WE CAME in that night, I felt bad for Chris and the way he nodded as Sarah gave him back the keys. Then again, I didn't feel sad or get upset or awkward or uncomfortable once at Jared's. We were trying, but we weren't there yet.

HATE TO HATE YOU

"Do you even remember how to ride a horse?" I asked Jared while he drove us to the address Chris had written down forever ago. I never had any intentions of coming, because horseback riding was something I associated with my dad, but Jared had shown up at school to take me out for the evening.

"It's like riding a bicycle," he told me, smiling way too much about something he never expressed the slightest interest in.

"I've never heard of that," I argued as he pulled into the dirt road that led to the stables.

"You like it though, don't you?" he asked.

"I haven't been since—" I was going to reminded him that I'd mostly avoided it for the past decade, but then I saw the reason for his imperturbable good mood. I wasn't even sure if the car stopped rolling, but I manually unlocked my door and rushed out, running straight into my brother's arms. I missed all of my siblings, all the time. I was used to seeing Sarah almost every day, so that was hard, but even she had moved out on me. I had never lived without Kyle one room away from me until I came to California.

Kyle looked the same from afar, albeit with a different haircut, but up close I could see the differences. He looked a lot like Jared actually, both of them built and tan. Kyle's blond hair would make him look like more of a beach bum, but with the buzz cut and muscles...strong was the word that came to mind. Maybe even fierce, or scary, if I didn't know him so well. It felt nothing like when he used to take me in his arms, but I was used to it from Uncle Jack and Jared, so it still made me feel safe.

"How come no one told me you were coming? How are you here?" I asked when he let go, knowing his next break wasn't until Christmas.

"I'm on the football team. We have a game against USC Sunday morning. Rest of the team's driving, but I took a plane so I would have more time with you."

"Are we actually horseback riding?" I asked after giving him another hug.

"How hard can it be?" Kyle was of the same mind as Jared, so I followed them to the horses.

"Peaches?" I read the name etched into the wood.

"Black stallion," Jared shrugged.

"Crumpet," Kyle tilted his head at us.

"Interesting." Jared looked at the three horses. I was guessing they were named before Chris bought them, but then again, it's not like I knew him enough to know if these names meant anything to him.

I used the little stepladder to get onto Peaches' saddle, but my brothers insisted they could do it without the 'kiddy' step. I waited outside for at least twenty minutes before they came out, and I was still not convinced they managed it without the step, or possibly each other's help.

It wasn't exactly like riding a bike. You weren't in control, which the horses knew, so they walked and galloped around, much to the amusement of the man who had unlocked the stables for Kyle. It was scary at first, but by the time we called it a night, I remembered why I had loved this as a kid, regardless of who was the one who brought me.

"Are you staying with the team or with us?" I asked when we got to the car.

"Rache..." Kyle looked at me like I was crazy. "I'm staying at Jared's."

"Oh," I realized that made more sense than coming to the house I was trying to get away from. "Can I stay there too?"

"That would involve letting the monster know I'm in town, which is not happening," Kyle turned me down.

"You're not going to see him the entire time you're here?" I asked, catching Jared's eye.

"Jealous?" Kyle smiled.

"I'll come pick you up bright and early so we can go surfing," Jared assured me.

"He says you'll forever be better than me until I get out there," Kyle boasted.

"You're acting like the minute you try it you'll be better than me," I reproached.

"But I love you for trying," Kyle teased, taking me in his arms.

"Be ready for six," Jared reminded me when we got to the house. It was a dreadfully early time to be awake, but Kyle was more than worth it.

I GOT READY FOR BED, so I wouldn't be tired for tomorrow and what I was hoping would be a jam-packed weekend. I was setting my alarm, about to crawl into bed, when there was a knock on the door.

"How was horseback riding?" Tracy asked with her warm smile when I let them in, putting herself between me and Chris. I was having trouble not feeling bad for the way he was calmly hanging back in the doorway, ready to flee if something he did upset me. It was happening less often now, but I didn't talk as much when he was around either.

"It was...it was perfect." I knew I couldn't tell them that another part of my heart found its way back to my chest, but that was how I felt.

"I'm glad." She smiled at me before taking Owen from Chris. "I went every weekend until the bump became a mountain." I smiled at her analogy for being too pregnant to ride.

"Ryan came over tonight. He has a premiere next week and a ticket with your name on it," Chris said cautiously. "We were going to go as well, but Tracy likes to avoid maternity dresses on the red carpet until—"

"We have exams next week." The fear took over when I realized he was going to suggest we go together, even if I would have loved to see Ryan's new movie. I had seen everything he had done, and this romantic comedy was right up my alley.

"Of course. Some other time," he pretended he believed the school excuse. I couldn't tell if he was a terrible actor who couldn't hide his disappointment, or an amazing one at playing crushed.

"But thank you for inviting me," I said as they headed out. I was feeling guilty that he had no idea his youngest son was in town. Kyle would be turning eighteen soon, which meant he would never be obliged to be around Chris like I was.

"Always," Chris assured me, then closed the door.

IT WAS FREEZING the next morning by the time we got to the beach, with what I felt was a serious risk of getting hypothermia, even with the wet suits. I went out with Jared first, because Kyle didn't believe I could actually stand up on the board, but once I proved myself by lasting forty-five seconds, I decided that was it for me in the water, and took the blanket Toby offered me.

"Not coming in?" I sat beside him on an extremely large beach towel.

"In the summer, yes. Once it gets cold I would rather drink my tea and watch."

"How long did you guys know Kyle was coming?" I watched as Kyle fell before even getting up to his knees.

"About a month or so? Jared initially told him he couldn't stay with us, but I didn't see the point in being cruel."

"You make me stay there," I pointed out. "And weren't you the one who told me I had it wrong?"

"I said I hoped you had it wrong," he corrected. "Do you think you do?" He turned away from them to face me.

"No," I reluctantly admitted. "I hate hating him, because I can see that he's trying, and he acts like he cares...but I can't reconcile the person I'm living with now and the guy who did that to us."

"I'm a big believer that people aren't black or white, they're somewhere in the middle, but it takes a special kind of person to do what he did. And I don't mean in a good way."

"I know."

"You think Kyle should be at the house with you?" Toby asked.

"I wish he was, because I could see him more and he'd be a great buffer. I'd be invisible all weekend...but I wouldn't be there either if I had the choice."

"You wouldn't?" he asked like he wasn't so sure anymore.

"If you gave me the choice right now, I would want to live with you guys, or back home with Sarah."

"But..." he pressed.

"But even if I wouldn't want to see him or talk to him, I think I would want him to be invited to your place sometimes, or to Katie's birthday, and then he would be there, and I would be upset and avoid him, but..."

"But you would still want him to be there," he understood.

"Just because I don't want him in my life right now...that shouldn't mean he isn't trying to."

"You think Kyle is missing out on him trying to be a part of his life?"

"Honestly, my life has become an emotional roller coaster."

"And you're still not interested in acting? I hear it's a great outlet..."

"Safer than painting at this point," I smiled, going there before he could.

We cheered for Kyle, who managed to ride a wave to shore, effectively beating the culmination of my month or so of progress.

WE SPENT all morning at the beach before going back to Jared and Toby's, where I made pumpkin spice coffees and Jared grilled steaks on the barbecue. After eating, we all went to their living room and sat on the couch to digest.

"What's the plan for Christmas?" Jared asked Kyle.

"I should be home."

"Chris invited everyone over here. He does it every year, but maybe this time we'll actually—" Jared tried.

"Count me out then." Kyle shot him down.

"Even if everyone else is there?" I didn't want to spend my holidays with Chris either, but I would be wherever my family was.

"The Lake House could be fun?" Toby suggested. Having Chris there would put a damper on his holiday as well.

Jared chose that moment to bring our plates to the kitchen, so I followed him.

"You don't have to clean here." He wasn't upset, just resigned.

"Habit," I argued, biting my bottom lip, trying to find a way to say what I was feeling.

"You okay?" he looked me over.

"I get it," I told him.

"Get what?" He put the plates he rinsed into the dishwasher.

"Why you keep pushing me to give him a chance. Why you won't let me live with you."

"He's your guardian," Jared agreed.

"I know, but I'm sure it would have been easy to let Uncle Jack or Sarah take me instead. You made me come here with him, knowing how I felt, because you wanted me to."

"You make it sound horrible, like I let you down..."

"You did," I told him. "I still hate mom for sending me to him, and all of you for letting it happen, but at the same time..."

"You would rather be in your shoes than Kyle's?"

"No," I said with certainty. "But maybe. It's like how no one likes going to the dentist and getting their teeth cleaned, but you should still go."

"I guess there are worse analogies you could have used."

"I hate feeling this way, and I wouldn't wish it on Kyle, but I would rather feel bad for hating him because he's trying to be better than to not feel bad because my dad is a monster who walked out of my life and never looked back."

"Do you believe that?" he asked about the monster part.

"Did he ever call you or visit you or do anything even remotely decent before you showed up on his doorstep?" I turned it on him.

"No, but—"

"There's not buts for that Jared. Christopher Glass is the amazing dad I had when I was little, he's the guy who took me in after my mom died, but he is also the guy who abandoned his family for almost a decade while he got rich and made himself a new family."

He opened his mouth as if to argue, but there wasn't anything he could say to that. I may feel bad for Kyle not being forced to get to know him, and I felt terrible turning Chris down every time he tried, but he did ask for it.

. . .

WE WENT OUT for ice cream and watched movies all night, so I finally managed to convince Jared to call Chris and say I fell asleep, so he would bring me back in the morning. He didn't like it, but I slept amazing on their couch, squished between my brothers and my cousin.

JARED AND TOBY were in their own beds when I woke up, but Kyle didn't have a choice but to stay with me or sleep on the floor.

WE DROVE to the stadium early so Kyle could warm up with his team, then watched them crush the opposition.

"You're getting close, aren't you?" Kyle asked when it was just the two of us. Toby was getting the car and Jared was trying to stuff Kyle's equipment into the bus he would be getting back to Virginia on. "You look to Jared when I say things, like I'm the one who doesn't get it."

"I think maybe I should give him a chance for real, not because it might help me get away from here," I admitted.

"You forgave him?" he looked betrayed.

"No," I said, maybe a little too quickly.

"Then what is it?"

"It hurts too much to keep hating him," I said simply, but it really wasn't simple.

He shook his head at my watering eyes, then asked, "If you haven't forgiven him, how can you even stand being in the same room as him?"

"I don't have a choice. I hate this person who is mean to him because of what he did when he's always trying to be nice and—"

"But he's not."

"I know."

"And you're not a mean person Rachel. You've got the biggest heart that you give away too easily," he warned. "If it'll make life easier for you, I can play nice, but I won't mean a word of it. We don't owe him anything. It'll be because I love you."

"Okay," I agreed, getting a hug that would have to last me until Christmas, before Toby showed up and Jared insisted on bringing me straight home. I wished it could have lasted forever, but I had an amazing weekend with my favorite guys.

❧ 24 ❧

BREAK ME ALL OVER

"Look, it's your dad," Nick told me while I was putting cookie dough on top of my frozen yogurt. Nick was back for our end-of-session exams, and this was his craving.

"Tracy went to a premiere with him the other night, and apparently debuted her bump." I put my froyo on the scale next to his.

"You said no?" He knew I had been invited, because I'd asked if he would be in town to go with me. Ever since Ryan invited me to his premiere, Chris was inviting me to similar events.

"I was invited as an afterthought, when I said I loved the lead actress. He didn't actually want me there," I dismissed it.

"Or maybe he did, and you were going to make your debut."

"No, he said he had extra tickets, so I could go with you or bring a friend from school. It would have been my first Red Carpet, but not a Big Reveal," I argued, looking up at the screen.

"Chris, you have a hit show in its ninth season, you play the lead in Blue Venom, and you and your wife are expecting Baby Number Two. Is it overwhelming?" the interviewer asked Chris.

"A little, but in a good way. We got lucky with Owen. He's a sweet, calm baby who loves meeting new people, and my wife is

213

absolutely incredible. She's an amazing mother, so I would say I'm more excited than nervous. Ask me again once the baby is here," he joked.

"People have told me you're not a real parent until you have more than one kid. Because the first one is easy, you just bring them around with you, but every new one is five times the baggage. Are you worried about that or are you looking forward to being a father of two?"

"I think as soon as you have one child you're a parent. More kids means more work, but from the first moment they put that bundle in your arms, for the rest of your life, they're all that matters. I love being a father and I am looking forward to it."

"Do you think Owen will adjust well to the new addition, or are you expecting sibling rivalry?"

"I think he will eventually love having someone at home to play with. Tracy and I both knew we wanted Owen to have lots of siblings, because there is so much to be gained from that bond," Chris said with a smile, before the interviewer asked about Blue Venom, and I realized Nick was staring at me.

"It's a beautiful day, why don't we eat these outside?" he suggested.

"They're done with the family stuff," I said like it didn't matter, before following him.

"Not mentioning you doesn't mean—"

"I know," I cut him off. "I'm fine."

"I want you to know I'm letting it slide because I can tell you want me to, not at all because I believe you."

"Duly noted," I assured him. We moved on to what he had missed at school and how the filming was going.

I WAS DOING homework in the living room with Owen, and Tracy was making delicious-smelling cookies when Chris got home a few hours later. By doing homework, I mostly meant leaving my books open while rolling the ball to Owen. His laugh and smile were infectious, but I stopped as soon as I heard the door.

"There's my big boy." Chris came over and grabbed him. "How was your day?" he asked me as I was closing my books, but I headed for the stairs. "What's with the cold shoulder? I thought we were getting along, you were actually talking to me." He looked exhausted and confused.

"That was a mistake. I fell for your act," I admitted, wanting to sound mean, but it came out as hurt. "I thought you were being protective of me when you got rid of the photographer who was following us last week, but now I know you were ashamed. I mean, I've hated you most of my life, and all those years, not once did I tell people you were dead. Even when Ted was there with us, every single day, helping us with homework and doing your job, even then I didn't forget about you. I was still convinced you were coming back. I told people my dad moved away for a while, which was stupid of me, because Ted was right there, and he loved me, and he wanted to raise me, and I should have let him and forgotten about the dad who didn't want me."

"Rachel, I..." He tried to understand what brought us back to the same arguments.

"Congratulations on baby number two. I'm excited for you and your wife, but the other four of us, that you've completely neglected in every sense of the word...you can't expect us to keep standing in the shadows, waiting for you to care about us again." When I finished, he knew exactly where this was coming from, and that he did wrong.

"I was ashamed of me, not of you." At least he didn't deny it. "How can I make this better?"

"You can't." I tried to be strong and cold, but my eyes were blurry.

"Rachel," he tried, reaching for me, but I spun on him.

"Why won't you let me go? Sarah has a spare bedroom and she cares enough to admit we're related. You don't want me here any more than I want to be here, so why can't you let me go?" I ignored the tears.

"Because I love you. And I'm sorry I didn't—"

"No, you don't!" I called him on his first statement. "The old you might have, and I think you want to, but you have a new life. A new family. And I don't fit."

"That's not true."

"Just let me go," I pleaded before Toby walked in, looking at Chris like he was ready to kill. I didn't tell him what happened, only that I couldn't be there tonight.

"HE DOESN'T DESERVE YOU," Toby told me once we were under the pier and I told him everything that happened. He had let me be sad and quiet during the drive, waiting until I was ready to ask me what happened.

"Which is why he doesn't have me." He looked like he didn't believe me, so I went on. "I said I couldn't trust him because he's an actor, and I was right. That's what I should have listened to. Because he can make you believe whatever he wants if you let him," I said bitterly.

"You're mad because he left you all over again."

"No, I'm mad because I realized that he never came back and isn't going to. I was starting to believe he had a valid reason for leaving, like the CIA or something, and he was trying to make up for it...I don't want the entire world to know I'm his daughter either...but it hurt that he pretended we don't exist."

"Well, if he's CIA..." He got a sad laugh from me. "I want to tell you you're better off, but I don't understand how anybody could ever be okay with making you feel like this. You're worth so much more."

"Next time I'll listen to you and Kyle and my gut."

"I wish we were wrong." He seemed surprised he meant it.

· · ·

Toby dropped me off just before curfew, because Jared would have brought me back if I tried to stay there. I looked over my history notes one last time to prepare for our essay final before getting ready for bed. I grabbed my phone to put it on the charger and saw I had a voicemail.

"Hey lovebug! I miss you." Haylie's voice made me smile and miss her as well. "Pete is playing at the Staples Center tomorrow, so I figured I would join him. If you're interested, I know a guy who can get you in real cheap. Not that I'm cheap. Anyway, let me know how many passes you need. And even if you don't want to come to the most awesome concert in the world, I want to see you. Hugs and kisses times infinity. Muah."

I immediately texted her back, in case it was too late to call, and went to bed feeling better than I had since the interview.

25

THE CONCERT

"Why are you smiling?" Nick asked when I got to school. I hadn't been in the best mood when I left him yesterday, and we had history and math exams today.

"Do you like Hartley?" I asked, getting a strange look from him. "They're this awesome band that my cousin's fiancé—"

"That look was because they're super cool and you'd have to be crazy to not know who they are," he cut me off to explain.

"They're playing the Staples Center tonight, and I have backstage passes," I said with a humongous smile. "If you want to come, of course."

"I'll have to check my schedule," he teased, meaning he would have to ask his mom. "But yeah, I'm in."

When we finished our exams, I brought Nick to the parking lot, where Haylie was waiting. As soon as she saw us, she rushed over to take me in her arms.

"You have a habit of running into people's arms, don't you?" Nick asked me.

"Only family." I hoped that made it less weird. "Speaking of, this is Haylie. She's basically my sister. And this is Nick."

"I don't need an introduction?" he raised an eyebrow.

"You're literally my only friend in California," I reminded him.

"Likewise," he assured me. It wasn't true, but most of his old friends either gave up on him for always being gone, or only wanted to hang out because he's famous.

"Pete's with the band, doing sound check and all that music stuff, so I thought we could go for supper, then meet the guys right before the...unless you want to watch the sound check?" she cut herself off when she saw Nick face light up.

"Can we?" he asked.

Hales looked like she'd been looking forward to a nice meal with good company, but I shrugged, so she settled for pizza and beer with the guys.

"How's living with your dad?" Haylie asked me, biting into her cheese pizza while everyone else was fooling around on stage.

"He might not be the worst human alive, but he's far from what a father should be. At least to me." I wasn't sure if I was being too harsh, but if he couldn't even own up to being our father, why should I give him a chance? "I see him with Owen and its exactly like what I remember, and he almost had me fooled, thinking I maybe had it wrong, but then he...I want to tell Owen not to get too attached, that he might be awesome now, but then he'll leave, and it will break his heart. Because if he doesn't...why would he stay with them when he left us?"

"Maybe he was an idiot and he grew up?" she suggested. "Whatever his problem is, he's the one who is missing out on all of the awesomeness you bring. I'm seriously feeling the withdrawal," she told me.

"What about transferring to Berkeley or Stanford?" was my proposal.

"Tempting, but it's Harvard." We got matching Harvard t-shirts when I was maybe five years old, because that had always been her dream, and I used to follow Sarah or Haylie, whichever sounded more appealing.

"I'm starving." Pete came and sat on the couch with us, grabbing a slice of pizza while Nick and the band did the same.

"How was sound check?" I asked Nick.

"Awesome," he answered with his mouth full.

"We might bring him on tour with us to do the woah," Pete teased.

"Everyone can come on tour," Ralph, the drummer, assured me when I was going to ask.

"Rachel can't sing," Haylie pointed out.

"Thanks for throwing me under the bus," I pretended to be hurt, but Nick was shocked.

"You can stay inside the bus," Pete offered.

"You're teaming up on me?" I reproached.

"It comes from a place of love and knowing it's better for people who love you to tell you than to find out in an arena with a billion people watching," Hales explained.

"Math isn't her strong suit," Pete told Nick, which earned him a playful tap from his fiancée, before they kissed.

"You have the coolest family ever," Nick told me.

"I really do," I smiled, knowing how lucky I was, but also how much cooler it once was.

"Beer pong?" Donovan suggested, playing with his guitar pick.

"They're underage," Haylie and Peter said at the same time before calling, "Jinx."

"They only act like teenagers," Donovan assured us. "Without alcohol?" he offered.

"I'm in," Nick shrugged, following him to a table. We played until their manager said they had to go get ready.

"Is it better here or out front?" Nick asked of our options.

"Both are pretty fun," Hales warned.

"We start out front and end up backstage," I explained.

"You guys do this a lot?"

"They're our groupies. Sorry, I mean band aids." Ralph was a big fan of Almost Famous, so he sort of meant it as a compliment, but we threw pillows at him for the comparison.

"Only if they're in our town, or one close by, or one we want to visit, or that time we toured with them for a week," I defended us to Nick, my smile spreading along with his.

"Be awesome babe," Haylie said before kissing Pete. The words sounded ridiculous coming from her mouth, but he was superstitious about good luck, and the time she tried 'break a leg', he almost did. Since then she says some random things like 'rock it' that give the rest of us a laugh.

NICK and I followed Haylie to our seats, since she had the passes and tickets. Once the show started, it was clear that Nick was into Hartley, but Haylie and I had him beat, singing along to every word, even with the variations that came with live shows.

We waited until the last few songs to go backstage, because there was a slow one he wrote for Haylie, that he always played at the end. We waited in the side curtains for him to look over to her, like he did whenever she was at his shows, and bring her on stage.

I felt Nick watching me watch them, so I laughed nervously and went back to singing along. He did the same, but I couldn't help but feel like the teasing was right, and this was more than just a friendship.

When Haylie's song ended, Pete kept her on stage and beckoned Nick and I over, so we were each sharing a mic with a member of the band. They let us do the woahs that Nick wanted to go on tour to do, but Haylie and Peter took turns looking over at me and laughing, because there was a reason the running joke was that I couldn't sing.

. . .

ONCE THE CONCERT WAS OVER, the guys came back to see us for a bit, then went out for drinks while Haylie insisted on driving us home.

"We could have come and not had any drinks," I pointed out once we were in Haylie's car.

"Don't you have a curfew? It's already midnight."

"Theoretically, my curfew is ten," I agreed. "But we're not on the best of terms because he wasn't the nicest person, so he can deal with me being however late I want to be."

"Probably not the best idea," Haylie warned.

"It's my turn to give him some trouble and he has to take it," I said with more confidence than I felt. "And I'm with family," I added. Mom always let us stay out late if we were with Sarah or Uncle Jack.

NICK and I had been talking about the concert, driving on the 101 when all of a sudden, I woke up and we were at Nick's.

"Rachel," he whispered, moving the hair that had fallen over my eyes when I fell asleep on him.

"Oh my God, I'm sorry," I said when I realized what I'd done.

"Don't worry about it," he assured me before I got out of the car to say goodnight to him.

"Was I asleep long?" I hoped I hadn't drooled or anything to make it even more embarrassing.

"Maybe ten minutes or so?" he shrugged with a smile. "But I like having you close," he added before leaning in, as if he might kiss me.

For a second, I wanted him to, and I closed my eyes to lean in, but then I saw Alex's face in my head and I felt like I was somehow betraying him. "Goodnight, Nick," I said instead, going in for a hug before pulling away from him.

"Goodnight." He only looked slightly disappointed. "Thank you for tonight, Haylie. It was awesome meeting you," he said through the open window on the passenger's side.

I waited until he was in his house, then got into the front seat with Haylie. "You know he was about to kiss you, right?" she pointed out.

"Yes, I got that," I agreed.

"And you didn't want to kiss him?" she asked like she was worried she misread the whole situation, but was sure she hadn't.

"Mostly yes," I admitted.

"But..."

"Alex." I shrugged my shoulders and bit my lip. There was also a part of me that kept thinking how mom had never met Nick. And she never would. Unless I went home to Lake George and married someone from school, I would spend the rest of my life with someone who didn't know my mother.

Haylie looked at me with sympathy before turning back to the road and driving me home.

"Want me to walk you in?" Haylie offered, wrinkling her nose and glaring at the house.

"That's okay. Text me when you get in." I leaned forward and gave her a hug before getting out of the car. I walked to the front door and saw the light in the foyer bursting through the window. It could have been someone being considerate and leaving a light on so I could find my way to my room, but I knew someone would be waiting on the other side. I had my key in my hand, but the door was unlocked.

Chris was sitting on the stairs, like he'd been there for hours. "Where have you been?" it wasn't like the time I hiked instead of coming to dinner. He asked it like I'd actually done something incredibly inconsiderate.

"Haylie brought me to Peter's concert. It finished a little late." I stopped in front of him at the foot of the stairs. I knew I should have texted him more than "I'll be out tonight," but I was mad at him for the interview. If he knew me as well as he pretended to, he would know that if Hartley was playing, I would be there.

"A little late? It is three hours past your curfew and I had no idea where you were. I was about to call the cops when Tracy got a hold of Ryan, who happened to be at the concert and saw you on stage. Do you have any idea how worried we were?"

"Next time, don't be." I would never speak like that to any other adult, not even my siblings.

I walked past him and was halfway up the stairs when he got up and followed. "That is not how this works. You can't turn the parenting stuff off when you get mad at me. I am still responsible—"

"Oh, so only you can do that?" I cut him off and turned to face him. "You're not my father." I glared at him before going into my room and slamming the door. I knew I could go to bed and try to ignore him while he kept yelling, but instead I put my back to the door and slid down until I was in a tiny ball on the floor.

"Don't pull that card with me, Rachel. I have been your father ever since the day I found out your mother was pregnant. I was in the delivery room when you were born, and I spent so many nights rocking you to sleep and checking on you when you cried because you wanted attention. Whenever you had night-mares or were sick or thought there was a monster under your bed, I was the one you ran to. It used to drive Sierra mad, but you were daddy's little girl, and that's what kills me about how we are now," he said from the other side of the door.

I waited a bit to see if he would go and leave me alone, but he didn't, so I stood up and opened the door. "If we were so close and you loved me so much, then why did you leave?" I asked, the tears flooding my eyes. I gave him time, but he couldn't come up with an answer. "It kills me too, because I remember. Every memory I have from before you left is with you. You were my entire world and then all of a sudden you were gone, and you broke my heart," I said the last three words deliberately. "Having your name on my birth certificate doesn't make you my father. And spending six years being there for me all the time doesn't make up for the nine years you were gone, building your career and a second family. That's not what a father does," I shot at him before closing the door and going back to my spot on the floor.

I sat there for a while, expecting him to argue more or to leave, but he stood on the other side of the door, for the longest time, so I could hear him breathing as I tried to stop crying. "I have always loved you Rachel. Always." He waited a bit for me to respond, but it brought more tears, so I stayed silent, and he left.

IN THAT MOMENT, I decided my heart had been broken too many times in the past few months and I couldn't take it anymore. Math had been our last exam, so I didn't need to stay. Or at least I had nothing to keep me from taking a few days where I didn't feel unloved and unwanted.

I went to my closet and filled my backpack with everything I couldn't bear to be without: some clothes, Alex's book, my sketchbook and a toothbrush. Then I put on Alex's jacket and tiptoed down the stairs. I wrote a note for Tracy and left it on the kitchen counter, to make sure they wouldn't call the cops on me, then called a taxi to an address a few houses down. I couldn't risk one of them having trouble sleeping and seeing me through the window.

I waited a few minutes to give the taxi time to arrive, then headed out into the night, hoping that I would never have to come back.

26

THE ESCAPE

It was pouring by the time I got to the hotel, so I ran to the revolving doors as fast as I could, getting in long before the doorman even opened his umbrella.

"May I help you?" the man behind the desk asked when I walked over.

"I'm looking for Haylie Harris? I'm not sure what room she's in. Maybe the penthouse?" I assumed they would be staying under her name to avoid being found, and she'd mentioned this tour was fancier than the last one.

"Is she expecting you?" he asked.

"Not exactly." I hadn't gotten the text to say she made it home, but unless she joined the guys for drinks, she was probably in bed sleeping by now. "You know what, I'll wait until she gets back to me." I got the feeling he wouldn't be telling me anything at this time of night, so I went over to the couches and called her phone. "Hey Haylie, it's me. I know you're probably sleeping, but I'm at your hotel, so call me when you get this," I left her a message, regretting that I didn't say something to let her know I was okay and it was only an emotional emergency. I didn't want to worry her too much. I should have gone to Jared's, because at least I knew where he hid his key, but I wasn't sure how he would have reacted. Not that he would have sent me back to be mean, but he probably would have called Chris to get his side. He would have wanted to bring me back so we could all talk about it and try to get along.

I pulled Alex's jacket closer to me and pulled my legs up to hug myself, figuring I would wait until Haylie woke up and got my message. Unless the desk guy was calling security on me. He didn't look at me funny after he hung up, so I was pretty sure I was safe for now. I was debating if I should take out the book and go to Narnia, or try to get some sleep, when Haylie stepped off the elevators.

"Rachel, what are you doing here?" she asked, followed by Peter. Both of them were wearing the hotel robes over their PJs. I was probably a sight to see, soaked with my eyes red and puffy from the crying I couldn't seem to stop.

"Can I stay here for a while?" I stood up as another batch of tears fell. I felt bad for waking them, but very grateful I didn't have to sleep on the couch in the lobby.

"Of course." She took me in her arms and Pete nodded to the guy behind the desk to let him know I wasn't a psycho.

WE TOOK the elevator up to the fourteenth floor, which we all knew was the thirteenth. Haylie waited until she had me sitting on the couch to ask, "What happened?"

"I let my guard down for five seconds and he broke my heart all over again," I shared.

"It's okay." She pulled me close. "You're soaking wet though sweetie."

"I'm sorry."

"Don't be. Let me go draw you a nice warm bath, then we can have teas and talk about it." She ran her hand through my hair while Pete stood there, looking helpless. "Or you can put some warm PJs on and go straight to bed," she offered when she saw how exhausted I was.

"You can go to sleep. I'm fine," I assured her.

"I have nothing to do tomorrow," she turned me down. We'd made plans to go to brunch and walk around the Grove. "We can start our Girls Day a little earlier."

"You don't have to take care of me. I just couldn't stay there anymore," I explained.

"I know. We'll figure it out tomorrow." She kissed the top of my head and led me to the second bedroom. She went to get me warm pajamas while Pete gave me a longer than usual hug. She came back and did the same, before they both went to bed.

I wished I'd said goodbye to Owen, because hopefully this was it. I could go home with Haylie to live with Sarah, and Chris could ship my stuff over. Even if it wasn't the best time, or way to do it, I definitely did not regret leaving.

I thought I would lie awake all night without being able to sleep, tossing and turning for hours, but as soon as my head hit the pillow, I was out.

I WOKE up to the sun shining, and a rhythmic breathing that was not my own. With my eyes still closed, I reached out and pulled Katie into me, like I did whenever she slept over. Something about wrapping your arms around a tiny child made everything seem like it might be okay. After all, if she trusted me to keep her safe, I must be doing something right. I moved her hair away from my face, then remembered that I was at Haylie's hotel, and Katie should be miles and miles away in New York.

I opened my eyes to confirm that it was her and not some stranger, then grabbed my phone and saw it was nearly one o'clock in the afternoon. I also had a lot of missed calls and texts, but I was not ready for those right now. I could smell peanut butter, bananas, and bacon, and hear voices from the next room.

"You flew here?" I asked Katie, who was staring up at me.

"We're on an adventure," she agreed.

"Are you hungry?" She nodded, so we got up and went to the common area of the hotel suite.

"Oh good, you're up," Haylie said as soon as she saw me.

"Surprise!" Sarah came over and took me in her arms, knowing the surprise was ruined when I woke up to her daughter in bed with me.

"You didn't have to drop everything and come here."

"Because you were coming to me next?" She knew me too well.

"It makes the most sense. I can take care of the munchkin and earn my keep," I teased, but she knew I meant it.

"Sweetie, I know you think it's awful living with him, but there's a whole lot you don't know—"

"I think I've yelled at him and cried enough that if he had a valid reason for being inconsiderate and mean, he would have let me know by now," I argued.

"We'll talk about it later." She didn't look convinced.

"For now, eat." Haylie handed me a plate.

"You didn't tell him where I am, did you?" I asked my sister, terrified he would be coming to bring me back.

"I woke up to a million calls this morning before flying here. I told him I was with you, so he knows you're safe, but I didn't tell him where you are."

"You should have let him suffer a bit," I argued.

"I know you don't mean that, you're only saying it because you're hurt, so I won't lecture you."

We had pancakes, eggs, and bacon with fresh fruit and three different kinds of syrup from room service.

PETER CAME BACK from a fan meet and greet as we were finishing, and almost immediately offered to take Katie to LEGOLAND.

"I don't like that look," I told Sarah when she closed the door on them.

"I want to understand what he's doing that's so terrible."

"You know how I told you I would try to be nice to him now, because Jared said he would let me move out if I did?" I asked and she nodded. "I tried to make things work, not just because it would help me get away from him, but because I was tired of spending my whole life missing him, and I wanted to see if we could have the relationship the rest of you seem to have with him. I wanted to not hate him anymore. So I let him in."

"Then what happened?" She didn't understand.

"He did an interview when I thought we were getting close and becoming a family. He basically told the guy he had no kids other than Owen and the new baby. I didn't necessarily want him to tell the world about me, but he didn't have to pretend we don't exist."

"If it was you, would you really..." Haylie stopped when I raised my eyebrows at her. "You were the one who always thought he was coming back."

"She used to tell Ted he could be her daddy for now, but only until her real one came back," Sarah remembered.

"Kyle told all his friends and his teachers that our dad died, and he was older, so people thought I was confused and not accepting the fact that my father died. Mom had to come to school and tell them I wasn't in denial and I didn't need therapy. Kyle was lying about the why, but he was right that our dad wasn't coming back."

"I remember that conversation she had with you after. I wanted to take you in my arms and..."

"If it was me, I would have told the truth," I answered Haylie's unfinished question, because mom had been the one who took me in her arms and held me while I cried over the realization that *he* was gone.

"I think he thought he was protecting you by keeping you out of the public eye," Sarah tried to defend him.

"Then why parade Owen and the new baby bump?" I asked.

"I'm team Rachel on that one. Even my mom admits we're related," Haylie had my back.

"Would you be mad like this if reporters came after mom died and Jared told the reporters he was an only child, and..." Sarah tried to ask a specific question, but wasn't very good at it.

"Would I still be mad at him for the interview if we didn't have a history of me hating him because he abandoned me?" I rephrased it for her.

"That is what I was getting at," she agreed.

"Maybe if I didn't feel so uncertain about his intentions, and if I didn't have abandonment issues, then I wouldn't be hurt by him publicly denying my existence. But if it was Jared, like you asked...I was going to say I wouldn't be mad at him, but I think it's because he would never do that to me. He might have asked them to respect our privacy or not answered any questions, but he never would've turned his back on us, or pretended we don't exist."

"Want me to bring you on stage again tonight and tell everyone you're my cousin?" Haylie offered.

"I don't doubt your love for me Hales," I explained the difference. "Or yours," I told Sarah before she could offer to do the same.

"And you don't ever have to. You live in my heart, Rachel. Even when you aren't calling me or texting me, I'm talking to Jared or Toby or...we are constantly calling each other to find out how you are."

"I know. I tell you something and Toby asks about it days later. It's like you have a weekly newsletter." I smiled at them.

"We should do conference calls. It would save so much time," Haylie teased.

"And actually let me be a part of them, right? You can talk to me instead of about me?"

"I can't make any promises. You're a problem child who got suspended and skips school." Sarah tried to keep a straight face.

"Toby kidnapped me," I defended the skipping accusation, since it was easier than why I got suspended.

"He called me before doing it. He doesn't talk to Chris, but he would have called mom before doing it back home, so he got my permission instead," she found it silly.

"And you gave it?" I was surprised.

"I have no worries about you and school," she assured me.

"I have excellent role models." I looked to them.

"You do," they both laughed, knowing they got amazing grades, but broke a few rules along the way.

"Our next newsletter was going to be Haylie updating us on you and Nick, because Toby is absolutely useless with that. Unfortunately, Haylie's voicemail was not as detail-specific as I wanted." She looked over to let me know it was inconsiderate of me to have usurped their gossip ring by running away.

"Go ahead, ask her." I waited.

"Not with you right there," she argued.

"You could also ask me if you wanted to know," I offered.

"You're awful at that. I want to know how he looks at you when you're not looking, and all the things you don't notice because you're just friends," She said like being best friends with a guy was a ridiculous concept she'd never heard of.

"You want to know about things like him trying to kiss me after I totally fell asleep on him while Haylie was driving us home last night," I gave an example of what she was looking for. I hadn't thought about the near-kiss with everything else going on.

"Yes, that is exactly what I want to hear about." Sarah looked to Haylie like she couldn't believe that wasn't the first thing that came out of her mouth while they waited for me to wake up.

"Well, that happened," I said simply.

"Is it the age difference that makes her not understand girl talk?" Sarah asked Haylie.

"Or is it because her best friends are always guys?" she suggested.

"Mom never talked about Alex like that. It wasn't until his mom told me she always thought we would end up together that I went over things we did and conversations we had. I realized he might have been thinking that too," I admitted. It wasn't just things he said, because I told him I loved him as often as I told my brothers. It was the way he looked at me sometimes, how he smiled when he saw me.

"And now Nick reminds you of Alex?" Sarah asked delicately.

"No...well, maybe a bit. But also, when he leaned in...I've never been kissed before," I confessed, looking to the two of them, who were way too excited for my comfort.

We talked about boys and normal life stuff until Pete came back with Katie, and another surprise in the forms of Jared and Toby. Having my family around me was exactly what I needed, but I knew they had an ulterior motive I wasn't going to like.

The guys brought Pink's hot dogs with them, so we sat around the coffee table and dug in while Toby brought Peter to his second LA concert, since it was on his way to work.

WE WERE STILL at the coffee table an hour after we finished eating, drinking coffees and talking. When Katie fell asleep, I went with Sarah to put her to bed in the spare room. I came back to everyone looking up at me like they were about to tell me someone died, which was not an expression I used lightly.

"What's wrong?" I asked, seeing mom's diary on the table in front of them. It looked older and more used than the one we found on her night table.

"Nothing sweetie, take a seat." Sarah pointed to the couch.

"Guys..." I waited for someone to explain.

"We thought it was time to tell you why dad left," Sarah admitted, which was the last thing I expected.

✤ 27 ✤

THE TRUTH

"What do you mean 'why he left'?" I asked, sitting on the couch like she wanted me to.

"The reason it was a lot easier for us to forgive him is because you were sleeping when it happened, but we were listening at the top of the staircase while they fought," Sarah explained.

"Until they found us," Jared amended. He and Sarah were on one couch, while I sat beside Haylie on the other.

"You were talking to him the whole time?" I felt betrayed and hurt, but it didn't make sense.

"No, we would never have done that to you. We grew up without him, like you and Kyle," Sarah assured me.

"It was only when I moved here and tracked him down..." he stopped when I shook my head.

"If he had a valid reason for leaving he would have told me by now. And even if it was amazing, how do you justify his abandoning us for the past decade? It doesn't make sense," I argued.

"That's what we didn't understand either," Sarah agreed.

"I don't care," I lied, but none of them believed me.

"The next few years will be hell for you if you don't know."

"Jared made me a promise. I tried. That means I have six months left until I'm free," I reminded them.

"Fine, then the rest of your life will be spent building up on regret until you eventually find out," Sarah rephrased.

"Find out what?" I was getting annoyed.

"That mom was the one who asked him to leave," Jared cut to the chase.

I paused, trying to digest this information. I looked to Haylie, who also seemed surprised, before deciding it didn't make a difference. "Because she saw through his act and knew he was an asshole. Either way, lots of couples get divorced, but parents shouldn't disappear."

"It wasn't like that Rachel; she broke his heart," Sarah argued.

"Like he broke mine? And yours? And—"

"I'm going to start at the beginning," Sarah cut me off, and I understood she meant the beginning of our parents. Which was probably the worst thing she could do, because I was not going to like him for stealing mom's heart and crushing it. Still, I listened. "Mom and dad grew up next door to each other and became best friends in high school. When they would tell the story, it was cute. He would say he fell in love the moment he laid eyes on her, and she would joke that she had absolutely no idea. She even had more of a crush on his older brother. Then dad asked her to prom, she said yes, and it was like a fairytale."

"I remember that story," I told her.

"That's how they would tell it," Jared continued. "They got married right out of high school, had us..."

"Then mom joined the police academy, had Kyle, had me...we were the picture-perfect family, like the one he has now, until he left to become an actor in Hollywood," I finished for him.

"You're not wrong, but you're not right either," Jared told me.

"Mom joined the academy and loved being a cop. She understood how dad could love a job so much he chaperoned parties and play visits and offered after school programs without compensation," Sarah shared.

"He used to teach drama at the high school, right?" I asked, unimpressed. I remembered what they were like before he left. It was the why that had me drawing a blank.

"Mom found her calling and discovered a world of possibilities."

"Are you reciting her diary entries?" Sarah didn't normally talk like that.

"I'm using her words to explain the parts that don't make sense to me."

"Like what?" I asked.

"Like how you can get married and have three kids before you realize you were never in love with the person you did it with." She was finally showing a bit of the pent-up anger I thought I was alone in feeling.

"They had four kids by the time he did something about it," I corrected.

"She's talking about mom," Jared said delicately.

"Are you saying she met someone at the precinct?" I asked, trying to put two and two together about her world of possibilities. I couldn't exactly feel my heart pounding, but my chest felt like it did when Kyle used to get pummeled to the ground at football games. It wouldn't go away until he got up and smiled to let us know he was okay. Mom was not the bad guy in the story, and I couldn't believe she would have done anything like that to someone she loved, or to us.

"There were guys and they flirted, but mom was married. She just realized she had married her best friend instead of waiting for someone to give her butterflies," Sarah explained, looking so uncomfortable. I wanted to argue, to yell at her to stop telling this lie, but I could see it was harder for her to tell than it was for me to listen to, so I tried to let her finish. "This was around the time she got pregnant with Kyle. Dad was thrilled, mom wished it wouldn't have happened so soon after starting her job, but it wouldn't have been a big deal if she hadn't had postpartum depression."

"She had what?" I had never heard anything about this. There was a woman from our church who had gone through postpartum depression after her first kid, and mom helped her out a lot, but she always did that. She never said anything about having gone through the same thing.

"It's a mood disorder that happens after women give birth sometimes. They can experience extreme sadness, exhaustion, irritability, the inability to take care of themselves and their family..." Sarah got into the medical symptoms, but it basically sounded like an extreme depression caused by having a baby.

"Dad tried, we tried, but we didn't know how to help her," Jared spoke up.

"But she got better." I figured it must have been written out of our history because it wasn't a big deal.

"She did. But it wasn't thanks to us. She was convinced she was an awful mother and that she would do something to hurt Kyle, so she left us, for what seemed like forever at the time, but it was probably only a few months."

"She left because she needed help, but then she came back," I was already defending her. I didn't mind hearing some ridiculous stories to help me forgive Chris, so we could all live happily ever after, but I would not let them bring down my mother in the process. Sarah's saving grace was that she looked as torn up about it as I felt.

"She did. She got the help she needed. But she didn't stay at the hospital while they treated her. She was with a guy she met at the academy." She waited for me to connect the dots, because Ted had been in mom's class at the academy, but I shook my head, not willing to accept that.

"It doesn't matter what we think happened, all that we know is that she came back, saying she missed us, that she was sorry. She asked dad if they could try again, if he could ever forgive her, and he took her back without hesitation." The way Jared described it was like he'd been there, like he was maybe the one who opened the door to let her in. As if he'd been hoping it was her every time the doorbell rang, like I had that first year after Chris left. I wanted to point out that Chris hadn't given her the chance to do the same, because he never came back or apologized, but I didn't think my voice would have worked.

"Things were still iffy when you were born, but once it was the six of us, we were back to that fairytale, with all of the traditions. We were the family everyone wanted to be," Sarah sounded relieved to be back to the story that made sense to her.

"The one I remember," I agreed. "Until it fell apart."

"Do you remember Uncle Jeff?" Jared asked out of the blue.

"No, but Chris mentioned he had a brother who was good at football." It was one of those things that I felt like I knew, but I couldn't remember meeting him.

"He was amazing at it," Jared agreed. "You can look him up if you want, but he had it all. He got a full ride to play football, got drafted into the NFL, endorsement deals, supermodel girlfriends..." he got a tiny smile, then went sad.

"How come no one ever mentions him?" I asked, looking around. This time, I was the only one who didn't know the answer.

"Because he died. And not in a good way," Sarah admitted.

"When do people ever die in a good way?" I asked.

"She doesn't mean him dying was bad. He did some bad things to get there. Part of his MVP lifestyle included drugs and lots of drinking in the offseason, but he freaked out one night. For no apparent reason, he shot two people in his hotel room before jumping off the balcony."

"You're making that up," I said because it was unbelievable, not because I thought my brother was lying.

"They did an autopsy and found the drugs, but they also think he was schizophrenic and may have seen them as part of his delusion. He had never been diagnosed, or followed, but it has genetic components, and the partying lifestyle is known to aggravate that." Sarah spoke like he was a patient, not a long-lost uncle. I had no recollection of him, but she looked like she was purposely distancing herself so it wouldn't hurt. "After that, there was something between them that they wouldn't tell us about. It was like mom blamed dad, he wasn't happy anymore, which made sense after his brother died, but he started drinking. Not lots, but he never used to before, and alcohol and drugs aren't good if you might be predisposed." I tried to remember this time when we weren't happy, but I couldn't. All my memories were of a happy family that loved each other until I woke up and he wasn't there anymore.

"And that's why she asked him to leave. Because he might shoot us and jump out a window." I liked the narrative where mom was protecting us. We didn't need to go into what she may or may not have done beforehand.

"A combination of factors," Sarah argued.

"From what we heard that night, dad was asked to test for a pilot. He had an agent and did little projects, then someone he'd worked with before recommended him, but he turned it down. It was a huge opportunity for him, but he didn't want to be away from us."

"Funny," I rolled my eyes.

"Mom called the agent back and said there was a misunderstanding, that he would take it. She told him we were holding him back, and he should make his dreams come true. This way, in case he did develop tendencies of the disorder, he wouldn't be anywhere near us."

"Would that make you leave Katie?" I asked Sarah.

"If I believed I was going to hurt her without meaning to, without being able to stop myself...I wouldn't be able to forgive myself."

"He looks fine now." Either he wasn't, so I shouldn't be living with him, or he was, and he should have come back and apologized way sooner, not waited for Jared to find him.

"Mom told him he was her best friend, always had and always would be, but she had never loved him the way he loved her. She apologized for it taking her so long to realize it, but she saw us at the top of the stairs and sent us to bed. Dad came a while later and kissed us goodbye, saying he would love us forever and not to blame mom," Sarah finished.

"Nothing else?" This explained why he left, but I would have expected him to come back.

"Nope. Which is why we hated him too."

"What did you find out to switch sides?" I asked Jared.

"That after mom told him to leave, he went to a lawyer to see about joint custody, or visitation rights, but he had less than a one percent chance of winning."

"Why? His brother was dead, it shouldn't have made an impact." I looked to Haylie.

"Schizophrenia is often predicted by having a first degree relative who has it," Sarah answered instead. "And dad had a similar outburst on his record."

"He shot people and jumped off a balcony?" I was used to assuming the worst of him, but it had all been emotional. I didn't think he would ever physically hurt me, or anyone else.

"Not similar, but angry," Jared corrected. "In high school, when dad was still considered a minor, but Jeff was eighteen and on his way to the NFL, dad took the blame for something he had nothing to do with. His brother would have been tried as the adult that he was, and it would have ruined his future, while dad only got community service."

"He would have had to prove your mom was unfit if he wanted to win against that," Haylie gave her legal opinion.

"No wonder mom was worried." It was a lot to process.

"Mom knew it was Jeff. She lied to help them cover it up, which is probably why she was mad at dad when it turned out it wasn't a one-time thing. Jeff had a mental problem he needed treatment for, so he wouldn't have killed people and died."

"I still have questions."

"I know," Sarah agreed.

"Is that everything? No more secrets?" I verified.

She nodded. "We weren't looking for reasons to hate him and

make him the bad guy, Rache, we were dying to get our dad back." She wanted me to understand why they were so ready to believe him, while I was struggling to accept it.

"How come you didn't tell me when you found out? Or when I was sent to live with him? Why wait until now?" I either wished they had told me sooner, or not at all.

"We couldn't do that to mom. At first it didn't matter that we knew why he left and you didn't, because he never came back. Then when Jared found out, I asked mom how she could do that, to deprive us of our father, and... I never wanted to have to tell you," she cut herself off.

"What did she say?" I pressed.

"She cried. She said she knew it was wrong, that she was the bad guy and she felt terrible about it. At first, she was scared, because she thought she knew Jeff, so she could be wrong about dad too, but...she eventually knew dad would never hurt us. They could have gotten a divorce and figured it out, with supervised visits or something. But she knew that if she did that, she would lose us. Kyle was the only mama's boy, the rest of us would have chosen dad at that point, if given the choice. She loved us too much to let us go."

"That's her excuse?" I tried to not be mad at her, or to stop the tears, but failed at both.

"She regretted it. What she did to him, what she did to us, having to comfort each and every one of us when we finally realized he wasn't coming home...but she couldn't regret keeping us safe and close."

"Does Kyle know?" I asked.

"We'll tell him at Christmas, or I'll drive out once I'm home. We just knew it was hurting you more to not know," Sarah explained.

It was late, so they pretty much sent me to go get ready for bed, knowing I had a lot to work through.

. . .

"ARE YOU OKAY?" Sarah asked when I came back.

"Not really." I was about to lie, but decided on the truth.

"I didn't want to tell you. I didn't like lying to you, but I would have been happy if you'd never found out. It seemed like the lesser of two evils."

"I'm so mad at her," I admitted. "And I don't want to be, and I hate myself for it, but ever since she died, everything keeps…"

"I know." She took me in her arms, because I was crying again.

"It's like so many things were a lie. Us being a happy family, him being the bad guy who ruined the fairytale…"

"That's why mom never talked to you about Alex like he was someone you might fall in love with. She saw the way he was looking at you, saw that you were oblivious, and it was like her and dad all over again. She didn't want you to settle for him because he was your best friend and he loved you. She wanted to make sure you felt the same of your own accord."

"No one invited me to the party?" Jared asked, finding us both crying.

"We're all going to be okay," Sarah decided.

"Mom raised us to make sure we would," Jared said the worst, but also the best thing.

The three of us sat on the couch and talked, not about the big things, but the little ones, that seem insignificant until they're gone.

THE CONFRONTATION

"Are you ready?" Sarah turned to me after Toby dropped us off in front of the gate. We'd all gone out to brunch, Haylie, Toby, Jared, Sarah, Katie, Peter and I, giving me a few more hours of family vacation before having to deal with everything, and Chris.

"No." I was never ready, but followed her anyways. Toby was taking Katie to cool kid places, and I wished I could be going with them instead.

"Does he know you told me?" I asked.

"You ran away and are willingly coming back," she pointed out.

"Did I have a choice?"

"Not really." She looped her arm through mine, so we took the final steps together. I was debating if I wanted to be formal and ring the doorbell, or if I should use my key, but Chris opened the door before we got to it.

I froze, all of my questions jumbled in my head, before Chris looked at us sadly and understood that Sarah told me everything.

"Come on in," he said after a sigh, stepping aside so we could follow him into the living room. I saw Tracy coming down the stairs, but she turned and went straight out to the patio instead of joining what would be a very heated, or at least emotional conversation.

"I guess you have a lot of questions for me."

"Only one." I tried to be strong and not cry. "Why didn't you fight for us?" The tears were blurring my vision, but I made him and Sarah cry too. I knew it sucked that mom stopped loving him and my heart went out to him for that, but it still wasn't a reason to give up on your children. Less than one percent was still a chance, and I was sure that if he got lawyers involved, mom would have given up to not put us through that. Basically, he could have done more.

Sarah was there as my moral support, so she didn't defend him, she waited with me for his answer.

"I wanted to, and I tried, but I couldn't do it. I have made mistakes Rachel, and not fighting for you is my biggest one, but I am not guilty of not loving you."

"You gave up?" I pressed, not accepting his cop-out of an answer. "Because you could have gone to court and tried. You could have said it wasn't you. I'm sure perjury is less frowned upon in this situation than whatever they think you did."

"You spend a lot of time with Haylie, don't you?" He gave a half-hearted smile.

"You're stalling instead of answering," I reproached. "Were you relieved, and it took too long for you to miss us? Or was that the excuse you came up with when Jared finally found you and —" Sarah put her hand on my arm, but it was Chris' sigh that stopped me from voicing more of my fears.

"There are things you kids don't need to know and—"

"That's the whole reason we're having this conversation. Because adults thought it would be better to protect me from the truth with a bunch of lies that made me hate someone who may or may not deserve it." Right now, I was thinking that he did, and Sarah didn't look so certain either, ever since he included her in the kids who didn't need to know things group.

"Sometimes it's worth it. To take the chance that someone

will hate you rather than hurt them even more with the truth."
He looked like he believed what he was saying and didn't understand that it was the last thing I wanted to hear.

"But the truth always comes out. I'm pretty sure it's better to
hear it from you than from someone else. I get that you didn't
want to tell me the other stuff because you didn't want me to
hate mom, or blame you for telling me, but she's not the one I
have to live with right now."

Now that Sarah knew she was in the dark on some things
too, she stepped forward, "Whatever it is dad, tell us. If you
don't, she will hate you, and you will lose us. You promised me."

"This isn't the kind of secret that makes things better. It
matters, and it hurts people. Once it's out, I can't take it back,"
he tried to explain his reluctance, but it made me feel validated
in needing to know.

"You're hurting people now," I reminded him. "Jared told me
I could leave if I tried to make it work but still hated living here.
If I can't trust you, and you keep this from me, I won't just hate
you for it, I will move back to Lake George and you will never
see me again." It wasn't a threat, it was a lifetime of lies and
secrets, and I was exhausted.

"You don't understand, Rachel...you don't want to know," he
warned.

"I do," Sarah argued. "And at this point, if you still treat her
like someone who doesn't deserve the truth, I will let her come
home with me. I won't make her stay here."

Chris looked like he was agonizing over the decision. "I love
you girls more than anything. You, Jared, Kyle and Owen...you
are my world, my reason for living...this thing...it changes
nothing."

"We get it," I assured him.

"You don't," he argued, but he was still going to share. He
sighed before asking, "They told you what happened after Kyle
was born?"

"Mom got postpartum depression, she stayed with a friend

while she got better, then she came home and stayed," I told him.

"Did you tell her how long she was gone?" he asked Sarah.

"I didn't know." Sarah was getting impatient. Neither of us liked this part of the story, and how long didn't matter, because it was a lot less than nine years.

Chris looked like he was struggling with whatever he had to say next. He looked guilty before admitting, "Sierra was gone for eight months."

"That doesn't make sense." Sarah was shaking her head at him.

"What doesn't?" I looked from one to the other, but their eyes were locked on each other, like he'd found a way to tell Sarah and she should now understand why he didn't want to tell me.

"Mom was there for my birthday," Sarah told Chris, not ready to believe him, but the look he gave her confirmed her suspicions. "She didn't leave right after he was born, it was a month or so after Kyle's first birthday," she told me.

I looked to them, not getting it, until it clicked. If mom left a month after Kyle's birthday, that meant she only came back in October, but I was born in March. And I was not a preemie. Mom would sometimes point out how I've been late since the day I was born, two weeks after I was due. "What are you saying?" I asked, using my fingers to confirm the math, but my tears were making it obvious that I understood.

"I didn't use a lawyer to try and get custody because I knew that even if it was almost impossible for me to win with the others, I would never get you," he said like it broke him as much as it was breaking me. "I didn't want to be the one responsible for you finding out, I didn't want you to feel..." He did what he'd spent a decade trying not to do.

"No wonder you left. I wasn't even yours." My tears stung my eyes before they fell. Sarah was trying to digest this new information and comfort me at the same time, but for the first time ever, my family wasn't making me feel better.

"Rachel, that is not how—"

"Does that mean Ted was my dad?" I tried to go over every memory, every conversation. Had he been nicer to me? Done anything to show that I was his? This exercise destroyed me, because while I think he treated all of us the same, like a dad should, I was horrible to him, and must have broken his heart. "I really am an orphan." I tried to remember what I'd said to him before mom drove him to the airport.

"No, you are my daughter," Chris raised his voice, which he hadn't done before. "Ted was the one she stayed with, yes, but he was a good guy, and he knew she was vulnerable and would hate herself for it. They didn't get together until after I was gone." He seemed convinced, but I doubt mom would have been completely transparent about all the details of her cheating on him.

"I'm nobody's then." I think it was worse than being Ted's, who at least loved me, even if I gave him nothing for it. Chris was talking, but I couldn't hear a word. Everything around me was a blur. Nothing made sense anymore. Everything about my life was a lie.

I didn't realize I was walking towards the door until Sarah took a step towards me. "Talk to me, Rachel," she asked.

"I have to get out of here." I was out of the door before the words were out, saying them more to myself than to her. I didn't know where I wanted to go, or what I wanted to achieve, but I knew that I couldn't stay there. It was the lie, it was the knowing, it was the fact that I didn't know who I was anymore.

MY FEET FOLLOWED their normal path up the hill, through the woods, until I reached the clearing. I was still too worked up to stop, so I continued up to Dante's view, then sat on a rock, completely exhausted. I tried to regain my breath, but my head was the bigger mess. I couldn't believe mom cheated on...well, the guy who was not my dad. That the guy I had been living with for months, whose absence I mourned for half my life, was nothing more than a stepfather, who let his actual children go so he wouldn't hurt me. None of it made sense.

I caught my breath and took Alex's book out of my backpack. Alex, who mom was worried I would hurt, like she hurt Chris. Or was she worried I would stay with him and be miserable, like she must have been if she chose this alternative? I took out the letter of her last words to me and paused, my hands shaking. I took a deep breath, that I swear smelt like her, then read:

"MY DARLING, beautiful, kind-hearted Rachel,

It seems silly to write this when I can hear you listening to music while you paint in the next room, but we lost Ted in a plane crash and it makes you realize that life is precious. That tomorrow isn't promised. And there are some things you need to know, if ever I die before telling you. Which will be the case, no matter how old you are, because these secrets are my deepest shame. I have made peace with my sins, but not with the pain they've caused others. I can hear you in my head saying it can't be that bad, that I must be exaggerating, and I absolutely love that about you. Your blind faith in those you love is why it took you years longer than the others to accept that Chris wasn't coming back, and to hate him. I'd been hopeful that you would never make that transition, because then maybe my sins wouldn't have been so unforgivable.

You see, your father didn't leave because he didn't love you. He didn't break my heart. I broke his. It was the pain of what I did to him that you saw every time I talked about him. It's why I have to change the channel every time I see him on TV, even if I am so proud of him.

If you're reading this letter, it means that I am gone, and you now have to live with a man you grew up hating, which was never my intention. He has never deserved it. I would love to be able to defend myself here, explain why I did what I did, but I'm afraid that I can't. I realized I wasn't in love with Chris the way he was in love with me. Still I stayed, because I did love him, as a best friend, in my own way, and because of you kids. Right now, I am your best friends and I love that, more than anything, but at the time, you thought your father hung the moon. Whenever you were sick or scared or sad or had a booboo, he was always the one you went to. To be honest, Kyle would have chosen me, but you, Sarah and Jared were enraptured by Chris.

I would have stayed in that make-believe fairytale forever. It's what I had decided to do, but Chris was turning down opportunities so that he could stay. Then something terrible happened to his brother. I could never imagine the Chris I knew ever hurting the children he loved more than his own life, but I couldn't have imagined Jeff doing something like what he did either. At the time, I was shocked, I was terrified, and I hated him for making me lie to protect Jeff all those years ago, when he convinced me his brother didn't deserve to go to jail. Maybe things would have been different if he had. I don't know, but it scared me.

I know this doesn't excuse what I did, but sending him away seemed like the best way to make sure you would all be safe, without a doubt. Chris would have the career of his dreams. And I could keep my babies. It was a heartless thing to do. I regretted it almost immediately. I wanted to try and make it right, but by then, Chris was in California with the contract signed, the boys already hated him, and I knew I would lose you for it.

I know this is too little, too late, but if I do die before you're eighteen, I am letting you live with Christopher. I consider it my attempt at righting the wrong I did all those years ago. I'm writing to ask you not to hate him, because it truly was my fault. He is a kind and caring man, and the most incredible father I have ever known. If I do have to miss out on the rest of your life, know that I love you more than anything in the world. It is a pleasure and an honor to be your mother, and I am so proud of the young lady you are becoming. You and your siblings will always be the absolute best part of me.

With all my love, forever and always,
Mom"

My tears had left drops on the paper, mixed with a few tiny raindrops, but the rain and the wind were picking up. I reached for Alex's book so I could put the letter back inside and get to the café for shelter, but the wind caught hold of the letter and ripped it from my hands. It landed in the muddy, overgrown forest part of the trail we weren't supposed to go to, but it was only a few feet away from me.

I put the book back in my backpack and left it on the rock, not willing to risk another irreplaceable item, and carefully stepped away from the beaten path, onto the mud. It had been raining for days now, so the ground was slippery. Normally I would have worn running shoes or hiking boots, but today I was in slip on shoes, which had once been cute, but were now covered in muck, providing absolutely no traction.

I bent to get the letter just as the earth shifted and my foot slid, carrying me down a slope. I managed to catch myself on a branch before reaching the ditch.

"Rachel?" I heard Chris off in the distance while I tried somewhat unsuccessfully to climb back up the slope. He was calling out to see if I was there, so I could hide by staying quiet as long as he didn't go to the end and look down to see me, or my bag on the rock.

"Rachel?" I could hear him getting farther away from me. I could call for help and hope someone heard, or I could let him help me. "Rachel!"

"I'm down here," I called, stubbornly trying to get up on my own.

"What are you doing? Are you trying to kill yourself?" he

asked in that upset tone parents use when you do something that could hurt you and they don't know how to express their fear other than by yelling at you. It was a big issue when Jared was training to be a firefighter and someone would tell mom about some heroic exploit he did.

"I slipped," I said simply, not wanting to defend myself, but I was in a bit of a mess. He was inching closer to the edge to grab my hand, but his shoes didn't look any safer than mine.

"There are storm warnings, Rachel, this is not the time to run off on your own and not answer your phone." He held on to a tree and offered me his hand.

"There's no service up here." I probably wouldn't have answered if there was, but he knew that.

"What were you doing off the path?" he asked after pulling me up to the top.

"I dropped this," I said it dismissively, but I grabbed my bag and carefully placed the letter between the pages of a textbook, hoping it wasn't destroyed.

"That's your—"

"She doesn't even mention it," I cut him off. "No name, no nothing."

"That's because you're mine."

"But I'm not—" I argued, the rain masking the tears running down my face.

"You are mine," he cut me off. "Sierra was the love of my life. No, she wasn't perfect, but she was so much more. When she came back and told me what happened, what she went through, I saw that I had failed her. I'm not going to say the Post-Partum made her do it, or that it was a mistake, because I don't know what happened. All I knew was that the woman I loved wanted to be with me, and she was pregnant, so we were pregnant."

"That's not how it works."

"I decided you were mine Rachel. Not that I would love you like you were, because I loved your mother. We decided, then and there, that you would be mine. When you were born, Sierra said you had my nose, and I told her you had my eyes too. I wasn't delusional, I—"

"You can't decide—" I tried to argue, but he wasn't having it.

"I did. Your birth certificate is the only thing that says otherwise, and that is purely for medical reasons. In every other way, shape or form, I am your father. They might not actually be my eyes, but you have my love of horses and peanut butter..."

"That's not a thing," I pointed out.

"Peanut butter is the only thing," he said as if I were crazy.

"This isn't funny," I argued in spite of the tiniest of smiles.

"No, it isn't," he agreed. "There are a million things I've done wrong. You have every right to hate me for them, but you need to know that you're hating your father."

"Why didn't you tell me everything when I moved in? Why did you let me hate you?"

"You would have hated me anyway, for making her the bad guy. It wouldn't have mattered if it was the truth or not. And I didn't want you to hate or blame your mother. I never did."

"Really?" I did not believe him.

"Maybe at first," he agreed. "But I was in a bad place. The lawyer basically told me that I could either destroy the family I claimed to love for less than a one percent chance of getting to see three of my kids, or I could get a judge to declare Sierra unfit to raise them and hope a judge granted me custody over Jack, which was just as unlikely, but also unforgiveable. Not to mention my brother's diagnosis terrified me. I did all kinds of research and nowhere did it tell me anything that could guarantee I wouldn't hurt you. I went to a bad place. A dark place. I didn't even recognize myself. I would call the house and at first Sierra would tell me she didn't think it was a good idea for me to talk to you guys that day, but eventually she just hung up. It took me a while to put myself back together and know that I would never do anything to hurt any of you. I tried calling, but my number was blocked, so I used a payphone. When Sarah picked up, she thought I was asking for her father, instead of saying that it was me, so she told me 'that asshole doesn't live here anymore'. Jared was with her, and when he asked who, she told him, and he added 'Good riddance'. Ted came on the phone and apologized, but Kyle called him daddy and it killed me. You guys had moved on, and going through what I should have done ages ago at that point, for you to spend time with someone you hated, and try to get you to warm up to me after I destroyed your lives...I couldn't do that."

"He said that to bug me," I admitted.

"What?"

"We usually called him Ted. I heard what Sarah and Jared said, so I told them they should have taken the message for when you came back. Kyle told me you weren't coming back and asked Ted to do something, calling him daddy, to show me that I should move on as well."

"I'm so sorry."

"You wouldn't have gotten me anyway, right?"

"I am sorry that I left you. That I didn't fight with everything I had for even the tiniest chance of not hurting you."

"I'm sorry I was mean. You were trying and I...god I was horrible when I told you what happened," I realized that if she was the one who broke his heart, my call would have broken it all over again.

"Ripped my heart right out of my chest," he agreed. "But I deserved it. And so much more." I could lie and tell him he didn't, but even if I was beginning to understand that there was a lot more to this story than what I had been told as a child, I could still see he made a lot of mistakes. "You were right. Loving you from afar is not the same as actually doing something about it. I don't want you to have any more doubts."

"Okay," I agreed. We stood there a moment, looking at each other and all the hurt and pain between us. I was glad it was raining so hard, because you couldn't tell that I was crying.

"Let's go home," he offered. I nodded before following him

down the path. It wasn't like everything was magically okay now, but I was beginning to feel like someday it would be.

HE HAD PARKED at the café, since everyone was driving around looking for me, but once we got back to where there was service, he received a dozen missed calls.

"What's wrong?" I asked, tensing up while he checked his voicemail. My phone was no longer in my pocket, so I assumed it died in the slope and I would never know how many times they tried to call me.

"Nothing's wrong, Tracy's in labor," he shared.

"Then let's get to the hospital."

I COULD TELL he would have sped there if I wasn't in the passenger's seat, but the windshield wipers were going at full speed and we still couldn't see more than a foot or two in front of us.

"It doesn't get easier?" I asked, seeing how white his knuckles were from holding the steering wheel so tight.

"Just as nervous and excited as when I drove your mom to the hospital for Sarah," he said, getting a smile. "She was the easiest delivery, a perfect little baby with all her toes and no complications. Before the epidural wore off, your mom told me that if it was that easy, I might get my bus load."

"You wanted a bus load of kids?" I asked.

"My best friend growing up had seven siblings and his house was one of my favorite places to be."

"Uncle Felix?" I asked. He used to bring his kids to the Lake House in the summer, until his wife got a job in Tokyo. They'd sent pretty flowers for mom's funeral with a picture of her smiling at my age, saying that's how he always remembered her.

"The one and only. He lived across from Sierra and she was always there, hanging out with his sister. Seeing her might have had something to do with it, but I loved how they didn't have to wait for friends to come over to play games or have adventures, there were already enough kids in the house to get up to all kinds of trouble.”

“It was awesome,” I agreed.

“I can’t imagine how hard it must have been for you, losing her and being torn away from everyone you grew up with.” He gave me a quick look before going back to the road.

“I’m thinking you might be one of the few people who can.”

“There were things I could have done to change my situation. You didn’t have a choice.”

“Were the other deliveries hard?” I brought it back.

“Jared’s was the scariest, because he had the umbilical cord wrapped around his neck, but you took forever. You were two weeks late and we were in the hospital for days. Plus, it was a snowstorm, so Jack was stuck with five kids, cooped up for nearly a week.”

“Sounds like fun,” I said it teasing, but I would absolutely love to spend a week cooped up with Uncle Jack, Sarah, Jared, Kyle, Haylie and Toby.

He shared stories like this the rest of the ride, his knuckles completely relaxed.

He parked in what I’m pretty sure was a tow away zone before we ran to the front desk, “Tracy Glass?” he asked, nowhere near the nurse’s desk, but she was used to it.

“Third door on your right,” she smiled.

I slightly jogged to keep up with his power walking, before we finally turned into a room and found Tracy in the bed with a nurse checking on her, while Sarah waited in the corner with Owen.

“Is this your daughter you were telling me about?” the nurse smiled when we ran in. I guess people frequently rushed into delivery rooms.

“Yes,” Tracy said without hesitation.

"And the husband?" he asked as Chris went over and kissed Tracy.

"The baby daddy," Sarah agreed.

"I'm so glad you're here," Tracy said, looking up to me.

"It's what family does," I assured her.

"Okay, I think it's time we start pushing." A doctor walked in as a big contraction hit.

"This is our cue." Sarah guided me to the door.

"Aren't you a doctor?" I asked.

"Not today."

SHE BROUGHT me to a waiting room and we sat in some of the more couch-like chairs. "It has been an emotional weekend," she sighed.

"Try three and a half months," I corrected.

"What happened out there?"

"I forgave him," I shared. "He isn't perfect, but neither was mom. He made some huge mistakes, but he loves us. And he's trying to make up for it."

"What happens now?" I could tell she was trying not to pressure me, either way.

"I can stay," I decided.

"Really?" she asked with a mixture of excitement and sadness.

"I love babies," I teased like that was the only reason, before going serious. "I'm sorry."

"For what?"

"I'm the reason he didn't fight for us. He didn't want me to be left out, so if I wasn't there, you would have had a dad. Or at least one who tried." I felt bad for them, but it would have broken my heart to stay home with mom while they all went to dad's, and I would have hated her for it.

"Out of all the people whose fault that is, you didn't even make the list," she assured me.

"Have you told Jared?" I asked, knowing she wanted to tell Kyle in person.

"I can if you want, but like dad said, it doesn't make a difference. You're my sister. End of story."

"I think I'm done with secrets," I let her know it was okay to tell him before Chris came out to introduce us to Tabytha Glass.

"I am going to smother you with love and kisses," I told her once it was my turn to hold her in my arms.

"She'll love that," Chris told me.

"You might not," Sarah warned.

"How so?" he was confused, but still smiling, like nothing could bring him down.

"She will babysit, change diapers, sing lullabies, feed her and make your life so much easier until the day you realize your daughter loves her more."

"All day, every day...eventually you can't help it," I defended myself.

"You're staying?" He turned to me.

"If that's okay?"

"That's perfect."

EPILOGUE

Sarah left after a few hours to get Katie from Toby, but the rest of us slept at the hospital, waiting for Tracy and Tabytha, so we could all go home together. I was on Christmas Break and Chris was on hiatus, so there would be more than enough hands to keep everything going smoothly. Still, Ryan was waiting outside when we got to the house, so Tracy asked him to feed his niece while she went to take a shower.

"He loves babies," she whispered to me before going upstairs, while Chris went to put Owen down for a nap.

"I read your paper," Ryan told me while feeding Tabytha.

"I'm sensing a joke, but I don't know what it is."

"On gun control and how the right to bear arms doesn't mean the same thing as it used to."

"My history final?" I asked, shocked.

"Ken showed it to me. You make some great points. And it was the perfect mix of historical evidence, facts, statistics and personal experience." I had talked about the shooting, but if I were to write it over now, I would research what happened to Jeff and include his story as well. "He said he asked and you didn't mind," he added.

"By Ken you mean Mr. Adams?"

"We went to acting school together. He was with me at the concert on Friday, so he took it out when I went over yesterday."

"Your friends sound like fun," I deflected.

"We took a break from all the partying to grade some papers," he teased.

"He wants me to publish it and start a crusade or something," I shared. Mr. Adams had written to my school email, raving about my paper and all of the things he thought I could do with it.

"You don't want to?"

"I don't want the attention it would attract."

"Why did you write it then?" Ryan asked. "No one puts that much effort into a school paper. Especially when you had to know Ken was giving you top marks no matter what."

"I'm one of those weird people who does put that much effort into every paper. But this one...it hit close to home, and I already did the research for myself, so it was easy to write."

"I think if something like that was easy for you, then you definitely have to do something with it."

"It can be my new year's project," I humored him.

"Ken will definitely hold you to that."

"Is Owen's giraffe in the car?" Chris came down the stairs and asked me, on his way out the door.

"Should be in the entrance on the bench." I had unloaded the car while Ryan got settled with Tabytha.

"That's not the only thing in the entrance." Tracy followed her husband, with Owen in her arms.

I looked over and saw Nick standing in the open doorway.

"You're still here!" I rushed over to hug him, but he had a weird look, so I stopped. I debated shaking his hand, but that felt worse, so I did nothing.

"I thought you had to be back in New York today?" I asked.

"We're on our way to the airport," he agreed. "You weren't avoiding me?"

"Why would I be avoiding you?"

"Because I tried to kiss you." His resolve died when the words came. "I left maybe a million messages and you never answered."

"That had nothing to do with you. I ran away, got an intervention, found out way more than I wanted to know, lost my phone down a ravine and got a baby sister." I nodded over to Tabytha.

"I was with you Friday night," he pointed out.

"It was pretty crazy," I agreed.

"You weren't avoiding me?" he confirmed.

"Nope, I wanted to call you, but you put your number right into my phone, so I don't have it anymore." I smiled. "You wanted to kiss me?" I asked, nervous, but a lot less than the last time I saw him.

He looked around and spotted Tracy and Chris before asking, "You wanted to call me?" instead of addressing my question.

"I did have a really crazy weekend," I reminded him. "And you said you love skiing, so I thought you might want to come to our Lake House some time. My siblings and I will be there until school starts up again, and I'm told the slopes are great in Tahoe."

"They're killer," he agreed. "Chris won't mind me staying over?" he asked, figuring the invitation to come over for supper didn't extend to staying overnight at our Lake House.

"Dad, is it still cool if Nick comes to the Lake House with us?" I asked.

"As long as his parents are okay with it," he called back.

"It really isn't up to him, because technically we own it now, but since he won't be there I thought it might be best to ask him before I invited you," I shared.

"Dad?" he raised an eyebrow.

"I'm trying it out," I shrugged. "I told you, things happened."

"I look forward to hearing all about it." He smiled like I surprised him.

"What were you coming to say if you thought I was avoiding you?" I asked.

"Oh, I was going to remind you how awesome I am," he shrugged.

"Believe me, I know. You've been my favorite part of most days," I let him know.

"Likewise," he agreed.

"You have to leave now?" I asked when his mom honked from the car.

"I was navigating to a private airport we were supposed to go to and I brought us here instead," he admitted.

"I'm glad she let you come in."

"She likes the way you make me smile. And do my homework," he shrugged with a smile, that I returned.

"Two of my many skills," I teased. "Before you go, I need your number," I remembered, going to grab a pen and some paper from the pad beside the phone.

I only brought one sheet, so he was having trouble without a hard surface to write on. I would have turned around so he could use my back, but I had an idea. "Oh, you can use the door," I said, probably way too theatrically, before closing it. It wasn't like Chris, Tracy and Ryan were staring at us throughout that conversation, but they were definitely listening to every word.

I felt silly as soon as we were alone on the porch, but before I could try to play it cool for Nick, he tucked a strand of hair behind my ear and leaned close, ever so slowly, giving me the chance to change my mind if I freaked out like last time. I finally closed my eyes and leaned in to bridge the distance between our lips. His were soft and tasted like peppermint, while I was very grateful that I had brushed my teeth when we got home after a night in the hospital.

"Second time's the charm," he smiled.

"Find me once you're back," I told him, not sure if we would still be here or at the Lake House.

"As soon as we land," he agreed, leaning in to kiss my cheek before running to the car so his mom wouldn't honk again.

I waved and smiled at them as they drove away, my lips still tingling long after they turned the corner and were out of sight.

I WAS ABOUT to go inside when Jared pulled into the driveway. He stepped out and for a minute, we both stood there, looking at each other. I wanted to run into his arms, but I knew Sarah had told him what we found out.

I took a hesitant step towards him, but it wasn't until he put his bags down and opened his arms that I rushed to him, still flooded with all of the emotions from the previous days.

"Sarah suggested we come here instead of Tahoe, so everyone can be together," he said when he put me down.

"That's it?" I asked.

"I couldn't care less about it, Rachel. You're stuck with me forever."

"And me," Toby added.

"You're staying too?" I asked.

"I can't spend another holiday without my family," he agreed.

"Do you like me better now?" I tried to lighten the mood.

"It wouldn't be possible to, munchkin." Toby stayed serious and gave me my hug before the three of us went inside.

"Do you want to meet Tabytha?" I brought them to Ryan, who was singing her a lullaby with a voice I wish he had recorded his album with.

"Absolutely." Jared came close and took his new sister from Ryan's arms, while Toby stood beside me, watching.

I put my hand on Toby's shoulder when Chris stood, knowing how I used to tense up.

"Tobias," my dad said with a head nod.

"Thank you for inviting me." Toby shocked me by stepping forward and shaking his hand.

"Thank you for coming," Chris was surprised he accepted.

"You found her," he said simply.

"I'm sorry I let you down, Tobias."

"Don't do it again." And like that, Jared came over to congratulate Chris and the six of us stayed in the room, with some awkwardness, but mostly okay.

I WAS MAKING coffees when I heard Haylie, Uncle Jack and Peter come in. She came to the kitchen to help me while the guys stayed with the baby.

"How are you holding up?" she asked me.

"A whole lot better." I gave her a smile.

"I'm glad it all worked out."

"You were Team Chris?" I raised an eyebrow, knowing she wasn't.

"No, I was completely on your side, one hundred percent... but if my mom ever cared enough to try and get back into my life, even after all this time and heartache, I would forgive her for leaving and take her back in a heartbeat."

"If he would have shown up on his own, even the day before she died, I probably would have too. But it wasn't his choice to come, and I was worried he would leave me again. I couldn't let him in and have him break my heart all over again."

"He had the choice," she argued.

"He could have said no, but mom chose him. And it wasn't like he was going to do that in a room full of people."

"The fine print the lawyer said didn't matter...he had to call Chris and see if he wanted to take you. If not, my dad would have taken you, because he was your actual guardian."

"And you didn't tell me because..."

"They didn't want you to have a way out. And your mom

didn't want you to have a choice either. She knew it would be hard at first, but she believed you'd be better off in the end."

"Parents," I sighed.

"You forgave him, right?" she verified.

"I did. They definitely did not have it all figured out, and they made some pretty big mistakes...but they both loved me. And it'll be nice to catch up on a decade of not having a dad."

"I wish you all the best."

"And it's your mom's loss Hales. You're amazing."

"Right back at you," she smiled.

I SAT BESIDE UNCLE JACK, who wrapped his arm around me and whispered, "You better never run into a hurricane again," in a warning tone.

"I ran out and then the hurricane started," I argued.

"Do I have to come here and..."

"You can come as often as you'd like," I smiled. "But I'm good here."

"I'm glad you're happy." He pulled me close.

TRACY CAME DOWN and took Tabytha, so I talked with Toby, Jared and Haylie, watching my dad and Uncle Jack laughing together.

"When did that happen?" I asked when Chris went to Tracy and his newest daughter, letting Uncle Jack come back to me.

"What?" he asked.

"Toby shook his hand, but you were laughing like..."

"Old friends?" he asked.

"How much did you know?" I asked, having recently come to the conclusion that adults thought lies protected children from hard truths.

"I didn't talk to him after he left, if that's what you're asking."

"But you know she asked him to leave?" He nodded. "And that my mom...that he chose to be my dad?" I rephrased it.

"I was a lot older than your siblings when it happened, and your parents were the only adults I hung out with other than my unit," was his way of letting me know he had.

"You lied to us too," I reproached.

"He was my best friend, and I would have helped him, but I saw you after he left, and I couldn't defend someone who would put you through that."

"Why are you nervous?" Jared asked while I paced, rocking Tabytha in my arms so it wouldn't look like I was anxiously checking the driveway.

"Sarah should be getting here any minute now," I said simply.

"Did you steal her strappy shoes?" he teased.

"He hated him more than I did last time I checked. What if he doesn't come?" I asked of Kyle.

"Sarah can be very persuasive," he reminded me. "And if he's not ready, we will go to the Lake House."

"Really?" I raised an eyebrow.

"We might hold another intervention once we're there, for peer pressure and to make sure she tried everything, but it's Christmas. I went many years without dad, but none without Kyle," he said simply.

"Cool." I nodded.

"That's not what you're worried about," he read me.

"To you, dad's story was an explanation that makes things better. For us, it's..."

"None of it is your—"

"I know that, on an intellectual level," I cut him off. "And I'm sure Kyle will too. But we messed things up just by being born and existing. Having Kyle made mom sick, and protecting me is what stopped dad from having a relationship with the rest of you."

"That was dad's fault, not yours," Jared let me know he also thought Chris could have done more. "And it wasn't that Kyle made mom sick. It's something that happens, but that usually gets treated. I don't know if mom was afraid to ask for help or if dad was too happy to notice, but none of it is on you two." I nodded as he said this, just as Sarah pulled into the driveway. Matt was in the front seat, but Kyle came out the back holding Katie, while they went to get the luggage from the trunk. "I'll take the baby," Jared assured me, opening his arms so I could transfer her over.

My first instinct was to run to Kyle, but I paused in the doorway. Katie rushed into my arms, completely unaffected by any of the bombshells. She was glad she got a few extra days of vacation, but that was it.

Kyle looked at me, and I could tell there had been tears, but he looked so sorry that I let go of my worry and went to him. "I'm so sorry," we both said at the same time, while he took me in his arms.

"What are you sorry for?" he asked.

"I'm the reason—"

"I meant you have nothing to be sorry for, Rache. If I hadn't been born—"

"Rachel wouldn't exist," Sarah cut him off. We both looked at her, about to argue, but she wasn't having it. "As horrible as it must have been for her, mom's post-partum is the reason we have you," she told me. "And I think that I speak for everyone when I say we would much prefer a world with the two of you in it, even if it means we didn't have the perfect childhood we thought we were going to. It was hard sometimes, but we're stronger because of it, and a lot closer than most siblings I know."

"We're strong, caring, decent human beings who will make it in the world and be incredible," Jared said with a smile from the doorway. We all looked back at him with that same smile, because it was, yet again, the best and worst thing anyone could say at that moment.

"Kyle." Chris stopped in his tracks, shocked, with Katie leading him by the hand. The past few months had probably convinced him he would never get to know his youngest son.

"Christopher," Kyle said, looking like he was still debating.

"When are you all heading to the Lake House?" Chris asked Jared, but kept his eyes on Kyle.

"We thought we might spend it here." Sarah looked to Kyle for confirmation.

"Really?" Chris was trying to contain it, but he looked like he could burst from happiness.

"It's where my family is." I could tell Kyle wasn't entirely comfortable with it yet, but Sarah had given him the option, and he decided to try it out.

"I am...more than happy to have you." Chris looked like he wanted to say so much more, but didn't want to overwhelm him, or do something to risk losing him again.

"This is me giving you a chance to prove that you deserve one," Kyle warned when he walked up the steps to Chris.

"Every day for the rest of your lives," Chris agreed before extending his hand, that Kyle shook.

I watched the handshake and felt like nothing realistic could make this moment any better. My heart was back together, except for the big hole for my mom, I had my dad, there was a baby, Nick and I kissed...it was a million times better than I could have expected our first Christmas without her to be.

I hugged Matt before we made our way inside, almost through the doorway when a cab pulled up.

"You married Mackenzie?" My dad asked Uncle Jack with a smile, recognizing her in the backseat.

Uncle Jack shook his head. "I thought she wasn't coming," he sounded confused as he went to greet her.

"He's afraid to lose her," I explained, so Chris wouldn't say anything to her about assuming they were married.

"It would be so much worse to never have her," he said like he knew it from personal experience.

I couldn't hear the conversation by the cab, none of us could, but we all crowded around the doorway and watched them go from smiling, to arguing, back to smiling, with maybe some tears sprinkled in between. I had no idea where this was coming from, but grabbed Kyle's hand, terrified this was Uncle Jack losing her.

"I was invited as 'Mackenzie plus date' to Haylie's wedding?" Mackenzie asked that part a little louder, looking hurt while she waited for him to explain. Uncle Jack moved closer to her and spoke softly, but she backed away.

"That was my bad. I needed her to know I wanted her there for her, not only as my dad's date," Haylie told us, looking as nervous as I felt. We inched as close as we could without making it too obvious.

"Because he wouldn't be you. Any other guy who would ask me out or want to be with me...I was never interested because they were never you," Mackenzie ensured that she and Uncle Jack could never go back to just being friends. He looked at her and said something I couldn't hear. Then he leaned in and kissed her, like he'd been waiting a lifetime to; the kind you see in movies.

"Eventually you get to a point where not making a move is how you lose her," Haylie told me wisely, her smile mirroring mine.

"Let's give them a minute," Toby suggested with a megawatt smile, ushering us inside.

I had said it before to convince myself, but watching everyone ahead of me, smiling and catching up, with Uncle Jack and Mackenzie finally owning up to their feelings...I knew without a doubt that we were going to be okay.

I hope you enjoyed Shards of Glass as much as I enjoyed writing it! If you did, it would mean the world to me if you could leave a review :)

And, if you're looking for a new read, although it's in a different genre, you might want to check out Prophecy, the first book in my urban fantasy series, The Owens Chronicles!

ACKNOWLEDGMENTS

This book would not have been possible without my mom, who read my first draft and advised against the 11 'kids' I had living in Sierra's house. She helped me brainstorm ideas, read every new version I wrote and spent days going through the final draft with me to make sure it was okay. She is my superwoman and my best friend.

To J.F. who talked me out of publishing anonymously when I worried nothing I wrote would ever be good enough. He encouraged me, let me pick his brain, listened to all of my frustrations and designed my amazing cover.

To Fay, who read my blog and insisted I should be a writer instead of an actress.

To Johnny, who listened to the entire story/did a developmental edit while we were parked on the 401.

And to Arsen, who let me ignore him for months while writing the final drafts, editing them and figuring out how self-publishing works.

Thank you, from the bottom of my heart.

ABOUT THE AUTHOR

Amanda Lynn Petrin grew up on the South Shore of Montreal with a big and supportive family. She studied Psychology and History at McGill University, then went into acting once she graduated.

In 2017 she moved to Toronto, Ontario, in the hopes of finding more opportunities. Instead, she discovered that you need to create your own. She has written, produced and starred in multiple short films, including Get-Together, All the Things, and Touched. Being an author was a dream she thought would never come true until she started doing the things that scared her. Her debut novel, Shards of Glass, was released in August 2019, and she is just getting started.

Find her at: https://www.amandalynnpetrin.com

ALTERNATE EPILOGUE

"And now if everyone could join the bride and her father on the dance floor for the father-daughter dance," Haylie's MC gave an open invitation. My cousin was absolutely beautiful in Mom's wedding dress, and she looked like she couldn't possibly be happier. Uncle Jack had supposedly been suffering from really bad allergies these past few days, but we all knew he was just going through a lot of feelings watching his baby get married.

"Could I have this dance?" My dad came over to the table where I had been telling Nick how Uncle Jack used to sing this song to Haylie every night when she was little.

"Absolutely." I smiled, bunching up the bottom of my bridesmaid dress in order to stand. Haylie was incredibly nice to make the dresses gorgeous, but they were of the poufy, princess variety. Which made them slightly cumbersome at times.

"Have I told you yet that you look so beautiful today?" my dad asked me as we swayed to the slow music.

"You might have mentioned it," I agreed. He had also suffered from allergies this morning when he walked into Haylie's hotel room and found me holding Tabytha while Tracy did my makeup. Sarah sent him out on the grounds that no guys were allowed to see the bride before the wedding, but he was as teary-eyed then as he was now.

"Every day as well, obviously, but..."

"I know," I assured him. "If you want to dance with Sarah or Tab for a bit, that's okay," I added, since I wasn't his only daughter.

"I am perfectly happy right where I am," he said, lifting his arm to twirl me before pulling me close.

We danced until the next song came on, one that was a lot faster, so most of the guys went to sit back down, leaving us girls to dance together. I couldn't help but smile every time I saw Haylie dancing to hip hop in a wedding dress, although I guess the rest of us looked almost as funny in our bridesmaid dresses.

"Have I told you that I'm really happy you guys worked things out?" Haylie asked, coming to dance beside me.

"No," I answered.

"I mean, I was completely on your side, hating him right with you...but to be honest, I kept thinking that if my mother had cared enough to try and get back into my life, even after all this time and heartache...I think I would have forgiven her for leaving," she admitted. The song had stopped, so she was walking me back to my table.

"I was terrified because I knew it hadn't been his choice to take us, it was in the will, and I was just so afraid that he would leave us and break my heart all over again, that I couldn't get close."

"It all worked out for the best though," she pointed out.

"And it's your mom's loss. Without a doubt. You're absolutely amazing," I said, giving her a hug.

"Right back at you," she said, lingering a second longer before taking Kyle's seat. "Did my little cousin ditch you again?" she asked Bridget. Haylie clearly intended for it to be a joke, since Kyle had 'ditched' her to be beside Pete during the ceremony, but with my brother shipping out in a week, Bridget didn't exactly appreciate it.

"He's playing big brother and prodigal son returning." She nodded over to where Kyle had Owen in his arms, talking to dad. Christmas had been a good starting point, but this week of wedding shenanigans was definitely bringing everyone closer.

"Picture time." Toby came over with a digital camera.

"We already did pictures. All morning," Haylie reminded her brother. We spent a pretty large part of the day with her photographer, taking pictures of us getting ready, on our way to the church, after the ceremony, at the reception...

"This is for our picture though. The family," he argued, with a look that told us it was non-negotiable. I guess we were already in fancy, wedding-themed costumes. "You're included in that," he added when Nick stayed at the table after we all got up.

"A little presumptuous, no?" Kyle joined us, lifting his hand that was holding Bridget's up in the air so she could twirl.

"Bridget too," Haylie said, but that just made the two of them smile.

"I guess you'll be doing a wedding theme this time?" Nick asked, understanding that this was like all the pictures Toby had in his trailer.

"And we were thinking Star Wars for this summer, so figure out who you're going to be," Sarah said while we were all taking our places.

"I'll be chewy," Mackenzie said, getting most of us to laugh. "That wasn't a joke," she argued, but Jack just kept laughing as he kissed her.

"Dad!" Kyle called when he realized he hadn't followed. Sarah, Jared, and I all exchanged a look. We thought calling him Chris instead of Christopher was progress for Kyle.

"I'll sit this one out," Dad assured us.

"Family means no one gets left behind," Toby argued.

"Tracy!" I called, letting her know she was needed as well.

Once we were all ready, Toby handed the camera to one of

Pete's musician friends, then came to stand between me and his sister. We did one with silly faces, one with us looking tough, which was obviously followed by one of us laughing, before we finally got one of all of us smiling.

"Perfect," I said when Toby showed it to us all for approval. It was a beautiful picture, and in the corner of the sky, flying into frame at the perfect moment, was a white dove on a rainbow.